THE HUMAN REVOLUTION

DAISAKU IKEDA

The HUMAN REVOLUTION

VOLUME FOUR

illustrated by Teikichi Miyoshi

New York • WEATHERHILL • *Tokyo*

This volume contains a condensed English translation of Volume 7 and Volume 8 of the original Japanese version of *Ningen Kakumei* (Human Revolution) as first published serially in the daily newspaper *Seikyo Shimbun,* Tokyo, and then in book form by Seikyo Press, Tokyo.

First edition, 1982
Second printing, 1983

Published by John Weatherhill, Inc., of New York and Tokyo, with editorial offices at 7–6–13 Roppongi, Minato-ku, Tokyo 106, Japan. Copyright © 1972, 1973, 1982, by Daisaku Ikeda; all rights reserved. Printed in Japan.

LCC Card No. 72–79121   ISBN 0–8348–0175–2

CONTENTS

v

BOOK EIGHT

PREFACE TO THE ENGLISH EDITION

THIS VOLUME, number four in the English-language edition of *The Human Revolution* (volumes seven and eight of the Japanese-language original), covers the period between 1953 and early 1955. It relates the vigorous development of Soka Gakkai made possible by Josei Toda, the second president of the organization, who firmly organized his plans and policies for propagation of faith in Nichiren Shoshu Buddhism. The growth of Soka Gakkai in this period was astounding. In 1953 alone, the membership grew from twenty thousand to seventy thousand households. Assuming the lead in this enthusiastic drive were the youth divisions.

At this time, though physically weak after a period of single-handed struggling to be of assistance in rebuilding Toda's business, I moved to the front lines of our propagation activities by becoming the leader of the First Section of the Young Men's Division.

In all times and places, youth always takes the initiative in pioneering a new age. In this volume, I lay emphasis on relating the way one young man, whom I call Shin'ichi Yamamoto, awakened to a sense of mission, devoted himself body and soul to the cause of spreading faith in the religion he embraced, and how, by doing this, he became a driving force in the popular movement for Kosen-rufu.

In connection with the preparation for this volume, I reread the two original volumes and felt as if I were reading my own diary for that period. Those were days of real hardship. For us, chilling winds swept over a land still frozen. Although suffering from tuberculosis, I was dizzyingly busy day in and day out. Toda's business was still unstable and would permit not even a brief letup in our efforts.

Although I have said we were still in the winter of our fortunes, the snow was beginning to thaw. Hope was starting to bud in my heart. I had made up my mind to live for our supreme goal of Kosen-rufu and the universal peace for all mankind that it promises. Furthermore, painfully aware of the expectations and affection my chosen teacher and mentor, Josei Toda, had for me, I launched boldly on a path that, though filled with labor, led to a glorious end.

The founder of Nichiren Shoshu, Nichiren Daishonin, left to all of his followers the great mission of Kosen-rufu, that is, the universal propagation of our faith. As part of his program to achieve that great goal, Josei Toda, after having emerged from a state of emaciation and physical exhaustion from prison, where he was unjustly held for religious beliefs until the last days of World War II, reorganized Soka Gakkai and vowed to see the membership reach 750,000 households. Determined to put my own youthful ardor to use in helping him fulfill that vow and realizing that, to do this, all of the organization's young members would have to join forces, I resolved to take the initiative. My enthusiasm struck a sympathetic chord in the minds of many other young members; and, before long, the whole membership, young and old, male and female, were united and eager to carry on Toda's revolutionary task.

Mingled with fond recollections in my reexamination of those youthful days, I find a solid awareness that I am free of regrets. Many young people are untrammeled but void of purposeful thought or activity. Their lives are rich but futile. My youth, however, was filled with hard work that was and remains a source of pride. For me, youth was a golden age filled with a combination of the sweat of hard work and tears of gratitude.

Another important aspect of our experience in the years covered in this volume was an increasing concern over the possibility of nuclear warfare. In 1954, the Japanese fishing ship Fukuryu-maru No.5 was exposed to fallout from test bombs exploded at Bikini atoll, and deaths resulted. With this incident, the movement against nuclear weapons gained impetus at home; even today, nearly three decades later, the fear has far from decreased. Indeed, it has intensified because of the development of neutron weapons.

All over the world a grass-roots awareness of the essential importance of averting nuclear war and ensuring lasting peace is spreading. But we must remember that peace is only possible as long as each human being entertains and demonstrates profound respect for the greater life that fills the entire universe and for life as manifest in each precious individual. Cultivating such respect for life is one of the vital roles of the Buddhism of Nichiren Daishonin.

The peaks of the twenty-first century are coming into view. Even now they await the triumphal songs of people who are are young today and therefore must bear the burden of the furture. Each year, the Nichiren Shoshu Soka Gakkai sets for itself a slogan indicative of the emphasis of the year's activities. For 1982, that slogan is "Year of Youth"; and it expresses our conviction that youth deserves stressing because of the role young people must play in the years and decades ahead. Believing that my own experiences as a young man can be of interest and value to the young men and women of later generations, I have issued this volume of *The Human Revolution*.

In conclusion, I would like to take this opportunity to thank

Richard L. Gage, for his help in preparing the translation, and all of the staff at Weatherhill, for their editorial assistance and advice as well as for their interest and encouragement. I will be very happy if this book provides a chance for people—especially young people—in many lands to come into contact with Buddhist teachings.

Daisaku Ikeda

BOOK SEVEN

1. CLOSER TO GRASS ROOTS

PRACTICAL action is the lifeblood of a religion. Without it and its vital force, a religion can only fail. But a true religion substantiated by down-to-earth, practical action inevitably generates a new motivating force to revolutionize history.

In the year 1953, the seven hundred and first year after the founding of true Buddhism by Nichiren Daishonin, Soka Gakkai grew more than it had in any previous year of its history: an increase in the number of member households from 20,000 to 70,000. Devoted, practical action on the part of the membership made these advances possible. To ensure that growth would continue, Josei Toda made some New Year's resolutions that promised epoch-making changes in the organization of the society.

On January 2, 1953, in a large room on the second floor of the Rikyobo lodgings situated at the head temple, Taiseki-ji, Toda and a group of top Soka Gakkai leaders and top staff members were listening to Takeo Konishi, who was explaining the schedule for the coming year. When he reached the rural membership campaign planned for the summer, Toda stopped him.

For years, Josei Toda had cherished a dream of expansion on

a truly national scale. Vigorous membership drives had been conducted in such areas as Osaka and Sendai; but this was far from his ideal of seeing Soka Gakkai flags flying over every town and village in Japan. One of the things that Toda vowed during 1953 was a full-fledged rural membership drive. He said to the gathering of the staff, "This summer, we plan to mobilize a much larger number of staff members in the rural campaign than we did last year. You will go to Osaka, Nagoya, and Kyushu as before; but this year I want you to make the campaign truly nationwide by adding Hokkaido to the list. This will cost a great deal, but we can no longer let things like money stand in our way. Besides, Soka Gakkai can manage a campaign of this kind now.

"New religions have mushroomed in the postwar years by making inroads in rural areas. The remote areas have been more important to them than the cities. Now we must move into the rural zones so that, eventually, we can outstrip the new religious organizations and sects. This year is going to be important, and I want you to remember that the summer membership campaign is one of the most important undertakings of this entire important year.

"A look at our own records shows that rapidly growing chapters—for instance, Kamata, Suginami, Tsurumi, and Adachi—made the greatest advances in rural areas. They did not plan it that way. It was only a natural result of attention to rural matters. And from now on, I want all chapters to lay heavy emphasis on rural areas.

"Harayama, you are chief of the Rural Supervision Department. I want you to make thorough and accurate studies of present strengths in local districts and work out detailed programs for the summer campaign."

With a grave nod, Harayama agreed and, after complaining about the nature of some of the work done in the past, requested cooperation and diligence on the part of the leaders and their branches in providing the accurate information needed.

After this pause, Konishi continued the briefing on the schedule, in which he gave a general outline of events, requested individual chapters to compile more detailed schedules, advocated the most meticulous planning in all undertakings, and mentioned hopes of purchasing a new building for headquarters during the year.

Excited and inspired by the challenge and promise that lay ahead of them, at eight o'clock, when the general discussion ended, everyone looked forward to the modest party they expected would follow. But they were to be surprised.

Assuming a stern expression, Toda turned to Miss Katsu Kiyohara and said, "Announce the personnel changes."

Miss Kiyohara rose and said to the startled group, "The following individuals are appointed to the following posts:

Yukio Ishikawa—chief of the Koiwa Chapter;

Eiko Ishikawa—chief of the Women's Division of the Koiwa Chapter;

Chisako Irie—chief of the Young Women's Division;

Shin'ichi Yamamoto—chief of the first section of the Young Men's Division;

Hisako Ishimura—chief of the second corps of the Young Women's Division."

This brief announcement, about which Toda had said nothing ahead of time, caught everyone unawares. At the usual Gongyo services at the headquarters on January 1, he had merely expressed gratitude for hard work during the past year, requested the staff members to work still harder in the coming year, and reminded them that he had already consecrated his own life to work in the name of the Gohonzon. All the way to the head temple, he had said little, and he had remained silent as Mrs. Tame Izumida read aloud from the *Gosho*. Personnel changes of this kind, especially coming at the beginning of the year, were like a bolt from the blue. And the most unexpected change of all was the replacement of Issaku

Tomiyama, who had served as the chief of the Koiwa Chapter.

After the surprising announcement, Toda thanked Tomi-yama for his hard work and then delivered the following stern advice: "You have been relieved of a burdensome post, but you are still a senior member and a leader in a major chapter. I want you to give the new chief your wholehearted coopera-tion. If you do not, it will indicate that there is no future promise for the life of your religious faith. You must now be courageous in faith and map a new course for your life."

When Tomiyama took it over in August, 1951, the Koiwa Chapter was playing a brilliant role in Soka Gakkai affairs; but in less than a year and a half it had fallen to seventh place in the total organizational rating. Holding himself responsible, serious, honest, and simple Tomiyama worked frantically, but to no avail. Things went from bad to worse. Toda became worried and tried to encourage Tomiyama, who was, however, too despondent and depressed to take advantage of the en-couragement. He soon began to hint of his wish to resign.

Though Toda liked Tomiyama, he had to give precedence to the welfare of the two thousand households in the chapter. The members criticized Tomiyama for lack of ability, vitality, and tolerance. Toda hesitated to make a decision. He did not want to hurt Tomiyama, but he knew that any organization is doomed to stagnation and possible ruin when its leader is in-competent and has lost the confidence and respect of his fol-lowers. Toda gave Tomiyama another chance, until the year ran out. But, on New Year's Day, 1953, he decided that, to-gether with making other personnel changes, he would have to replace Tomiyama.

He selected Yukio Ishikawa as the new chief of the Koiwa Chapter in order to give the young man further challenge and thereby stimulate him to develop and mature still further. Ishikawa was only twenty-eight. It was risky to appoint him to such an important office. But Toda decided to take the risk and, to help Ishikawa bear the heavy burden, Toda appointed his wife, Eiko, chief of the Women's Division of the same chapter. The way in which this young couple carried out their new tasks would soon reveal the efficacy of the training to which they had been subjected.

Toda had long felt the need to put Shin'ichi Yamamoto in a front-line position, where he could grow and develop. For this reason, he put him in the office of chief of the first section of the Young Men's Division. The appointment was made official on January 2, 1953, Shin'ichi's twenty-fifth birthday.

At this stage in his life, the young man had overcome all hesitation. He was prepared to face whatever struggles the future might hold with determination and courage. His new duties in the society were a vital challenge for him.

Toda was eager to have the installation ceremonies for the new Koiwa leaders and for the new officers in the youth divisions as soon as possible. Ishikawa said that he would need time to notify the chapter, and that January 10 seemed a reasonable date. But, insisting that the membership was unwilling to wait that long, because each day was vitally important, Toda instructed Ishikawa to hold his own inauguration on January 5 and the other installations on the following day.

Although at first he was at a loss to know how to accomplish everything in such a short time, Ishikawa suddenly remembered that all of the district and group chiefs were on hand at the head temple for the New Year's pilgrimage. As soon as the staff meeting was over, he hurried to see each one, to notify them of the personnel changes and in this way to prepare for his own inauguration. On January 4, a fine sunny day, Toda left the head temple for Tokyo.

On January 5, he invited the top leaders to a dinner party at a Chinese restaurant. As everyone enjoyed the gaiety of the event and the fine food—brought in course by course, in the Chinese fashion—singing started. Some members sang old favorites from the nineteenth and early twentieth centuries. Others sang country songs or songs that were popular at the time. Then Akio Nakamichi stood and, in a fine, clear voice, began to sing an unfamiliar song that expressed a combination of courage and graceful pathos.

"The sad autumn wind blows on Mount Ch'i.
Ranks of clouds are dark on Wu-chang Plain.
Patterns of fallen dew are thick;
Though horses fatten on dried grasses,
The banners of the army of Shu have lost their luster,
And the sound of drums is heard no more,
For the prime minister lies dying.
The prime minister lies dying."

This is part of a poem by Bansui Doi (1871–1952) called "A Star Falls in the Autumn Wind on Wu-chang Plain." It describes a grave crisis in the life of Chu-ko Liang (181–234), a famous strategist, and the hero of the Chinese novel, *Tale of Three Kingdoms*, which was compiled in the fourteenth century and relates events of Chu-ko Liang's own time.

On the previous evening, as he was reading from the collected poems of Bansui Doi, Shin'ichi Yamamoto had come upon this verse, of which he had once been very fond. Rereading it, he found that he was still deeply moved by its epic and tragic style. Later in the evening, when friends came to congratulate him on his recent promotion, Shin'ichi treated them to sukiyaki and, on the spur of the moment, recited this poem for them. Akio Nakamichi, who was one of the party, said that he knew a musical setting and sang it for his friends. All of the others liked the song and the words but found the content difficult to understand. To help them, Shin'ichi explained the meaning as he understood it.

"Chu-ko Liang, though basically a man of peace, was a great strategist, who almost never lost a battle. He assisted a famous general to found the Shu Han state and to become its emperor. But, in the moment depicted in this poem, he is dying on the windswept plain of Wu-chang, where his troops have been waging a losing battle. Because of his own prestige and the fear that his name inspired in the hearts of his opponents, he decided to keep his illness a secret. Lying in bed, he thought of the grave battle situation and of the great trust placed in him by the emperor. A man who believed in the rule of righteousness, Chu-ko Liang found it painful to know that war brings immense suffering to the ordinary people. Loyal to the emperor, he was nonetheless agonized by the frustration of his current situation. He was alone in the infinite expanses of heaven and earth. . . ."

His friends listened as Shin'ichi told them what the poem meant. Nakamichi said that he, too, had always liked the song, ever since he had first heard it in military preparatory school, but that he had never realized its meaning was so profound.

Shin'ichi then remarked that Chu-ko Liang must have been a man of immense integrity and tenacity of purpose; and, as he said this, he suddenly saw a similarity with Toda, who had been fighting all alone for the great cause of Kosen-rufu. Excited by the idea, he said, "Nakamichi, I want you to sing the song for Mr. Toda tomorrow." It was agreed; and, before the young men parted, grateful for the happy evening, they once again sang "A Star Falls in the Autumn Wind on Wu-chang Plain."

On the following day, Akio Nakamichi sang as planned. He began the second stanza:

"Waking or sleeping, he respected
His lord's last words.
With burning mind and worn body,
How many years he bared himself in service!
Now rain sounds on the fallen leaves.
And, if the great tree once should fall,
What then would be the fortune of the House of Han?
The prime minister lies dying."

Even though most of the people in the room, while enchanted

by the lovely melody, were confused by the elaborate Chinese references of the lyrics, Toda sat rigid and attentive until the lines "Now rain sounds on the fallen leaves. / And, if the great tree once should fall, . . ." At this point, his eyes became moist. He lowered them thoughtfully, occasionally raising them to the ceiling as he listened to the third stanza.

> "Though some may question his success,
> He was true until his body's demise.
> The countless cold stars
> Of the Milky Way's brilliant
> Silver river shine upon
> The hero's lonely anguish,
> Reacting to his valor.
> And even demons wail
> In the autumn wind."

By this time, the solemn mood prevailing in the room was the result less of the song itself than of Toda's profound reaction to it. At the last stanza, he raised his handkerchief to his eyes.

> "Ah, in the wailing autumn midnight
> Of Wu-chang storms rage and dews weep.
> Lofty the light of the
> Clear river of silver stars;
> Clothed in tones of mystery,
> It beams faintly on heaven and earth,
> Bringing thoughts inestimable.
> And today, more than a thousand years later,
> Chu-ko Liang's name shines still."

Silence filled the room at the conclusion of the song. Though they did not fully understand the meaning of the lyrics, everyone present was moved, yet puzzled, by Toda's obviously emotional response. Suddenly he said in a subdued voice, "Please sing that wonderful song again for me."

Nakamichi began, and Shin'ichi Yamamoto quickly rose to

join him. Their young voices resounded through the sun-filled room, and, when they had finished, Toda asked them to repeat the song again. They willingly complied. Then, first Toda himself, then, one by one, all the other people there began to sing, too. As finally the entire group was singing, Toda no

longer tried to restrain the large tears coursing down his cheeks. The group repeated the song six times. Though its meaning gradually became clearer, the audience still did not understand it completely. Toda rose and began to explain it.

"A song must be heard as much with the heart as with the ears. There are two levels on which this song can be interpreted. First, there is the obvious one: the great strategist Chu-ko Liang is dying, as his army is on the verge of losing an important battle. This song describes his anguish in a way that awakens sympathy. But the thing that moves me more deeply is the ordeal afflicting a man of responsible nature who has been awakened to a great mission and who must carry it out alone. On his deathbed and in the face of impending defeat, Chu-ko Liang felt no resignation and much more than remorse. Never for a minute did he abandon his noble tenacity and integrity. It is the tenacity of purpose portrayed in the poem that struck a responsive cord in my heart and moved me to tears.

"Perhaps you will see what I mean better if I analyze the poem, stanza by stanza, in relation to things that are closer to all of us than ancient Chinese history. For instance, in the first stanza, we find words that could be applied to Nichiren Daishonin's agonies at the time when his true Buddhism was in danger of collapse. He alone was deeply concerned about its fate. And still today, in all of the jealousy and strife within and without Nichiren Shoshu, who is able to play the prime minister's role that Chu-ko Liang plays in the poem?

"The second stanza pertains to the man who has staked his own life on the mission of carrying out Nichiren Daishonin's will. He cannot forget the words of his lord, even in sleep. Those words are his mission. He is the great tree. And, if that great tree should fall, what would become of Nichiren Shoshu? My own body is wracked with sickness. But, if I succumb, what will become of the cause of Kosen-rufu? I alone am aware of our great and noble mission. I could not give in to death, even if I wanted to. And I cannot think of the future of the Nichiren Shoshu without tears.

"The third stanza refers to the turbulent period of the Three Kingdoms, Chu-ko Liang's time, when demons wailed in the autumn wind. And demons wail today, in our own time, too. Deprived of faith in Buddha or the gods, people suffer in agony. We may dream of the peaceful world that will come to be when Kosen-rufu has been attained, but it is still only a dream. None of the leaders who struggle for power today has the lofty determination to build a truly peaceful world. In our time, as in Chu-ko Liang's, merciless strife is the rule and not the exception.

"In the fourth stanza, which was not included in the part sung here today, the poet asks why Chu-ko Liang gave up his idyllic life among farmers and friends at Nan Yang—where he could have enjoyed himself as he had done twenty years earlier—in order to serve his country. The answer is that Chu-ko Liang recognized such service as his mission and as the only way to save the people of the country from suffering. My own circumstances were similar. I could have gone on working happily, enjoying my sakè and a merry life. Why did I choose this incredibly difficult life? Why do I work with you day and night for the realization of my mission? It is strange!

" 'Though some may question his success, / He was true until his body's demise.' The man portrayed in this stanza is completely free of earthly ambition. No common ambitions can inspire the desire to bring eternal salvation to the suffering masses in a turbulent age. Such is the greatest possible undertaking. From my own standpoint, I do not care whether people question my success. Consecrating myself to the cause of Kosen-rufu is the only way. I am a common mortal, but no one can fathom my thoughts. Perhaps only Nichiren Daishonin is aware of my intentions. But he is aware, and his awareness—the only thing I have—gives me courage.

"In the last stanza, a song of frustration, Chu-ko Liang dies, though his name continues to shine today. Frustration is permissible to Chu-ko Liang, but not to me. If Kosen-rufu is not achieved, the entire future of mankind will be dark indeed. If I knew there was someone to take my place in this work, I would not care what happened to me. But at present there is no one. I have no alternative but to live with this reality and to continue being devoted to my mission, no matter how hard it may be, and no matter what other people say or think. My sole strength is the knowledge that Nichiren Daishonin realizes and that he is watching over me."

A more intimate, deeper Toda than they had ever known had delivered these moving remarks. And, as they sang the song again, many people in the room wept with the knowledge of what it truly meant to him and to them. With the conclusion of the song, the New Year's banquet in the Chinese restaurant ended, but the new year and its activities were just beginning.

At five-thirty in the afternoon of the same day, Toda attended ceremonies to transfer the leadership of the Koiwa Chapter from Issaku Tomiyama to Yukio Ishikawa. As the symbolic flag was handed to the new chief amid loud applause, Toda instructed Ishikawa to fight courageously, so as never to disgrace the chapter banner. Following brief remarks by outgoing chief Tomiyama, Ishikawa made a spirited, youthful inaugural speech, in which he vowed to devote himself to the chapter, to leave district affairs to district chiefs, and to expel the devils of worldly desire and authoritarianism that he believed were responsible for the chapter's stagnation. Ishikawa's remarks were followed by a speech by his wife as the new chief of the chapter's Women's Division and by messages of encouragement by the chief of the Koto General Chapter, the head of the Guidance Department, and the chief of the Kamata General Chapter.

Then Toda mounted the platform and began to speak in an intimate tone of voice, suggesting that he was addressing his comments directly to each individual present.

"No one knows better than I how hard Tomiyama worked to make a success of this chapter. And it grieved me deeply to see that no one—not even the district and group chiefs—cooperated with him. I thought the matter over for a long time and finally, in spite of my deep sympathy for him, decided to appoint a new leader.

"I have always loved the Koiwa Chapter. I still do. And that is the reason I have made this personnel change. I have entrusted the chapter flag to Yukio Ishikawa, and I intend to allow him to do as he sees fit.

"To be perfectly frank—and I want you to understand this

thoroughly—it won't matter if none of you follows him. Yukio and I have risen together with the chapter flag in our hands, and, if everyone else falls away and we are left alone with the banner in front of the gates of this temple, it will be enough.

"But, if you want to make improvements and progress, take the Kamata Chapter as an example of what ought to be done. In contrast to your group, it is thriving and prosperous. It turns out so many men of ability that, no matter how many of them we draft into the headquarters, Kamata always has more. Its resources of efficient, talented personnel are apparently inexhaustible. It seems to be overflowing with the rewards of good works and faith.

"But what about you? Dismal and lax! The appointment of the new chief is going to be a turning point, however. All of you, and especially the district and group chiefs, must devote yourselves courageously to our cause. I want you to turn out as many fine, hard-working men as you can. Headquarters needs them. Rise up and fight majestically with the hearts of kings. If you fail in this, if you do not revolutionize your lives, I will be unable to regard you as my disciples any longer. Don't complain idly about your new chief. Join him, march forward, do your very best."

Ishikawa had told the chapter what the cause of their trouble was, and Toda had exhorted and encouraged them. Ishikawa was grateful for Toda's affectionate consideration of his position as new chapter head. The meeting was one of the truly unforgettable moments in his life. Senior leaders and all others present were deeply moved. The way was paved for the recovery of the ailing chapter.

When the meeting was over, and the members began to depart in small groups, Toda went out into the wintry evening, made gloomy by signs of impending rain or snow. A cold wind blew across the Sumida River.

In the evening of the following day, the corps banners of the Youth Division seemed to glow with history and tradition as they were entrusted to Shin'ichi Yamamoto, new leader of the first section of the Young Men's Division, and Miss Hisako Ishimura, new leader of the second section of the Young Women's Division. Everyone present was filled with pride and a profound sense of responsibility as they observed the proceedings. After being sworn in, Yamamoto and Miss Ishimura expressed their determination to live up to all of the expectations that the Soka Gakkai Buddhist force had for them.

Listening to Shin'ichi Yamamoto, Toda felt mixed emotions. He was proud of his beloved disciple. He had full faith in his ability to take on this new, important responsibility. But he was sad to see Yamamoto moving away from his side into fields of wider duty. He was like a father who wants his son to succeed but is sad to see him leave home. Still, Toda knew that Shin'ichi was now mature, and that it was impossible to keep him by his side forever. This was to be a year of major significance for Soka Gakkai. It might be that the success of Kosen-rufu depended on what would take place in the next twelve months. Shin'ichi was ready for greater religious duties, and the organization was in intense need of him.

Although for a number of years, Shin'ichi, in spite of his weak health, had been undergoing intensive, special religious training with Toda, he had been forced to spend the majority of his time on the affairs of Toda's business enterprises, which had undergone one crisis after another. Most of the old employees of the credit cooperative had deserted. The business had gone bankrupt, and Yamamoto had helped to liquidate it. Then he did the work of several men in his efforts to make a success of Toda's other firm, the Daito Shoko Company. Although physically weak, he worked perpetually in the hope that success in Toda's businesses would be useful to the mission of Soka Gakkai. These duties kept him away from religious work, however, sometimes for days on end; and members who did not understand the full situation even accused him of forsaking his faith. Shin'ichi's selfless efforts eventually saved the company, which was now on so secure a footing that the young man was at last able to devote himself full time to the religious duties for which he had been trained. His hard work in the business field, though exhausting, had given him an excellent background in administrative affairs and had fortified his will power and character.

Toda had complete confidence in him. Shin'ichi revered and trusted Toda. The two were bound together by the spiritual bonds of teacher and disciple. And, as he listened to Shin'ichi's words, Toda thought, "We will fight together for the attainment of Kosen-rufu. I will watch over you wherever you go. Fly, Shin'ichi, into the boundless skies."

It was cold outside, but the room where five hundred members of the Youth Division were gathered was warm indeed when, after speeches by other leaders, Toda rose with a stern look on his face and began to speak.

"Soka Gakkai is growing, but with only 20,000 households, we are still a long way from my goal of 750,000 households. Kosen-rufu must be attained at all costs. If, by the time of my death, that goal has not been reached, don't hold a funeral for me."

Toda was repeating the shocking words he had said at his own inauguration on May 3, 1951. Shin'ichi Yamamoto immediately realized Toda's intention. He had said nothing about the Youth Division inauguration ceremonies. Instead, he had begun his remarks with a restatement of his vow. In this way, he wanted to impress upon Shin'ichi and the others the gravity and urgency of their mission. Toda was tormented to think that his own goal might not be fulfilled, that it would be regarded as no more than a fanciful dream. The recent personnel changes were made in the hope of stimulating greater growth of the membership.

Toda went on to explain that personnel changes had been made in the Youth Division leadership in the hope of preparing for increasingly demanding future activities. He added that he would need large numbers of trained, devoted, and efficient men to use whenever and wherever he needed them, and that the Youth Division must accept the responsibility for training them. He added that he had appointed young Ishikawa to the top position in the Koiwa Chapter and that from then on he fully intended to put young people in other leading posts throughout the organization. He then said that they must fortify themselves by studying the doctrines of Nichiren Shoshu. They must not complain that they already had enough to do. Instead, they must readily face the challenge ahead and work hard in order to be equal to their great task. Finally, he told them that they must do their best every moment of every day if they wished to be the kind of young activists who can accomplish the apparently impossible. Toda knew that a religion is worthless without faithful adherents to practice, guard, and transmit it. He knew that he required adherents like the members of the Youth Division, and that they had to practice their faith daily. For a Buddhist, the crucial moment is not something that comes suddenly; it is embodied always in the present moment of existence, because cause and effect are simultaneously operative in their ultimate manifestations at all times.

All of the young people present were deeply moved by Toda's words and resolved to practice their faith daily as he advocated. Section chief Kazumasa Morikawa, who was master of ceremonies, closed with the following words: "Let us all pledge to take President Toda's words to heart and to strive for the realization of our great goal. The time has come for the Youth Division to play a vital role. Let us fight courageously as crusaders for Kosen-rufu."

Thunderous, wholehearted applause greeted these words. And as an epilogue, in response to Toda's call for courage and effort, Shin'ichi led the assembly in singing the song "A Star Falls in the Autumn Wind on Wu-chang Plain."

Personnel changes in the Koiwa Chapter and the Youth

Division initiated what turned out to be the most sweeping organizational reshuffling of key officers in seven years. Up to this time, Toda had concentrated on training the top leaders of the organization, but he now switched emphasis to the lower levels, and especially to the district chiefs, among whom a new group of talented men was beginning to emerge.

At the first district chiefs' meeting, held in the Kanda headquarters on January 27, Toda took the podium and said: "In order to help us reach this year's goal of converting 50,000 families, I have decided to train district chiefs to be able to accept the responsibilities of chapter chiefs. I feel that this is the only way to please the Gohonzon; and, for this reason, I have convened this conference. But to enable the district chiefs to work to the best of their abilities, the chapter chiefs will have to achieve true dignity, both physical and spiritual. Because the role of the district chiefs is going to grow in importance, from now on the headquarters will issue policies and administrative instructions directly to them.

"But this elevation in importance must not tempt district chiefs to be domineering. Some people tend to react in this way to increased authority, but we will not tolerate it in any of our leaders. District chiefs must earn the respect of their members. And they and the chapter chiefs must keep a watchful eye on the religious progress and way of life of each member under them. Failure to do this disqualifies them as Buddhist leaders.

"There are going to be further wide-scale shifts in personnel this year. I want all of you to realize that what we are doing is for the sake of Kosen-rufu. The time has come for us to rise. I want complete devotion from all of you. There is no room in our organization for grudges or jealousy over personnel changes."

This brief speech made such a deep impression on the staff members that some of the district chiefs spontaneously rose and expressed their determination to fight with all their might for the attainment of the goal. This pleased Toda, because it showed that these young leaders eagerly responded to his call and that the districts were preparing themselves for the great membership drive scheduled for that year.

The remainder of the meeting was devoted to one of the question-and-answer sessions that had already become a tradition in the organization. The first question submitted was: "What is the most important thing for a leader to bear in mind at all times"?

Toda replied as follows: "The need for constant proper guidance in relation to faith. To be sure of having the needed guidance, leaders must be constantly in contact with headquarters. This contact will enable you to remain abreast of the latest policies and to remain in harmony with my general sqiritual stand and my intentions on specific issues. All of you who have received proper guidance in faith, propagation of the faith, and character development have, as you well know, improved greatly."

The second question was: "What is the key to growth for a district?"

To this, Toda answered: "There are several things that determine success, but the most important is devotion in worshiping the Gohonzon and in performing morning and evening Gongyo services. Leaders must be dignified but compassionate in their treatment of individual members. For their own good, you must be able to point out members' shortcomings. Since all officers of this organization exist for the benefit of the people and for the sake of the Supreme Law and Kosen-rufu, you must always be kind, generous, and magnanimous to your fellow members."

The third question was one of special interest to all the district chiefs: "What is the best way to regain people who have lost faith?"

Toda replied: "People backslide for their own reasons, grave or trivial. (I might say that most of the reasons are usually trivial.) Nonetheless, from the viewpoint of the persons holding them, these reasons are sufficient to make them waver and then depart from their religious faith. As leaders, you must keep your eyes always open for the least signs of wavering and must at once discuss the problems besetting your members. Once they begin to talk, the rest of the problem is usually easy to solve. You need only to awaken them to the knowledge that, no matter what the reason, they are wrong to forsake their religious faith. They will usually see that their reasons are not as important as they thought they were and will once again return to the practice of their faith. Let me repeat: the important thing is to get the doubtful members to talk about their problems. Then you must be sympathetic, patient in teaching, and generous with your time and effort in showing them exactly where they are mistaken."

After still further questions, all of which revealed the eagerness of the district chiefs to learn and develop, Toda, with a look of happy pride in the attitude of these young men, said: "All of you chapter chiefs must be on the lookout for talented, efficient men. We are in critical need of them. This year, the membership is going to grow tremendously, and we require plenty of capable people at the district-chief level who can be available for work as top officials when the time comes.

"Right now, the number of district chiefs is no more than sufficient to the needs of our rural membership. But we must think of the future—three, five, or ten years hence—when our society will have expanded so rapidly that a huge number of staff members will be needed. Furthermore, to keep a constantly growing organization in good order, the officers we have now will have to mature still further. Proselytizing is a very important part of your duty. But you must not let it so completely occupy your time that you fail to pay enough attention to your own growth and development. To be competent leaders in the Buddhist force, you must mature spiritually.

"You will find it necessary to make personnel changes at your own level, just as I have made them within the top echelons. In making decisions, do not be arbitrary. Do not rely solely on your own judgment. Always ask the advice and counsel of the people who are concerned with the issues. In this way you will be able to make a correct, impartial decision. Turn to headquarters for advice on personnel matters when you need it. We will always help, since we lay primary emphasis on competence and ability in appointing staff members."

The greater responsibility invested in them gave the district chiefs increased initiative in the drive for Kosen-rufu. They were no longer considered mere lesser members. The campaign was steadily moving closer to the grass roots.

2. A PRIEST'S COURAGE

WHILE these important organizational changes were being made, an event was taking place in a small, obscure village in northeastern Honshu that, though totally unexpected, was to be highly significant. The following letter, addressed to Teiichi Kato, reached the Tsurumi Chapter of Soka Gakkai on January 20, 1954.

"Dear Teiichi,

"The situation is getting worse about removal of those heretical statues from the temple. The parishioners object and are gossiping and trying to convince everyone that I ought to be removed from my job at school. They say that the local children ought not to be entrusted to a teacher with a philosophy as dangerous as mine. I may be forced to resign.

"To make matters worse, somebody is scheming to have me officially punished. I have just been summoned by the police and am about to leave for the police station. I have no idea how long they will keep me or when I'll be allowed to come home.

"I am prepared for the worst. But I am proud to undergo even one-thousandth of the sufferings that Nichiren Daishonin went through seven hundred years ago. Still, I am worried about my family and our faithful members.

"Perhaps this is because my own faith is weak. All of my wife's relatives belong to other religious sects. I have tried unsuccessfully to bring them to Nichiren Shoshu, and they have come to hate me. Since I have been abandoned by all the local parishioners, I wonder if my wife and children will be able to survive without me. I depend on the Gohonzon and the faith of Soka Gakkai. But I ask you to do all you can to help my family if anything should happen to me.

"I shall now offer this letter to the Gohonzon, recite the Lotus Sutra, and chant the Daimoku. Then I'll report to the police. I have firm faith in the benevolent protection of the Gohonzon and will express my belief without fear.

"Please give my best regards to President Toda.

Yours,
Gensho Hisakawa."

Upon receiving this letter, Kato, a member of the Youth Division of the Tsurumi Chapter, reported at once to his section leader, and the two of them went directly to the Ichigaya branch of headquarters to seek Toda's guidance on the matter. Though Toda was unacquainted with both the case at hand and with Hisakawa, he responded at once to the urgent plea for help by sending four Youth Division members to the distressed priest's temple, Myofuku-ji, in the village of Kanagami, in Fukushima Prefecture.

Teiichi Kato and Gensho Hisakawa had met in 1952, when the young Soka Gakkai member had been enthusiastically conducting membership campaigns in rural districts and, in connection with them, had visited Kanagami several times. Hisakawa was surprised that the Soka Gakkai campaign had reached his remote village, and he was very much impressed with Kato's zeal. For his part, Kato always visited the temple Myofuku-ji when he was in Kanagami. Soon he and the priest had become good friends and conducted membership drives together. As a consequence of their work, by January, 1953, seven Kanagami families had joined Nichiren Shoshu. Hisakawa came to look forward with pleasure to Kato's monthly visits. Symbolic of the spirit of unity between the clergy and the laity, the two men walked forward side by side in their efforts to spread an understanding of the true Law.

Their friendship grew at just the time when a nationwide scandal was being caused by the priest Jiko Kasahara, who, though defrocked by the head temple, continued to conduct a campaign of vilification and slander against Soka Gakkai and the high priest of Nichiren Shoshu until he was finally silenced and humiliated. [For a full account of this incident, see *The Human Revolution*, Vol. 3, pp. 69–89.] Kato, who, as a member of the Youth Division, had taken a vigorous part in the struggle with Kasahara, related all the details of the incident to his friend Hisakawa, who at once saw that Soka Gakkai was just and right in castigating the heretical priest.

The heresy of Kasahara awakened in the mind of Hisakawa an awareness of heresy in his own temple, in the form of numerous Buddhist statues that for hundreds of years had been the objects of mistaken worship. No one knew precisely when the statues had been brought there, but Hisakawa decided that they must be removed, for the sake of the purity of true Buddhism. He explained to the parishioners of Myofuku-ji that Nichiren Shoshu, the true and orthodox sect of Nichiren Buddhism, could not allow these statues in the temple compound and could under no conditions sanction worship of them. But the local people, who had revered these figures for centuries, in ignorance of the nature of true Buddhism, opposed the removal.

Perhaps the remoteness of Myofuku-ji from the head temple accounted for the laxness of other priests in continuing to house these heretical figures for so long. From very ancient times, beside the main hall of the temple there had stood another hall, enshrining the statue of the Bodhisattva Jizo (or Kṣitagarbha, who was believed to ease childbirth pains) and a great number of other statues, including a set of the Thirty Guardian Deities. Gensho Hisakawa was the first priest in the history of the temple to attempt to restore orthodoxy by removing these figures. His decision had been inspired by Soka Gakkai's drive to purge Nichiren Shoshu of such impure elements as the wicked priest Jiko Kasahara.

To provide some background information on the way in which Myofuku-ji came to be polluted by heretical statues, it is important to sketch briefly the history of the institution and of the priest who founded it. According to tradition, the temple Myofuku-ji was founded by a priest named Nichizon, a disciple of Nichimoku Shonin, who became the third high priest of Nichiren Shoshu. Nichizon was born in 1265 at a place called Tamano, in Rikuzen, which is now Miyagi Prefecture. While still a boy, he entered the temple Chokoku-ji, which belonged to the Tendai sect. Then, on August 13, 1283—one year after the death of Nichiren Daishonin—he was granted an audience with Nichimoku Shonin and was accepted as a disciple. In the following year, Nichizon accompanied Nichimoku Shonin to Mount Minobu, where they both studied under the second high priest, Nikko Shonin.

When Nikko Shonin left Mount Minobu forever, Nichimoku Shonin and Nichizon went with him. Nikko Shonin founded Taiseki-ji, the head temple of Nichiren Shoshu, in 1290, and Nichizon built a subtemple called the Kujobo on the main temple grounds.

One day in the late autumn of 1299, Nikko Shonin was expounding the profound teachings of true Buddhism to a group of priests. Instead of paying close attention, Nichizon, who was in the group, was intently watching leaves falling in the autumn wind from a distant pear tree. Apparently sensing arrogance and impurity in Nichizon, Nikko Shonin suddenly roared, "You there, stand and leave the room at once. If you were truly desirous of propagating the Supreme Law, you would not allow your attention to be diverted from my lecture by falling leaves."

This severe reprimand meant expulsion from the sect. This punishment may seem harsh, but the great, clear-sighted Nikko Shonin had seen deep into the heart of Nichizon and had found there traces of his old Tendai training. These impurities had made it impossible for Nichizon to commit himself whole-heartedly to a cardinal Nichiren Shoshu principle: a nation that slanders the true Buddhism will be deprived of the help of guardian deities and will meet with disaster. Nichizon had secretly doubted this principle, and Nikko Shonin perceived the doubt through the man's feigned devotion.

Nichizon, who was stimulated to action by this punishment, spent the next twelve years traveling and converting old temples to Nichiren Shoshu or founding new Nichiren Shoshu temples. After he had thirty-six such temples to his credit, he returned to Nikko Shonin to implore forgiveness for his past sins. According to tradition, Nikko Shonin not only reinstated Nichizon but also inscirbed thirty-six Gohonzon scrolls at one sitting and gave them to him for the temples he had converted or founded. (No historical verification is available for the figure thirty-six for either the temples or the scrolls.)

In 1333, Nichizon and Nichigo, both disciples of Nichimoku Shonin, who was by then high priest, accompanied their master on a trip to Kyoto to remonstrate with the emperor for ignoring the true Buddhism. On the way, Nichimoku Shonin died, at the age of seventy-four. The disciples continued on their journey, carrying with them the ashes of Nichimoku Shonin's cremated body.

Nichizon remained in Kyoto and was later granted a piece of land in the Rokkaku Aburakoji part of the city, where he founded the temple Jogyo-in in 1336. This was the origin of the sect known as Kyoto Yohoji.

In spite of all of his close associations with Nichiren Shoshu,

Nichizon always entertained doubts about some of the cardinal doctrines. Certainly, in the late years of his life, he formulated heretical theories about the use of statues in temples. In all likelihood, the temple Myofuku-ji was founded by him and therefore fell under the influence of his attempts to compromise the purity of true Buddhism with false teachings that were prevalent in his time. And this may be the explanation of the continued presence of heretical statues in the temple and, consequently, of the incident that erupted in 1954.

The following is the story told about the way in which the temple was converted. In 1303, when Nichizon was nearing a village called Kumagura on his way to Dewa, a young acolyte suddenly appeared from behind him and pleaded for help. "An epidemic is killing everyone in our village" he said. "I beseech you, reverend sir, to come with me and save our people by means of your benign powers."

Nichizon had already passed the acolyte's village, but he agreed to retrace his steps if he could be of any help. He followed the acolyte, who carried Nichizon's baggage on his shoulders. When they arrived at Myofuku-ji, which was in the village that was their destination, the acolyte led the way into the hall enshrining a figure of the Bodhisattva Jizo and, after they had entered, suddenly vanished like a ghost. Mystified, Nichizon approached the custodian, who was in the hall at the time, and asked where the acolyte had gone.

"Our temple is too poor to afford acolytes," was the reply.

Still more puzzled, Nichizon looked carefully around and saw his baggage, which the acolyte had been carrying, on a table in front of the altar.

This story became very popular in the local region. People in general prefer attractive fiction to historical fact, and this tale of the vanishing acolyte probably accounts for the reverence that the Jizo Hall enjoyed for over six centuries and for the twentieth-century refusal of the local parishioners to agree to the removal of the statue and the other heretical figures for the sake of orthodoxy and purity.

Having risked his life and endured great hardships during his service in the Army Air Corps during World War II, Gensho Hisakawa was prepared to put up with the difficulties confronting him when, in August, 1946, he became chief priest at the run-down temple, Myofuku-ji, in the remote mountains of Fukushima Prefecture. With only twenty-two parishioners, the temple was so far from affluent that making ends meet was a grave task. Hisakawa tried to improve his lot by reclaiming a dry, reed-choked riverbed and tilling it for small crops. To eke out his living still further, he took a job as a teacher in the local primary school. His situation was hard and uneventful. It probably would have remained that way if Soka Gakkai had not launched the vigorous membership drive that found its way even to his village, and if the Kasahara incident had not occurred, to reveal the great dangers inherent in heretical thought and action.

These two things woke Hisakawa to the threat of heresy in general and especially of the heretical objects of worship in his own temple. At first, he attempted to convince the parishioners that the statues had to be removed if the temple were to be restored to orthodox purity in Nichiren Shoshu. But his appeal met an adamant refusal: the parishioners claimed that the presence of these statues had enabled the people of the village to remain faithful for six and a half centuries. Believing that this was false, Hisakawa set about removing some of the statues on his own. But he hesitated to touch the figure of the Bodhisattva Jizo.

When he confronted the parishioners with his intention of cleansing the temple of this statue too, he started what amounted to a small-scale religious revolution between the forces of a 650-year-old tradition and his own determination to be true to the doctrines of Nichiren Buddhism, even if it meant excommunicating recalcitrant parishioners.

Matters were rapidly coming to a head. The parishioners organized a committee of representatives to go to the head temple to petition permission to keep the statue of Jizo at Myofuku-ji. In the written document they submitted to the head temple, they accused Hisakawa of arbitrary actions and repeated their assertion that the presence of the statues had enabled their ancestors and them to be faithful to Nichiren Shoshu. They concluded with a threatening statement to the effect that refusal of their petition might drive them to take drastic steps.

Back in the village of Kanagami, other parishioners were at work to undermine the standing of the priest. Some of them requested that the village education board dismiss him from his post in school, since they considered his religious philosophy too dangerous for the ears of the very young. Others went so far as to ask the police to take judicial action against Hisakawa, and the local newspaper devoted considerable space to the entire series of events.

The committee members who had gone to the head temple returned with orders that Hisakawa must defer further action until he had official instructions from the Taiseki-ji administration bureau. These instructions were promised in the near future. Though nothing could be done by either side, rumors continued to circulate throughout the village. And, on January 18, the day on which he wrote his appeal to Soka Gakkai and his letter to Kato, Hisakawa was summoned to the local police station.

This was the state of affairs when Kazumasa Morikawa, Takimoto, Sakita, and Kato, the four Youth Division members dispatched by Toda on January 20, arrived in the snowbound village of Kanagami. Mountains, fields, houses, and roads lay under a thick blanket of snow; and their shadows, advancing slowly in the bitter cold, were the only interruptions in the immaculate winter white.

To their immense relief, when they entered the priest's quarters at Myofuku-ji, they saw Hisakawa seated by the fire with his family. He had not been detained by the police, and he greeted this unexpectedly prompt aid from Soka Gakkai with tears of gratitude. The young men sat down for cups of hot tea and an immediate discussion of the steps they should take. They all agreed that nothing could be done about the statues until official word from the head temple had been received. But, since they had made the long trip from Tokyo, the visitors wanted to do something to be of help. Takimoto suggested that it would be a good idea to approach the parishioners individually. Since there were only twenty-two of them, this small group of trained, disciplined, and courageous young men could easily visit them all, if the task were divided up. Sakita, who was noted for his sincerity and sound common sense, said, "The fact that they sent representatives to the head temple leads me to think they might come around to our way of thinking if we talked to each of them alone and quietly."

But Hisakawa, who had remained largely silent until then, objected almost desperately: "No. They fly into a rage whenever the Jizo statue is mentioned. They're nothing but boneheads"

Eager to go ahead with attempts to persuade the parishioners, Morikawa smiled and said, "Maybe we can soften up those boneheads."

After lunch, they set out in three groups: Hisakawa and Morikawa, Takimoto and Kato's elder brother, who lived in Kanagami, and Sakita and Kato. Patiently and earnestly, each group interviewed the parishioners and, by referring to Nichiren Daishonin's *Rissho Ankokuron*, (*The Security of the Land Through the Establishment of True Buddhism*), attempted to show why the heretical objects of worship must be removed from the temple compound. (For many of the local people, this was their first contact with the true essence of this great writing.)

At a discussion at the temple in the afternoon, the small band compared the results of their interviews. One thing seemed both certain and encouraging. Though the parishioners might be

stubborn and even violent when in a group, approached individually, they appeared more tractable. Only three of them had openly and immediately refused to entertain the idea of removing the statues. The majority indicated that they would go along with everyone else. One young man had said that, though he understood the priest's viewpoint, the time for removing the statues had not yet come.

Encouraged by their modest initial success, the young men forgot that people who are sensible individually become unreasonable in groups. The Youth Division members began to hope that continued talks and attempts at persuasion could result in an amicable conclusion of the issue. Since they had not themselves yet seen the controversial statue, they went to the Jizo Hall for a look at it.

Next to the hall stood a shack that the local parishioners had erected as a watchhouse, because they suspected that something might happen to the statue if close observation were not maintained. No sign of life was forthcoming from the shack as the small group drew near.

The young men found nothing in the aged, stained statue of the Bodhisattva to detain them, and so they left the Jizo Hall to return to the priest's quarters. Suddenly they were stopped in their tracks by the frantic beating of an alarm drum from the watchhouse. Obviously someone had been on guard there all the time, and the furor of the drumming was clearly a prearranged signal that something untoward appeared to be about to happen to the Jizo statue.

Suddenly villagers were heard rushing to the temple. An old woman with a towel wrapped around her head and a look of militant fury on her wrinkled countenance was the first to speak up. "You rotten priest! I suppose you've burned the Jizo!"

Then a crowd of about a hundred people, all excited and angry, gathered in front of the temple's main hall. Among them were some parishioners and many more children and laborers unrelated to the temple but curious to know what was going on.

"You won't get away with this!"

"Drag that priest over here!"

"Beat him up!"

"Kill him!"

Morikawa and Takimoto found it impossible to calm the shouting, cursing crowd.

"If he burns the Jizo, we'll burn him!"

No attempts to convince the people that the statue was safe

and sound had any effect. The members of the Soka Gakkai Youth Division stood around Hisakawa, protecting him from the wild acts of the enraged mob.

Then, noticing the time, Hisakawa called out for everyone to join in evening Gongyo services. He turned his back on the crowd, entered the main hall, sat upright in front of the Gohonzon, and with prayer beads in his hand began the service. The members of the Youth Division followed his example.

Deprived of an object for their shouts and curses, the crowd dashed into the Jizo Hall, where they began Gongyo services of their own, as if in rivalry with the ceremonies being conducted in the main hall. This provided a short truce; but, when both recitations had ended, confrontation was renewed in front of the main hall.

Morikawa addressed the mob: "Rest assured no one will so much as lay a finger on the statue until instructions are received from the head temple."

Takimoto said, "Anger and voilence are no way to solve this problem. Why don't you send some representatives to us so that we can talk the matter over? We're willing to go on discussing for as long as it takes to reach an agreement."

But the people paid no heed.

"Don't think you're so smart, you little whippersnappers!"

"What did you come here for, anyway?"

"Why don't you go back where you came from?"

Then they threw Takimoto and Morikawa down into the snow as they rushed into the main hall, forcing Sakita and the Kato brothers into the priest's quarters, where Hisakawa's terrified children clung to their mother. They did not dare to touch Hisakawa. He sat unperturbed in the main hall, protected by the sanctity of his clerical robes. Nonetheless, in their fury, the crowd surrounded him and poured out accusations and imprecations.

Just at this moment, two police officers rushed in. Their uniforms and weapons had an immediate effect. Suddenly there was silence. A gray-haired old man, who apparently had influence in the village, spoke briefly with the police officers, then turned to the now moping crowd.

He said, "I propose that we remove the statue. Its presence in the building is causing the trouble. And, if things get any worse, there will be hardship for the whole village, not for this temple and its parishioners alone. Mr. Hisakawa, be good enough to put the statue in our custody."

Though the crowd was stunned to silence by this sudden proposal, Hisakawa agreed at once, with the provision that the villagers write a statement of receipt of the statue, in order to prevent future complications.

Though made in a spirit of caution, this request inflamed the crowd. "Why should we give you a receipt for something that belongs to us anyway?"

Once again the police tried to pacify the crowd, but it was by this time in a frenzy. Exasperated by futile arguments, some of the mob went into the Jizo Hall and came out with the life-size figure on their shoulders. They left in triumph, and the rest of the crowd immediately ebbed away behind them.

Only the five young men from Soka Gakkai, Hisakawa, and his wife and children remained, smiling in the cluttered and damaged temple. Ironically, in its rage, the foolish villagers had taken away the statue and thus had purified the temple of heresy. They had accomplished what Hisakawa had been unable to bring about.

After the happy little group had cleaned up the mess made by the disorderly crowd, they relaxed around a bright fire and discussed the many events of the day. Tired and pleased, the young men from Tokyo and the priest and his family slept soundly that night, as deep moonlit snow gleamed silver in the outside world around them.

On the following day, the Youth Division members visited the principal of the local school and learned that, as long as his teaching methods were sound and correct, Hisakawa was in no danger of losing his post. In spite of the principal's sane attitude, however, many of the teachers refused to discuss the matter. They did not want to become involved.

The next step was to go to the offices of the local and regional newspapers to give a correct account of the incident and to request that the press refrain from printing distorted interpretations. This was necessary, because newspapers over the country were already giving attention to the dispute over the Jizo statue in the obscure temple Myofuku-ji.

The major newspaper visited by the young men was in the nearby city of Aizu Wakamatsu. On the evening of the day of their visit there, they called on the Nichiren Shoshu temple Jitsujo-ji, where they received a noncommittal and indifferent greeting from the priest. When the subject of the incident at the Myofuku-ji temple came up, he changed the subject and generally tried as hard as possible to avoid mention of it and of Hisakawa.

For a while they were puzzled, but the Youth Division members later learned the cause of the priest's peculiar attitude. Before becoming head priest at Jitsujo-ji, he had himself been priest at Myofuku-ji, and his father had served there before him. Neither of them had done anything to purify the temple of the heretical objects of worship.

From Aizu Wakamatsu, the young men took a night train back to Tokyo. Upon arrival, they immediately reported to Toda, who decided at once on a policy of unconditional support for Hisakawa. After making contact with the head temple's administration bureau, he instructed the newspaper *Seikyo Shimbun* to carry full coverage of the incident, in order to inform the nationwide membership of the truth.

Admiring the courageous priest and realizing that in his isolation from his defiant parishioners he would need all the help and moral support he could get, Toda invited Hisakawa to Tokyo. On February 4, for the first time in his life, Hisakawa visited Soka Gakkai headquarters, where Toda welcomed him warmly and assured him that Soka Gakkai would stand behind him in his struggle to preserve the purity of a Nichiren Shoshu temple. Toda made it clear that the struggle was an important one.

The next day, at Toda's suggestion Hisakawa visited the temple Jozai-ji, in Ikebukuro, where he had an interview with Seido Hosoi, chief of the General Affairs Department of the head temple, who greeted him cordially and briefed him on the policy of the department, "Let the parishioners go their own way until they return to ask for forgiveness. But you must select representatives from among them as soon as possible. We think that you ought to take on the additional duties of chief priest of the temple in the Koriyama district. You will have to obtain the endorsement of the secretary for membership drives in your area. Remember, you have nothing to worry about. The head temple is with you."

Moved to tears by the kindness of this leading priest, Hisakawa apologized for the trouble he was causing and said that, when the parishioners returned to the temple, he intended to awaken them to pure, true faith and to have them all make a fresh start as members of Soka Gakkai. In addition, he said he intended to launch a membership drive in the Koriyama district. While alone in his village, Hisakawa had felt alone and isolated, but the support of all the people he met in Tokyo—especially that of Toda and Hosoi—renewed his courage.

During the lectures, meetings, and other Soka Gakkai functions he attended at headquarters and at such places as the important Koiwa Chapter during the following few days, Hisakawa had a chance to observe firsthand the progress that the society was making toward Kosen-rufu. What he saw inspired him with further ambition to emulate the efforts of Soka Gakkai in his own village.

On February 7, Hisakawa joined other members of the society in their monthly pilgrimage to the head temple, where he was granted an audience with the high priest, Nissho

Mizutani, who, with a look of warm compassion in his eyes, said: "What you are doing is just and right. I hope you will continue to be brave, no matter what persecution you may encounter, and that you will persevere courageously in your struggle."

Hisakawa was overcome with gratitude, and in the evening, at the Rikyobo lodgings, he expressed his feelings and explained his future plans to a meeting of several high Soka Gakkai officials.

"I intend to resign from my teaching job, so that I can devote myself entirely to my duties as a Nichiren Shoshu priest and command the respect and obedience of my parishioners. For about five months, my family and I can live on my severance pay from the school. During that time, I intend to convert one hundred households to Nichiren Shoshu. Once I have received permission to serve as a chief priest in one of the several Nichiren Shoshu temples in the city of Koriyama, I want to extend my membership drive into that urban region as well. I hope I can call on you for continued support. I cannot hope for any assistance from my parishioners, but I want to carry out my task in cooperation with Soka Gakkai members. Though this has been a trying experience for me, it has been instructive as well. From now on, I want to march along the road to Kosen-rufu with the society. The kindness, understanding, and inspiration I have met here from all of you and from the high priest and Seido Hosoi have deepened my conviction to do all within my power for the sake of our cause."

Though in good spirits when he left Tokyo, Hisakawa was to suffer sharp disappointment upon arriving in Kanagami. During his absence, the vindictive villagers had taken every opportunity to harass his wife and children, who had been literally ostracized from local society. On the pretense that they were temple property, donated by the village, some of the parishioners were bold enough to deprive the priest's family of utensils and other articles of daily use.

No suitable way of dealing with the Jizo statue had yet been found, and it lay on the floor of the village assembly hall. The wrathful parishioners frequently gathered in the hall in the presence of Jizo to denounce the priest. They could not see why he had raised objections to these pieces of sculpture, when other local priests had tolerated them for centuries without a word of protest. From the purely secular viewpoint, their interpretation of the situation may seem sensible. But, in the mouths of believers in Nichiren Shoshu, their remarks were gross heresies. It was just these heresies that blinded the villagers to the true meaning of Hisakawa's attempts to restore purity to the temple and to lead them back to the true faith.

Their blindness was so great that some of them made frightening, insane statements: "The Gohonzon in the temple is nothing but a piece of writing. If it should be destroyed, you can always write a new one—as many new ones as you want. But the Jizo statue is irreplaceable."

A few—but only a very few—of these half-mad people crept surreptitiously to the temple at night with small gifts of food. But the majority, frustrated at the head temple's refusal to heed their ultimatum, attempted to take out their anger in small, vicious acts against Hisakawa's family. For instance, they heckled the priest's children as they passed through the village on their way to school. Soon the children asked to be allowed to remain at home, so as to escape this kind of painful embarrassment. When Hisakawa returned home and learned this, he shoveled a different path, by-passing the village and leading to the school. But drifts and fresh snowfall soon obliterated the new path, and the children were back in their former unpleasant predicament.

One day, as Hisakawa was cleaning the old Jizo Hall, a crowd of about a hundred parishioners and local villagers who had been persuaded to join them charged into the temple and threatened to have the priest arrested for trespassing. They insisted that the Jizo Hall and the land around it be reregistered as village, not temple, property. Without the consent of the high priest of Nichiren Shoshu and the chief priest of the temple—Hisakawa himself—such an act would be patently illegal. Nonetheless, the villagers insisted, and, when he refused, kicked and pushed Hisakawa. They called the police and tried to have the priest arrested on a trumped-up charge of trespassing. When the police officers arrived, they saw at once that the charge was groundless and suggested that a fence be built around the Jizo Hall, cutting it off from the main temple building.

Everyone accepted this suggestion. On the morning of February 14, the fence was up, all of the articles associated with the heretical statues were removed from the temple, and Myofuku-ji was restored to a purity it had not known for centuries.

Still not content, the parishioners attempted to force Hisakawa to make reparations for the statues he had already disposed of. But he refused to do so. "I disposed of them on the grounds of the true Buddhism of Nichiren Daishonin. I have an endorsement for such action from the head temple. And there is no reason why I should comply with your profane demand. If you think you are right, file an official complaint with the proper authorities."

Then the enraged parishioners began to shout to be shown the endorsement. They threatened to break ties with the temple if their conditions were not met. But, refusing to back down, Hisakawa said, "Go ahead and break with the temple, if you dare."

Their bluff had failed. The disgruntled parishioners went away. On that very evening, Hisakawa decided to request permission from the head temple to break ties with them.

Although the Myofuku-ji incident was relatively minor and in no way affected the activities of Soka Gakkai, it inspired increased unity between the clergy and the laity and stimulated a greater desire to put the teachings of Nichiren Daishonin into actual practice. Because of his courage and integrity in the struggle against heretical objects of worship, Hisakawa helped to dissipate the air of stagnation that had prevailed in some temples over the past several centuries.

On April 18, trouble over the Jizo statue flared up in one more violent, but final, episode. Having decided to leave his rebellious parishioners to their own devices, Hisakawa, with Toda's assistance, took on responsibility for the members in a town called Haramachi, which was quite a long way from Kanagami. He enjoyed the new work, since most of the parishioners were members of Soka Gakkai. But the distance and the several changes of trains often made it necessary for him to remain away from home overnight.

Apparently aware of his absence, on the night of April 18, about two dozen of the rebellious parishioners gathered at the Jizo Hall to try to make things so unpleasant for him and his family that Hisakawa would be forced to resign his position at Myofuku-ji. Willing to go to desperate lengths, they agreed to take collective responsibility for the punishment that might be meted to them if they should be caught. They remained in the hall until the silence of sleep fell on the entire village; then they rushed out and began throwing stones at the windows of the Hisakawa house and banging loudly on the walls. Some of them shouted for Hisakawa to come out—they knew of course that he was away—and threatened to kill him if he showed his face.

In her terror, Mrs. Hisakawa did the first thing that came to her mind: she gathered her children and dashed into the innermost room of the house, where she began to chant the Daimoku. For about an hour, the gang of hooldums broke windows and jeered, while the priest's small family chanted and waited.

At last, to Mrs. Hisakawa's great relief, the mob went away, shouting triumphantly. On the following morning, after no sleep, she tried to clean up the broken glass and debris. She entertained the idea of reporting the raid to the police, but decided to wait until she had talked the matter over with her husband, who was due home on the twentieth.

But, as she was about to go to bed that night, the mob returned and took up the attack again, breaking what few windowpanes remained intact. Mrs. Hisakawa, who had been chanting the Daimoku, felt that things had gone too far. After instructing her children to remain in concealed, protected corners, she went swiftly to the back door and, under the cover of virtually complete darkness, ran to the village police station as fast as her legs would carry her. The local police reported to their headquarters, which immediately sent a riot squad.

Before long, a siren was heard wailing in the distance. At the sound, the gang of parishioners turned tail and scattered in all directions. By the time the five-man riot squad arrived at the Hisakawa house, there was no one there but the priest's children.

During their investigation, the police collected stones and shattered glass as evidence. Then, moving out into the grounds, they were astounded to find hanging from an electric-power pole near the temple a life-size straw effigy of Hisakawa with about ten bamboo spears stuck in it.

On the twentieth, in their battered house, Mrs. Hisakawa wept as she told her husband what had happened. He praised her for the bravery with which she had stood up under the frightening ordeal, but she said that all her strength and protection had come from the Gohonzon and from chanting the Daimoku. Hisakawa went to the main hall and began a long Gongyo service. As he knelt, it suddenly dawned on him that this was the one hundredth day since January 8—the bitter cold day when the trouble had reached a head—and he recalled a passage from Nichiren Daishonin's *On the Buddha's Behavior*, in which it is said:"Then you will have to face the punishment of Bonten and Taishaku, the gods of the sun and the moon, and the Four Heavenly Kings. One hundred days after my exile or execution, and again on the first, third, and seventh anniversary, there will occur what the sutras call 'internal strife'—rebellions in your clan."

On that very same day, because of the abundance of the evidence, the police had no choice but to interrogate every member of the gang who had caused the disturbance and to request Hisakawa, as the victim of the violence, to make a deposition. Though the parishioners had not wanted it to happen, the affair was now in the hands of the law-enforcing authorities. Weak with fear of what would happen to them and to their families if they were charged with criminal offenses, they requested influential people in the village to intercede with the police to have the charges dropped. But this was impossible.

On April 30, in the name of High Priest Nissho Mizutani, the Administration Bureau of the head temple Taiseki-ji expressed full approval of Hisakawa's request for permission to excommunicate the parishioners who had rebelled over the removal of the Jizo statue. Representatives of the Soka Gakkai Youth Division showed their support of Hisakawa by making a two-day visit to the village and informing the parishioners of their expulsion from the parish. This put an end to the Myofuku-ji temple incident. But it should be said here that many of the parishioners who were expelled on this occasion later repented and, making a fresh start as members of Soka Gakkai, devoted themselves to the practice and protection of true Buddhism.

3. A STEADY PACE

IN JANUARY, 1953, the number of families converted to Nichiren Shoshu reached the surprising figure of 2,600, or four times the figure for January of the preceding year. The organizational shuffle that Toda had initiated at the beginning of the year continued, as Hiroshi Izumida was relieved by Koji Morikawa of his extra duty as chief of the Finance Department, as new chiefs were appointed to the women's divisions of the Bunkyo and Shiki chapters, and as district officers of the Koiwa, Osaka, Sendai, Nakano, and Shiki chapters were changed.

In that same month, Toda started a round of visits to important chapters to pave the way for the forthcoming nationwide summer membership campaign. On January 31, he visited Osaka to present the chapter with a new flag. Osaka, the second largest city in the country at the time, was important to Soka Gakkai, even though its chapter was still not fully developed. They were readying for a full-fledged forward drive and had converted five hundred households in the preceding six months.

Some people can accomplish in a few days what others require ten days to do. Although he was in Osaka for only two days on this occasion, Toda carried out a dizzying round of duties, including lectures on the *Gosho*, discussion meetings, personal guidance, and other activities. Being aware of the large number of people who lived in the city and of the unhappiness and ignorance of true Buddhism in which most of them lived, Toda proposed that the chapter members struggle together to banish misfortune, poverty, and illness from Osaka and to put their chapter on a level with the chapters in Tokyo.

On the final day of his stay, after he had presented the new flag, and when he saw that some free time still remained, he gave the assembled group a stirring lecture on the *Hoben* chapter of the Lotus Sutra. This presentation, which made the living philosophy of true Buddhism accessible to ordinary people, uplifted the members of the audience and provided them with an unshakable basis on which to cultivate faith and religious practice. They pleaded with Toda to give a similar lecture on his next visit. He willingly promised to do so. Until the very last minute on the train platform, members of the Osaka chapter thronged around Toda, singing Soka Gakkai songs.

A pilot at the controls of a complicated organization, Toda was indefatigable. In March, he traveled to the well-established Sendai Chapter, which was older than the Osaka Chapter. He delivered a lecture on the Three Great Secret Laws and called on the members to devote themselves as followers of the Bodhisattvas of the Earth to the cause of Kosen-rufu. The questions in the succeeding question-and-answer session impressed him with the high level of study and knowledge they revealed. Though his two-day stay in Sendai was packed with discussion meetings, private interviews, and personal guidance, he found time to give detailed attention to the wedding of a local district chief and a leading member of the Young Women's Division.

At the end of the month, he flew to Kyushu to present a new flag to the Yame Chapter, in Yame County, Fukuoka Prefecture. Since the time of the first president, Tsunesaburo Makiguchi, this small chapter had continued to operate mainly due to the efforts of the Tayama family. Makiguchi had always made the home of this family his basis of operation during his frequent guidance visits. In the summer of 1952, the Soka Gakkai membership campaign increased the Yame Chapter to 200 households. But no able new leaders had been forthcoming, and Toda had left the chief position in the hands of Mrs. Mitsuyo Tayama, to whom he presented the flag. He then held a guidance meeting that seemed to reinvigorate the entire chapter.

On the way back to Tokyo, he stopped for three days at Osaka for discussion meetings, guidance on personal as well as religious problems, the first meeting of three hundred staff members, and finally the promised lecture on the *Juryo* chapter of the Lotus Sutra.

In Tokyo, as well as in the outlying chapters, Toda was busy. On February 15, he attended the second general meeting of the Shiki Chapter, held at the Kawagoe Civic Hall, in Saitama Prefecture; on March 1, the second general meeting of the Tsurumi Chapter, attended by a thousand members, including some from Fukushima and Gumma prefectures; and, on March 15, the second general meeting of the Koto General Chapter, including members from the Koiwa, Hongo, Mukojima, and Joto chapters.

The unity between master and disciples was shown by these meetings to be growing stronger daily. In comparison with the general meetings of previous years, the ones held in 1953 were characterized by zeal and organizational solidity and by a steady, serious response to everything Toda had to say. Gone was the frenzied, excessive excitement of former years, and in its place was resolution to move steadily toward attainment of Kosen-rufu.

Toda's vision for 1953 was beginning to materialize, as the number of converted households exceeded 3,500 for February and March. He expressed his heartfelt gratitude in the speech he made at the monthly leaders' meeting in March, which was held at the Education Hall.

"In spite of your tendencies to be disobedient, temperamental, greedy, and unintelligent, I love all of you as if you were my own children. Your sincerity truly moves me. Nichiren Daishonin is constantly observing you; and, if you carry out your efforts to save the masses and to bring peace to the world, you will be rewarded, no matter whether or not other people pay attention to the meritorious things you do. In matters of faith, it is essential to take a long-range view and to see everything in proper historical perspective. You may be content that your rewards will be forthcoming as long as your efforts are sincere. Tonight, let me thank you for what you have done to increase our membership."

With these words, Toda, their leader—who often seemed blunt or gruff of speech, but whose love and concern for all underlay his every word—bowed in deep gratitude to the assembly of followers of the Bodhisattvas of the Earth.

The Young Men's Division now numbered 2,000 members. When it had been founded only eighteen months ago, on a day of torrential rain, there had been a mere 180 members. All of the men had worked hard, sometimes going without food and sleep, to expand the division; and the results of their efforts showed at the first general meeting held in the Education Hall on April 19.

On this occasion, the usual testimonials were replaced by presentations of thirteen scholarly reports by young men who had studied subjects ranging from the Nichiren Shoshu object of worship to Christianity, communism, nationalism, and revolution, as well as other religions and philosophies, and the mission of the Young Men's Division in terms of world history. Toda's face betrayed his pleasure at these discourses when he addressed the group of about seven hundred selected young men.

"Your papers were most impressive. If the late president Makiguchi were alive to hear them, he would be very moved. I am very deeply moved by the very thought of his presence.

"People my age and the ages of your parents tend to be conservative. You young people are the progressives. And it is your ardor and progressiveness that will determine the fate of mankind."

He went on to show that youth had played the most important role in spreading all of the leading philosophies and religions, including the teachings of Sakyamuni, Jesus Christ, Marx, and Lenin. Young people have always been the motivating force for great changes in world history, and they will be the leaders in the transformation of Japan through the propagation of the true Buddhism. In the next section of his talk, Toda showed that Buddhism, far from being opposed to scientific thought, has its own splendid scientific learning.

"Buddhism is the highest of all philosophical investigations of ways to make man happy. The Gohonzon, the embodiment of the fundamental force of the universe, shows how to apply philosophy to daily life and how to change human destiny."

Then he made comments on communism and capitalism and said that he had no preference between them since both are related only to the political and economic aspects of human life. "Our supremely important philosophy of life transcends politics and economics. The happiness we can bring through our religious philosophy has a timeless value. It surpasses communism and capitalism, which are ephemeral. It will guide all branches of science in the future, and you will be leaders in the movement."

Appointed leaders of the philosophy of life destined to bring happiness to humanity, the young men were stirred with dignity and pride and with a sense of mission. They realized that pure, enduring faith and perseverence toward self-improvement are essential to the noble attainment of Kosen-rufu.

When the affair of the heretical priest Jiko Kasahara, which had caused a storm of controversy within Nichiren Shoshu for six months, finally ended with a letter of admonition to Kasahara from the high priest, Toda immediately requested and received permission to repair the long-neglected, five-story pagoda at Taiseki-ji. He then solicited donations from the membership for the work. Six months later, restored to its original splendor, the tower rose in vermilion and green majesty among the fresh verdure of the surrounding forest. All of the buildings in the head temple compound face south except for the pagoda, which traditionally faces west in symbolic representation of the belief that true Buddhism will spread from the east to the west. The pagoda was physical evidence of the ardent wish of Toda and his followers to protect and spread the Supreme Law.

On April 28, Toda and about thirty-five hundred Soka Gakkai members hastened to the head temple to participate in a two-day memorial service to celebrate the completion of the reconstruction of the pagoda. Toda arrived at seven-thirty in the evening and went directly to attend a meeting of eight hundred members of the Young Men's Division at the temple Myoren-ji, about a mile from the head temple. The enthusiastic young men greeted Toda with a chorus of the song "A Star Falls in the Autumn Wind on Wu-chang Plain." Section chief Kazumasa Morikawa conducted the informal meeting, at which much of the conversation centered on reminiscences of the night one year earlier, when the same young men had exacted an apology from Jiko Kasahara for his malicious war-time connivances with the militarists and for his attempts to impose heretical teachings on the faithful of Nichiren Shoshu. Toda explained to the group that the true significance of the Kasahara incident lay in its demonstration of the way in which the true Buddhism will prevail over heresy. The hour-long meeting of question-and-answer discussion flew by. At its conclusion, the young men put Toda on an improvised palanquin, and sixteen chosen members carried it toward the head temple. They sang about Wu-chang plains as they walked along, and their voices echoed toward the lower slopes of Mount Fuji, soaring darkly in a veil of moonlit spring mist.

At the main gate, six hundred members of the Young Women's Division met the procession and joined in the singing. Toda got off the improvised palanquin, only to have to get on it again to be carried to the Treasure Temple. Though he was exhausted from overwork and in ill health, he did not allow anyone around him to know that this was the case. In front of the Treasure Temple, he got off, knelt in silent prayer, then turned to the young people and said: "I am deeply touched by the way you have carried me all this way. I want to take this chance to renew my often repeated pledge of dedication of my life to the cause of Nichiren Shoshu and the universal propagation of the true Law and to express my hope that you will share my determination and march forward with me toward the supreme goal."

A great shout of "We're with you always, Mr. Toda!" soared through the giant cryptomeria cedars and into the night sky.

When he returned to his room in the Rikyobo lodgings, though totally exhausted, Toda was exhilarated. The response of the young people in front of the Treasure Temple (where the Dai-Gohonzon was enshrined at that time) reassured him that, though it would require decades, the great task of achieving Kosen-rufu would be accomplished. Moreover, Shin'ichi's first son had been born that very day. Though they had been together all day, they had had no chance to share their happiness.

Shin'ichi alone knew of Toda's exhausted state. Not wanting to tire him further, the young man started to leave, but Toda stopped him: "Don't go yet. Stay a little longer."

"But you're so tired."

"A few minutes more won't make any difference. After all, we've got something to celebrate."

Taking out a brush and opening the folding fan he always carried, Toda wrote a short poem on it.

"A misty spring moon
Shares my happiness
Over the birth of
A child."

At the splendid ceremonies on the following day, after Gongyo and the Daimoku, the high priest read a message of congratulations and glorification and gave Toda a letter of appreciation. After still further congratulatory messages, Toda took the rostrum.

"The attainment of Kosen-rufu, the sole aim of Soka Gakkai, is of paramount importance today, because the peoples of Japan and of the entire Orient suffer in the depths of misery from which we must save them. The restoration of the pagoda is only a small contribution to the cause. I am embarrassed to be so warmly thanked and praised for having done so little. But I am prepared to do ten thousand times this much. And I ask all members of Soka Gakkai to share my resolution and to continue our fight for the worldwide spreading of true Buddhism."

A wind that had risen during his talk carried Toda's words to all corners of the temple. Toda reflected that Nichiren Shoshu was now standing firm and ready for a great forward leap. As he thought of the things that had happened in the year since the seven-hundredth anniversary, he saw that, though still modest, the results of the efforts of the society held great promise of steady future growth.

4. INTERPRETATION
FOR OUR TIMES

CREATIVITY of the highest kind set Josei Toda apart from the general run of human beings. It is true that he can be conveniently put in a number of categories—educator, businessman, man of religion, leader of the masses—but his creative originality was so great that he transcended all categories. Many people have abilities and marked traits of character, but Toda was truly rare. And even more rare was his ability to put his creative powers to practical use in great accomplishments. In the search for the source of the basic characteristic in Toda's personality, inevitably the sublime, solemn moment of enlightenment he experienced in a prison cell during World War II must be stressed. He often spoke about that mysterious moment, which was the result of intensive readings of the Lotus Sutra. It changed everything for him in the latter part of his life. But the actual reading of the sutra, though important, was only an expedient. The nature of the enlightenment itself was the attainment of correct understanding of Nam-myoho-renge-kyo, the essence of Sakyamuni's Lotus Sutra as distilled by Nichiren Daishonin in the *Ongi Kuden*.

When he was enlightened to the great truth of Nam-myoho-renge-kyo, the scales fell from Toda's eyes. The sufferings and difficulties of the first half of his life were settled. With complete lucidity, he saw the joyful future and his own tremendous misson: Kosen-rufu, the universal propagation of faith in the true Buddhism and the salvation of all mankind.

Upon his release from prison, Toda set out to share this great experience, the source of his own creative originality, with other people and to use it in the reconstruction of Soka Gakkai, which had largely dispersed, owing to persecutions by the militarist war-time government, and which had suffered deeply because of the loss of the first president, Tsunesaburo Makiguchi (who had died in prison, where he had been thrown because of the strength of his pacifistic principles and his religious faith).

At first, Toda concentrated on lectures dealing with the Lotus Sutra. Though, in the beginning, he had only four people in his audience, gradually the number increased. In spite of Toda's eagerness to have them understand, his first students were immature and needed a great deal of help. To assist them, Toda called on commentaries written by scholars of the Tendai sect to clarify points in the sutra. But this policy had the bad effect of coloring everything he had to say with the Tendai philosophy instead of the teachings of Nichiren Daishonin. For this deviation Toda was punished with business failure.

But hardship only helped him see where he had been wrong and to make amends. After 1951, when he was inaugurated as the second president of Soka Gakkai, all of his lectures were completely free of Tendai influence. Once he had returned to the *Ongi Kuden* of Nichiren Daishonin for reference and enlightenment, he was able to institute a new series of lectures with total confidence.

These lectures uplifted and invigorated his audiences, because they were delivered from the standpoint that true Buddhism and the actual life of today are one and the same thing.

Toda had the innate, uncanny ability to go directly to the hearts of his listeners and to explain the most abstruse Buddhist terminology in a way that was absolutely clear and understandable. In this way he opened their formerly blind eyes to the truth. It was—as he often said himself—his mystical experience in prison that enabled him—and only him—to waken the force of universal life that is embodied in Nam-myoho-renge-kyo and is latent in all people.

The original series of lectures had dealt with the Lotus Sutra chapter by chapter, from beginning to end. In the new series, Toda adopted the difficult, but more promising, plan of concentrating on two vitally important chapters: "Expedience" (*Hoben*) and "Measuring the Merits of the Tathagata" (*Juryo*). Those two chapters are of particular importance to an understanding not only of the life of Josei Toda but of the true meaning of Nichiren Shoshu philosophy.

As the popularity of the lectures on the chapter called "Expedience" increased, the meeting place was changed from time to time, until finally it was necessary to use the newly-completed Toshima Public Hall, which held up to two thousand people. One evening in that auditorium, Toda, seated behind the speaker's desk, on which there was nothing but a microphone and a pitcher of water, startled his audience with a bold opening statement: "The difference between the Buddhism of Nichiren Daishonin and the Buddhism of Sakyamuni is immense. What is this difference? The following passage in the *Ongi Kuden* gives the answer."

Noticing that very few people in the audience had copies of the *Gosho* with them, Toda said, "I suppose you think the *Gosho* is too expensive. But remember, once you have one, it is with you for the rest of your life. It does not change with fashions, the way law books do. Trying to study the doctrines of true Buddhism without a copy of the *Gosho* is like being a samurai without a sword."

His light humor put the audience at ease. Toda always used

similar techniques to relax his listeners and to prepare them for what he had to say. Mrs. Tame Izumida, who sat on the platform next to him, read the pertinent passage from the *Ongi Kuden*.

"About the chapter 'Measuring the Merits of the Tathagata Who Devotes Himself to Nam-myoho-renge-kyo,' chapter sixteen of the Sutra of the Lotus of the Supreme Law. As is said in the ninth volume of *Hokke Mongu*, the term 'Tathagata' is an ordinary word for all the Buddhas of the universe and the three worlds of past, present, and future, the two Buddhas, the three Buddhas, the true Buddha, and Buddhas in their transient manifestations. The chapter on 'Measuring the Merits of the Tathagata' is so called because it sets forth all the merits of all the Buddhas of the entire universe and the three worlds of past, present, and future.

"According to the oral teachings of Nichiren Daishonin, the title of this chapter is vitally related to Nichiren Daishonin himself and pertains to the contents of the chapter entitled 'Divine Powers.' The term 'Tathagata' represents Sakyamuni and all of the Buddhas of the universe and the three worlds of past, present, and future. In particular, it means the fundamental embodiment of the Buddha: the three bodies of the Buddha.* According to the opinion of Nichiren Daishonin and his disciples, today the term 'Tathagata' is interpreted to mean all sentient beings, but especially the followers of Nichiren Daishonin. If this is true, the triple body of the Buddha, the fundamental embodiment of the Buddha, is equated with the faithful votaries of the Lotus Sutra in the Mappo era. And the glorious name of the fundamental and triple body of the Buddha is Nam-myoho-renge-kyo. This is the essence of the content explained in the words 'three important things.' "

At the conclusion of the reading of this difficult passage, the members of the audience were confused. Seeing this, Toda at once set out to make things clear for them.

"Before I deal with this wondrous revelation, let me bring to your attention an important point of caution. There are many commentaries on the Lotus Sutra, but all of those that depend on Tendai doctrines only and fail to take into consideration what is said in the *Ongi Kuden,* the oral teachings of Nichiren Daishonin, are worthless. I had an unpleasant experience myself when I tried to teach the Lotus Sutra through Tendai teachings. The danger is great of a person's orally professing allegiance to Nichiren Shoshu while mentally being overly influenced by Tendai doctrines. As Nikko Shonin, the founder of Taiseki-ji, says in his 'Twenty-six Articles of Admonition,' 'Without complete understanding of the teachings, do not study Tendai

*The three bodies or natures of the Buddha are the essential eternal body, the body gained as a reward for past merits, and the transformation body, by means of which the Buddha can assume any form he needs for the omnipresent salvation of other creatures.

doctrines. Believers must concentrate on the *Gosho*, and only when they have free time should they listen to Tendai teachings.'

"On the basis of my own experience, I advise you not to read Tendai. Of course, I doubt that you would read the teachings, even if I told you to. And I further doubt that you would understand them if you read them. The best thing to do is to stay away from them and, if anyone asks why, tell them that I told you to.

"I am the only lay person alive today who can lecture without mistake on the nature of the Lotus Sutra, and I do so on the basis of a thorough knowledge of the true Buddhism of Nichiren Daishonin. In your study of the sutra, you must concentrate on the explanations found in the *Ongi Kuden* and in the *Kechimyaku-sho* (Treatises of the Lineage) of Nichiren Daishonin. The passage quoted by Mrs. Izumida from the *Ongi Kuden* is the basis of this lecture on the chapters 'Expedience' and 'Measuring the Merits of the Tathagata.'

"Earlier I said that there is a great difference between the Buddhism of Sakyamuni and that of Nichiren Daishonin. I shall now explain what I mean. The title of the sixteenth chapter of the Lotus Sutra, as given by Sakyamuni, is 'On Measuring the Merits of the Tathagata of Myoho-renge-kyo' (the Sutra of the Lotus of the Supreme Law). The title as given by Nichiren Daishonin in the *Ongi Kuden* is, as you have already heard, 'On Measuring the Merits of the Tathagata of Nam-myoho-renge-kyo.' In Sakyamuni's title, the word 'Nam' (devotion) is missing. Nichiren Daishonin went to pains to add it, because he considered it very important. The Tathagata of mere Myoho-renge-kyo is superficial. The Tathagata of Nam-myoho-renge-kyo is the profound, essential Buddha. In other words, since Tathagata is an epithet for any Buddha—one who has come all the way and is enlightened—by adding the word 'Nam' to the name of this chapter, Nichiren Daishonin makes it clear that the Buddha of which he is speaking is not the same as the one Sakyamuni had in mind. 'Measuring the Merits of the Tathagata' means estimating the immense merits of the fundamental, profound Buddha of the Mappo era.

"No matter what religious sect he may belong to, any person who reads the *Ongi Kuden* thoroughly must clearly see the difference between the Buddhism of Nichiren Daishonin and that of Sakyamuni. But all too many people do not see this difference, simply because they lack the Gohonzon.

" 'The triple body of the Buddha, the fundamental embodiment of the Buddha, is equated with the faithful votaries of the Lotus Sutra in the Mappo era.' This is a tremendously important passage. The fundamental and true embodiment of the Buddha, which has never been created by anyone, is a unity of the eternal body, the reward body granted for past merits, and the transformation body. The *Ongi Kuden* says that this fundamental embodiment is the same thing as the faithful votaries of the Lotus Sutra in the Mappo era. There can be no doubt whatsoever that, in saying this, Nichiren Daishonin had himself in mind.

" 'And the glorious name of the fundamental and triple body of the Buddha is Nam-myoho-renge-kyo.' This means that the Tathagata, the fundamental Buddha of the Mappo era, is none other than Nichiren Daishonin. 'And these are the three important things of the chapter "On Measuring the Merits of the Tathagata of Nam-myoho-renge-kyo." ' This means that what has been said about the Buddha of the Mappo era is the foundation of the Three Great Secret Laws. I have gone to some length over this point, because I want you firmly to understand and to remember that the Tathagata I am discussing in these lectures is Nichiren Daishonin, the true Buddha of the Mappo era.

"Now I shall discuss the chapter 'Expedience.' Some people say that lies can be expedient. The expedience treated in true Buddhism had nothing to do with—and can have nothing to do with—such an attitude.

"In Buddhist terminology, expedience refers to three methods of teaching the true Law. The first expedient method (*hoyu*) is designed to lead to Buddhism someone who has no knowledge or experience of it. The second expedient method (*notsu*) consists in telling the person who has been led by the initial method that the Buddhism to which he has been introduced is not the true Buddhism. He is then ready for the third method, which is instruction in the Lotus Sutra. This expedient is called *himyo*, which means that it is secret, or known only to the Buddha, and wondrous, in a way incomprehensible to ordinary human intelligence. The wonderful truth of *himyo* teaching is that all ordinary people are Buddhas; that is, that they have the Buddha nature inherent in them. This is a revolutionary idea, even within Buddhism, since all of the sutras preached before the Lotus Sutra had treated the Buddha and all other sentient beings as distinctly different. In the *Ongi Kuden*, Nichiren Daishonin explains this on the basis of several illustrative parables found in the Lotus Sutra."

Toda then discussed the parable of the rich man and his son, in the fourth chapter—"Understanding Faith"—and the parable of the man who labored desperately for a living because he was unaware that he possessed a priceless jewel, in the eighth chapter —"The Five Hundred Disciples Receive Predictions." Through these tales, Toda made it clear to his listeners that only the Buddha knows the true meaning of life, but that, on the basis of correct and powerful faith, it is possible to experience a human revolution and to alter fate. Everyone in the room was compelled to see that this was true in the daily experience of life and that the knowledge held great promise for the future. Toda continued by having Mrs. Izumida read the opening of the chapter, "Expedience." Everyone was familiar with the text, since it is part of the Gongyo service that each performs every morning.

"At that time, the World-Honored One, who had been in deep meditation, quietly arose. He then said to Śāriputra, 'The wisdom of all the Buddhas is indeed profound and infinite.' "

"The entire meaning of the text," said Toda, "depends on the way in which we interpret the words 'at that time.' This phrase is not a reference to an hour, a season, or a year. It is certainly nothing like the "once upon a time" of fables and fairy tales. In the sutra, 'at that time' means the time when sentient beings were eager to have the Buddha preach them a sermon and when the Buddha appeared and fulfilled their request. Just as a product sells when there is an eager market for it, so the Law of the Buddha spread because sentient beings were longing for it. The meaning of 'at that time,' then, is 'at the right time.' It is the time when Sakyamuni preached the first part of the Lotus Sutra."

Next Toda explained the two ways in which Buddhism may be interpreted: the *kyoso* (literal) method, or the interpretation in the light of the teachings of Sakyamuni; and the *kanjin* (essential) method, or the true interpretation in the light of the teachings of Nichiren Daishonin. He showed that the tendency today is for the general public to adopt the literal method, to consider Buddhism to be limited to the teachings of Sakyamuni, and to remain ignorant of the truth that Nichiren Daishonin's Buddhism has been established not only for the present but also for the everlasting future.

"Now let us examine this passage, first from the literal and then from the essential standpoint. Read in the literal fashion, 'at that time' means the time when people attained Buddhahood through the arduous stages of self-development, leading through the ten stages to the stages called Learning and Absorption, which precede the Bodhisattva stage. At that time, the World-Honored One, Sakyamuni of the first half of the Lotus Sutra, arose quietly from deep meditation and turned to Śāriputra, one of his ten (or twenty-one, according to some reckonings) leading disciples and reputedly the wisest man in India.

"Interpreted in the essential fashion, however, the passage reveals a quite different content. It goes like this. 'In the Mappo era, the World-Honored One embodying the fundamental and hidden universal law, Nichiren Daishonin, rose quietly from deep meditation in the Lotus—that is, from the essence of the universal life-force that has no beginning and no end—and turned to Śāriputra . . . ' Just as the Śāriputra of Sakyamuni's time was the wisest man in India, so that person to whom Nichiren Daishonin, the Buddha of the Mappo era, addresses himself is the wisest of that era. And that means each one of us. Perhaps we are not all that wise in ourselves, but our faith in the Gohonzon gives us the wisdom of the Gohonzon; and that is greater than the wisdom of Śāriputra. The extent of our wisdom depends on the strength of our faith. So you see, if you have faith, you are not so stupid after all.

" 'The wisdom of all the Buddhas is indeed profound and infinite.' Now, in all nine—or twelve, as is sometimes said— parts of all his teaching except the Lotus Sutra, Sakyamuni employed a dialogue method, in which he answered questions put to him by others. He never initiated a sermon. In the second chapter of the Lotus Sutra, 'Expedience,' however, he speaks up in praise of the wisdom of all the Buddhas without anyone's having addressed a remark to him. This must have been surprising—indeed, later Śāriputra asks him why he extols the wisdom of the Buddhas without being asked about it.

"In the literal reading, this passage means that the wisdom of the Buddhas is profound, in that it penetrates to the ultimate depths of truth, and is infinite, in that it extends throughout the universe of the Law. In spatiotemporal philosophical terms, this means that the wisdom is temporally profound and spatially infinite. It permeates all space and time. From the essential viewpoint, on the other hand, the only wisdom that can be profound and infinite is Nam-myoho-renge-kyo.

" 'The way of their wisdom is difficult to understand and hard to enter. Neither those who have heard and heeded the Buddha directly nor those who have attempted to attain Buddhahood on their own can understand it.' If the wisdom of the Buddhas is this difficult, it cannot save the unenlightened masses. Obviously, Buddhism interpreted in this way has remained the affair of aristocrats and learned intellectuals. But, in the essential interpretation of Nichiren Daishonin, the way of wisdom is the way of faith.

"Faith, too, is difficult to understand and difficult to enter. Those of us who attempt to win other people to Nichiren Shoshu know exactly how hard it is to acquire faith. But the way of wisdom is the way of faith, because faith, once attained, becomes wisdom.

"Sakyamuni taught that even those people who had been close to him and had heard the teachings directly from him and those who had striven to attain enlightenment on their own and for their own sakes only could not understand the wisdom of the Buddhas. Essentially this means that understanding comes only with faith. People today who feel that they are enlightened because of a superficial knowledge of philosophy and science correspond to the two classes that Sakyamuni said could not understand. Members of the intellectual class tend to fall readily into such mistaken security in assumed enlightenment. For the way of wisdom of the Buddhas is indeed difficult to understand and to enter.

"I am by no means totally opposed to science. On the other hand, I cannot sanction the notion that science is the answer to everything. It is true that scientific knowledge has done much good by providing us with comfort and conveniences. On the other hand, it has done great harm by producing such monstrosities as nuclear weapons. I reject the notion that scientific development alone brings happiness. And there are other people who see things my way, though at present mapping a suitable course of action is difficult.

"True happiness is possible only on the basis of a true life philosophy, our philosophy as embodied in the Gohonzon. Truly worshiping the Gohonzon brings us into a state of harmonious union with the object of worship and the reward in such a state is true happiness. Those who pursue scientific knowledge and learning blindly correspond to the people in the chapter 'Expedience' who heard the teachings directly from Sakyamuni and who sought Buddhahood for themselves alone. They will never enter the way of wisdom and will consequently remain unhappy.

"People whose minds are attuned only to intellectual pursuits find it difficult to give themselves fully to faith, as they must if they are to find true happiness. For instance, a friend who is a popular novelist once came to me in despair. His child was near death, and he was at a loss to know what to do. I suggested that he chant the Daimoku, and he took my advice. But, to perform the chanting, he locked himself in his study. This is not a demonstration of faith. How is it possible to be embarrassed or shy about Nam-myoho-renge-kyo? The more a person is given to theorizing and rational thought, the more difficult he finds it to enter the realm of faith. Should you encounter such a person, I want you to try to convince him of the truth of our Buddhist faith. But you must not threaten or say things to cause adverse emotional reactions."

At the completion of this exposition of the chapter "Expedience," Toda's audience was well on the way to understanding clearly the distinction between the literal interpretation and the essential interpretation of Buddhism. The lecture on the chapter entitled "Measuring the Merits of the Tathagata" took four sessions. During it, their understanding of this point was perfected.

"In both the literal and the essential interpretations, there are objects of worship," said Toda at the beginning of his lecture series on this part of the sutra. "For those who accept the literal interpretation, the objects of worship are the usual statues of Sakyamuni, Amida, and other Buddhas and Bodhisattvas. But these objects are useless in the Mappo era. In our time, the only object of worship that can become a source of abundant life-force and later human karma is the essential object of worship: the Gohonzon.

"In the first part of this chapter there is a line that, in the literal version of Tendai Buddhism says, 'Since I became a

Buddha.' This is generally accepted to mean since Sakyamuni became a Buddha. The essential interpretation of Nichiren Daishonin is different. According to it, the text means, 'When by myself, I attained the three bodies of the Buddha (essential body, reward body, and transformation body).' The essential body is the basic life-force that is a condition for Buddhahood. The reward body represents the wisdom of the Buddhas that we ordinary creatures can receive. Nichiren Daishonin appeared in this world in his transformation body and during his mission attained the other two bodies. And, for this reason, the essential interpretation of this passage, is, as I have explained it: 'When, by myself, I attained the three bodies of the Buddha.'

"To make it easier to understand, I can relate these three bodies to myself—as they can be related to any of us. My universal or essential body is the entity or life-force that I represent. My limited abilities to lecture on the Lotus Sutra are my reward body—or my wisdom. And my physical body, which is now fifty-three years old, is my transformation body. Nichiren Daishonin said that every person can attain these three bodies on his own by chanting Daimoku to the Dai-Gohonzon. This is as it must be. Buddhahood cannot be taught. Though a person who has studied the Lotus Sutra and the Law asks me to teach him Buddhahood, it cannot be done. But, as Nichiren Daishonin says, if we worship the essential Gohonzon and chant the Daimoku faithfully, we can all attain the three bodies in one. And this is the meaning of the lines from the chapter 'Measuring the Merits of the Tathagata':

" 'Countless ages have passed. I have taught and led to the way of Buddhahood countless creatures. For the sake of saving sentient creatures, I have taught Nirvana. But I have done so as an expedient. And I myself have not entered Nirvana but remain here, always teaching.'

"In the essential reading, this passage means that the existence of Nichiren Daishonin in the unified three bodies of Buddhahood has continued infinitely with the universe. He was not born a Buddha only seven centuries ago. He did not attain Buddhahood through studying at the monasteries of Mount Hiei. He has existed with the universe. Like it, he has no beginning but has always taught the Law.

"Life-force is eternal. But, if this is the case, what is the need for death? In the Nirvana Sutra, Maha-kasyapa, one of Sakyamuni's leading disciples, asks: 'You have taught us that life is eternal. But now you must die. Have you taught us something untrue?' Life is eternal, and Nirvana is an expedient. The Tendai interpretation is that Sakyamuni had to teach Nirvana in order to give sentient creatures a reward to strive for. But this is unconvincing.

"Death is essential. Furthermore, it is part of the Supreme Law that we be ignorant of the hour of our deaths. Dying is part of the system, like aging. When a person reaches the age of seventy and his work in this world is over, it is time to die. The life-force manifest in him will return in another manifestation. It is one with the universe and has no beginning or end. But this return is not reincarnation. It is a continuation of life from the world of the present to the world of the future. I can illustrate my meaning in this way. Think of the stick of incense you light each day for Gongyo services. It gradually burns from a long stick to a short one. But no one would think of saying that the short stick is a reincarnation of the long one. Our life is beginningless and endless, like the universe of which it is a part. But Nirvana—that is, death—puts an end to one manifestation only to allow that life to return to this world renewed in different manifestations.

"In that remanifested life are contained all of the conditions carried over from previous manifestations. This is what is called karma, and explaining it is one of the most important principles of Buddhism.

"It is only human to ask why we should be held responsible for things that happened in previous lives when our own lives have been given fresh manifestation. But the fact is that we are responsible for them. Past karma is the cause of present fortune or misfortune. It is past karma that explains why some people are poor or unintelligent, whereas others are rich and clever; or why some fail in business, no matter how hard they try to succeed. Since life is continuous, we are responsible for past lives. If we fail to take this into consideration, we will be unable to solve the most important questions confronting us.

"Here is a simple illustration of this complicated issue. Science tells us that, in a relatively brief cycle, all the cells of the body are replaced by new ones. Physically speaking, a man is not the same man he was ten years ago. But, he is unlikely to to get away with evading debts on the grounds that he is not the man who contracted them since all of his cells are different. Similarly, though our life is born into a new manifestation, it is still responsible for the acts of past lives and will be responsible in the future for acts committed in the present life.

"This presents a grim practical picture. But there is something that can be done about it. Nichiren Daishonin said, 'You are lacking in virtue and are much defiled; but, if you worship the Gohonzon, all of your past misdeeds, no matter how wicked, will be absolved, and you will be rewarded as if you had done something good.' In other words, the important thing is deep faith to bring about a human revolution of the life-force at its deepest level. Many of you are not wealthy. This means that you may have been thieves in previous lives. (Maybe there are a lot of former thieves in this room.) But Nichiren Daishonin says that, if you worship the true Gohonzon of the essential interpretation, all of your past evil will be removed; and you will enjoy as great a reward as if you had given a large amount of money to charity. But he insists that the revolution depends on the intensity of your faith.

"Now I return to the still unanswered question: If life is eternal, why must we die? The Lotus Sutra says Nirvana is 'an expedient, but actually I have not entered Nirvana but am always here teaching.' In short, death does not exist. The

Buddha is always here preaching in this world of hardships and endurance. But for us, teaching takes the form of constant striving for the sake of spreading faith in the true Buddhism. That is our sutra. The loftiest sutras, however, are those uttered by the Buddha.''

When a lecture went well and ended somewhat early, Toda always welcomed questions and dealt with each one thoroughly. One evening, a man in his thirties, wearing glasses and dressed in a frayed suit, said—in a voice that showed he had worried about the question for some time—: "The passage on 'Instructions to the Adherents of the Fuji Sect' in the *Gosho* says that Nikko Shonin severed ties with five senior priests for several reasons. One was their tendency to regard the Gohonzon as nothing but a mandala and to bury it with the dead. The collected letters of Nichiren Daishonin show the great value he put on the Gohonzon. Why should these senior priests, who had been trained directly by Nichiren Daishonin, have handled the Gohonzon inscribed by him so carelessly?''

Thanking the man and smiling, Toda explained: "Those five priests did not actually study long enough with Nichiren Daishonin. They were devoted to him and were so eager that they started immediately to try to spread faith in Nam-myoho-renge-kyo. They did not take sufficient time to learn the supreme doctrine directly from Nichiren Daishonin. Furthermore, like most other Buddhist scholars in their day, these five men tended to interpret the Lotus Sutra in the literal fashion.

Nichiren Daishonin first allowed Nam-myoho-renge-kyo to sink in. Then, after he went to Sado, the Gohonzon emerged. These five men totally lacked understanding of the establishment of the Gohonzon after Nichiren Daishonin's trip to Sado. Only Nikko Shonin, founder of the head temple, who was true to the principle of constant service to his master (*jozuikyuji*) and who remained constantly at his side, understood the Gohonzon and its value.''

The discussion continued with a comparison between the present and the Kamakura period.

"Since means of transportation were primitive then, the Daishonin had a difficult time conducting guidance work. It was an age that had never heard of Nam-myoho-renge-kyo. People of such an age, even if they understood Myoho-renge-kyo, remained uninterested in it.

"These five men were pillars of the community in their regions. But, enlightened only to Nam-myoho-renge-kyo, they remained unenlightened to the Gohonzon. This is why Nikko Shonin scolded them, saying that if they understood Nam-myoho-renge-kyo there was no reason for them not to understand the Gohonzon.

"Nikko Shonin rebuked these priests, but he did not expel them from the sect. What they had done was shocking, but it was in line with religious customs at a time when images of Amida or other Buddhas were buried with the dead. Nikko Shonin had the Gohonzons collected and brought to him at once.

"To help you understand that the object of worship of Nichiren Shoshu is different from those of other religious sects, we urge all Soka Gakkai members to read Nichikan Shonin's *Sanju Hiden-sho* (Treatise on the Threefold Secret) in which these points are explained."

The man who had asked the question was not satisfied: "According to a biography of Nichiren Daishonin, two of the five priests—Nissho and Nichiro—accompanied Nichiren Daishonin on tours, during which a large number of people were converted. Furthermore, Nichiren Daishonin was extremely cautious about the kind of people to whom he gave Gohonzons. He considered the nun Oama Gozen unworthy. In his 'Reply to Nichinyo Gozen' and in 'The True Object of Worship,' he explains the doctrine of the Gohonzon in great detail. Today, even I do not find it impossible to understand.

Therefore, I cannot see how such distinguished followers as the five senior priests failed to understand it."

Toda replied, "Your question is fair and brings us to a very important point. During his lifetime, Nichiren Daishonin underwent severe persecutions. Though none of the men who were against him, including the high official Hei no Saemon and the regent, were awed by the presence of the great Buddha, when he died, suppression moved into a second, more virulent, phase. The five senior priests were actually so frightened for their lives that they tried to disclaim being disciples of Nichiren Daishonin and announced that they were followers of the Tendai sect."

Toda wanted to lay special stress on this historical incident and to point out possible parallels warning of future dangers. He delivered another series of lectures on the *Gosho* at about this time for the general membership and the staff. The meetings, open to everyone, came to be called the "Friday Night Lectures" and gained such overwhelming popularity that the Toshima Public Hall, where they were held, was always overflowing with people eager to hear what Toda had to say.

5. GUIDANCE AND GROWTH

THE YEAR 1953 was one of those crucial turning points that occur in the history of an organization—one of those relatively brief periods that are more important than decades, in terms of achievement and value. In that year, the fervor to increase the membership from 20,000 to 70,000 reached a peak. Toda, who knew that this goal had to be reached if his larger goal of a total membership of 750,000 households was to be attained during his lifetime, continued to exert utmost caution in planning and in selecting leaders. But, though enthusiasm produced startling results throughout the total organization, problems afflicted some of its parts.

For instance, the Kamata Chapter, the largest in the nation, had added members rapidly during the first three months of the year, but slowed down thereafter. The cause was the failure of the staff members to keep pace with chapter expansion. The situation was worse with the Bunkyo Chapter, which had fallen from a leading position to the level of the least rapidly growing chapter in the entire organization.

In 1952, Koichi Harayama was shifted from the post of chief of the Bunkyo Chapter to that of director of the Regional Supervision Department. Until that time, Mrs. Haruko Taoka had been a group chief in the Bunkyo Chapter and one of its most capable and effective leaders in membership campaigns. Indeed, she had sometimes brought into the organization almost half of the chapter's monthly total of new members. Toda had been keeping his eye on her.

Suddenly, one day, Toda called Mrs. Taoka to his office. "What do you think of the idea of becoming chief of the Bunkyo Chapter?" he asked her. All the way to the office, she had been running over in her mind the many questions and problems she wanted to discuss with Toda. She had not expected anything like this sudden offer of promotion. The responsibility seemed too great, but her hesitation only gave Toda the opening he wanted. "There, I know you can do it. It's all settled," he said. Mrs. Taoka was incredulous, but Toda remained calm and casual. He had so much confidence in her that he took her acceptance of the job for granted.

Although she decided that she would have to accept and do her best so as not to betray his confidence in her, Mrs. Taoka was worried. Would she, a woman, be able to fill the shoes of Koichi Harayama, one of the most efficient members of the entire staff?

Upon returning home, she immediately told her husband what had happened. Kin'ichi Taoka, a taciturn man, was a member of Soka Gakkai, but he devoted more time to his business affairs than to his religious life. When he heard that his wife had become chapter chief, he let the matter rest with no more than a remark to the effect that she had taken on too great a responsibility at a time when she already had enough to do. She replied, "I know it's too much for me. But Mr. Toda must have his reasons, and I must do the best I can. I hope you will help me." Kin'ichi, who did not share his wife's fervor for membership drives and other religious activities, remained noncommittal, saying only, "I don't know how much help I can be."

From the very next day, Mrs. Taoka began to work hard,

holding meetings with group and unit chiefs, discussing plans for chapter expansion, and conducting discussion meetings. But, no matter how hard she worked, she encountered one difficulty after another. The members would not cooperate with her, and her experience as acting chief was of little help.

While other chapters recorded phenomenal increases in membership, under her leadership, the Bunkyo Chapter made one of the worst showings of all Soka Gakkai chapters: sixty-nine familes in January, seventy in February, and—slightly better—eighty in March.

Mrs. Taoka was dejected and embarrassed when she attended a monthly leaders' meeting at the end of March. She wished the meeting would end as quickly as possible, but it was followed by a senior-officers' conference, where, as one of the few women, she suffered still greater embarrassment. Though her fellow chapter chiefs tried to cheer her, none of them had any good suggestions for revitalizing the Bunkyo Chapter.

Her success as a group chief had probably made Mrs. Taoka a little too optimistic about her chances as a chapter chief. Even though when she had accepted the post she had entertained misgivings, in the back of her mind she believed that the members would cooperate with her, enabling her to make a decent showing. But things had not turned out as she had expected. After a few months, she was a despondent failure, who alternately thought of suicide and blamed Toda for having put her in such an awkward position.

After the next meeting, Toda, who was never a man to overlook changes of the kind he observed in her, said to Mrs. Taoka, "Remember, I appointed you to the post, and I am still behind you. Don't let temporary defeats get you down, Haruko. Come to see me in a few days; we'll see what can be done."

A few days later, Mrs. Taoka went to the headquarters in Ichigaya. A woman of strong character and mental capacity, she was resigned to do whatever Toda ordered. She would listen to his reprimands and would then quit or continue in the post, according to his instructions.

At the conclusion of her lengthy explanation, without a word of blame or criticism, Toda gently said that he understood and that, though he could not come to her rescue himself because of his heavy schedule, he would send her one of his most trusted men, Shin'ichi Yamamoto, to help her and the chapter out of difficulty. Since she had barely ever heard the young man's name, Mrs. Taoka thanked Toda but without overwhelming enthusiasm. Noting this, Toda said, "Shin'ichi is not in the limelight yet. What he does is not widely reported. But he is highly intelligent and capable. More outstanding than anyone you have met. He has my fullest and deepest confidence. From the standpoint of faith, obey Shin'ichi and take his advice."

Finishing this brief remark, Toda suddenly asked, "How is your husband? Is his business running smoothly?" With a slight sense of guilt, she murmured that all was well. Toda said no more, but the matter of her husband's apparently flagging religious faith weighed on Mrs. Taoka's mind long after she returned home. Perhaps Toda had been suggesting that she would be a better chapter chief if she managed to persuade her husband to be more diligent and to assist her. Indeed, he had been no more than a spectator during her trials and defeats of the past few months; and she felt she should have done something to bring him to share her own ardor.

After careful consideration, on April 20, 1953, Toda made further personnel changes. Hisao Seki, chief of the Youth Division; Hiroshi Yamagiwa, chief of the Young Men's Division; and Kin'ya Takimoto, section chief, were appointed joint secretaries of the Kamata Chapter. As acting chief of the Bunkyo Chapter, Toda appointed twenty-five-year-old Shin'-ichi Yamamoto, who only three months earlier had been made first section chief. All four of these young men, who had been trained directly under Toda's own wing, were immeasurably valuable to him and were an immense support in all areas of membership campaigns.

In a few days, Shin'ichi attended a meeting of the Bunkyo Chapter group chiefs at the Taoka house. The way this meeting was conducted indicated the low condition to which chapter

spirit had dropped. Shin'ichi, who was unfamiliar with the neighborhood, had been ineptly directed and had lost his way. Though the meeting was scheduled for much earlier, when he still had not arrived by seven in the evening, the group chiefs sat dumbly waiting. It never occurred to any of them to go out in search of the wandering acting chief.

But, at length, the doorbell rang. Sensing immediately an air of dejection—perhaps brought on by poor recent achievements—Yamamoto set out to dispel it. "Well, I have been on a wild goose chase. I've stumbled around for hours looking for this house. It really is in a kind of labyrinth. I even went into somebody else's house thinking it was the right one. But no matter; I'm here now."

His bright voice and enthusiastic manner and the humor with which he related his embarrassment at the wrong door brought smiles and eased the tension.

Next Yamamoto officially opened the meeting by kneeling before the Gohonzon and chanting the Daimoku. The others joined in, but their voices were not in unison. Yamamoto stopped, rang the worship bell, and started again. Still the voices lacked life and did not blend with each other. Yamamoto started again and again, until finally union and vigor were achieved.

Lack of solidarity was Yamamoto's acute diagnosis of the stagnation and lackluster performance of the Bunkyo Chapter. And, as soon as he detected it, he at once let the group chiefs know in words that were stern though warm:

"In all struggles and in everything, including chanting the Daimoku, unity—togetherness—is the key to success. Once we are all together, our collective capacity multiplies, and we can perform unimaginable feats. Let's get together right now and set our immediate goal for this month at two hundred new households brought into the membership."

Everyone in the room was dumbfounded. Given their performance in the past few months, how could they convert this staggering number of new households—unless people from other chapters lent them a hand?

Yamamoto saw the incredulity on their faces and said, "I assure you, if you work together, act with determination and joy in your work, and do what I tell you, this goal is completely within your abilities."

He then turned to the surprised Mrs. Taoka and asked to be introduced to each of the people present.

When introductions were over, Shin'ichi Yamamoto engaged each person in individual conversation about group conditions, family life, and other matters and gave them personal guidance when it was needed. In this way, he quickly grasped the overall situation. He found that the chiefs were a fine group of people and that matters were not as bad as he had feared. To the marvel of the others, the young man set out briskly to outline operations scheduled for the coming month and, before long, the group chiefs found that their minds were functioning in tune with his quick actions.

With a great burden off her own shoulders, Haruko Taoka felt that, under the leadership of this energetic young man, the Bunkyo Chapter might catch up with the others. She remembered Toda's instructions to obey Shin'ichi from the standpoint of faith and silently resolved to do as she had been instructed. Her resolution seemed to convey itself to the other people in the room, who took it as their own. In a few days, they all realized that they were going about their religious work not only with greater confidence but also with joy.

At the time, rivalry was strong among Soka Gakkai chapters. It was strange that a young man from one chapter could completely win the confidence and affection of the entire membership of another. But Shin'ichi's sharp intelligence and warm, amiable personality won the day. He visited the Bunkyo Chapter headquarters two or three times a week. Some of the groups of the chapter were located as far away as Sagamihara and Yokosuka, in Kanagawa Prefecture, but Shin'ichi found time to visit them all, as he worked methodically to reinvigorate the lagging organization. Thanks to his efforts, signs of life began to appear in monthly achievements. In September, 275 new households were converted. The number rose to 431 in December, and the Bunkyo Chapter was out of its embarrassingly bad position.

One of the important outcomes of Yamamoto's efforts was a change in the attitude of Mr. Taoka. The chapter chief's husband was in the habit of coming home early in the evening. But, on nights when there were chapter meetings, he had his supper early and slipped out of the house. This evasiveness made it difficult for Shin'ichi to talk with him; but one evening he cornered Mr. Taoka and engaged him in conversation. He explained that he had long wanted to have a talk and that he was grateful for the hard work Mrs. Taoka was doing.

From this conversation, Shin'ichi learned that, though devoted to the faith and sometimes a private participant in membership drives, Mr. Taoka was put off from more active work by what he considered the arrogance of several of the officers. But Yamamoto's friendliness went a long way toward changing this opinion. From that time forward, whenever he went to the house, Yamamoto made a point of talking with Mr. Taoka, who warmed to him and no longer ran away at meeting time.

To Mrs. Taoka's great happiness, Yamamoto's consideration proved to her husband that not all the officers were arrogant. Gradually he took a more active part in chapter work, helped his wife with her tasks, and, in a few years, took over from her the position of chapter chief.

Through effective practical measures and constant lecturing, with quotations from the *Gosho* on the vital importance of faith in everyday matters, Shin'ichi Yamamoto laid the groundwork on which the Bunkyo Chapter was later to grow into one of the most significant in Soka Gakkai.

During the same year, as the Bunkyo Chapter was being revitalized under the guidance of Shin'ichi Yamamoto, all kinds of important events were taking place in the rapidly growing Soka Gakkai.

As usual, one of the most important was the annual general meeting, held on a fine spring day, May 3, at the auditorium of Chuo University, with fifty-five hundred people in attendance. The Myofuku-ji incident had led Nichiren Shoshu priests to understand the role of Soka Gakkai better and to wish for closer ties between clergy and laity. Consequently, a large number of priests from Nichiren Shoshu temples all over the nation attended the meeting this year. In the morning, the high priest made a special speech, fifteen believers delivered moving testimonials, and representatives of the Young Men's and Young Women's divisions, chapter chiefs, and other leaders made resolutions and reports. The spectacular membership campaign being mounted throughout the country at the time inspired this meeting with an air of fervor and resolution that grew stronger as the proceedings advanced. Toda saw what the people were feeling and realized that the great transformation he had dreamed of for many years was about to take place. To help it along, he was contemplating further personnel changes that would make things run better and more smoothly.

In his morning lecture, Toda clearly explained that the Buddha of the Mappo era is called Nam-myoho-renge-kyo. At the time of the delivery of the Lotus Sutra of Sakyamuni, this Buddha assumed the form of the Bodhisattva Jogyo (Viś-iṣṭacāritra) and then was born into the world as Nichiren Daishonin for the salvation of mankind. The power of the Buddha Nichiren Daishonin is as great as the universe and indeed is to be identified with the universe.

Next Toda explained the relation between religion and science. The two do not contradict each other; it is only that their fields of operation are different. Science deals with phenomenal aspects of life—matter, society, psychology—and with their various ramifications. Religion, on the other hand, is concerned with life in its eternal, all-encompassing aspects. He next showed that the force of life that is Nam-myoho-renge-kyo is the source of the constant change inherent in all life and that Nichiren Daishonin, the Tathagata from the infinite past, born into the world in the Mappo era, possesses this force of life. Nichiren Daishonin was a great scientist in terms of the eternal aspects of life. After he made public the results of his scientific research in this field, he inscribed the Dai-Gohonzon, the one thing that is capable of generating cosmic life-force and enabling all human beings to attain happiness.

Toda concluded his talk with a comment on the duty of Soka Gakkai to spread true Buddhism in other countries. It is said in the *Kembutsu Mirai Ki* (On the Buddha's Prophecy) of the *Gosho* that the true Buddhism shall travel from the east to the west; that is, from Japan to India. This means that true Buddhism must spread beyond the bounds of Japan. Ensuring this propagation is the mission of Soka Gakkai, and Toda called on all present to devote themselves to its fulfillment.

In his afternoon talk, Toda discussed the need to pay attention to one's own success and happiness as well as to religious activities. He compared faith in true Buddhism to the planted seed that quickly matures into a tree with abundant foliage and fruit. Although the members of his audience were still at the stage at which the tree was only growing, Toda promised them that they would know happiness by the time it had come into leaf. He said, "The heart of faith is respectfully accepting the Gohonzon and planting a tree that will become a Buddha. In other worlds, it is planting a seed of Buddhahood in the field of the mind. It is invisible to the eye, but, day and night, all good gods protect the seed with all their powers.

"The seed will germinate. Finally, the developed tree will put forth branches, leaves will be abundant, flowers will bloom, and fruit will develop. All of this takes place in a short time. At the field stage, no matter what you think of it, the plant will grow tall. This is called the circumstance of becoming a Buddha. Without going this far, however, when leaves are abundant, a human life can be very happy.

"You are still at the stage where it is uncertain whether buds have emerged. No good will be forthcoming if the buds are eaten by worms. If weeds are allowed to grow rank, the buds will rot.

"You must weed the fields of your minds. This is *shakubuku*. Chanting Daimoku morning and evening is fertilizing the fields.

"People whose lives manifest no merits have neglected their

weeding. You have already planted the seed in the fields of your minds. Now you must become happy by constantly fertilizing and weeding the fields."

Patience is essential. Toda estimated that the attainment of true happiness requires about fifteen years, though the person who is diligently faithful can expect to notice improvement in his way of life in about seven years.

Increasing membership meant a growing need for temples in which to carry out initiation ceremonies (Gojukai). Toda knew this, and he had already worked out a plan for building large temples throughout the nation, but for financial reasons, he decided to start with smaller projects. First, he set up a branch of the temple Byakuren-in, in a rented building in Tsurumi. But when this proved unsatisfactory, he bought a house in Oyama, Sagamihara, Kanagawa Prefecture, had it remodeled for use as a temple, and donated it to the head temple. This was the first temple ever built by Soka Gakkai. It was called the Myoen-zan Shokei-ji, and ceremonies to celebrate the installation of the Gohonzon were held there at one o'clock in the afternoon on May 31, 1953. About a hundred people, mostly members of the Bunkyo Chapter who lived in the Sagamihara area, attended to hear messages by Nissho Mizutani, high priest of Nichiren Shoshu; Josei Toda; and other leaders. Following recitations of the Lotus Sutra, High Priest Nissho read a lengthy message of felicitations, in which he said that Soka Gakkai efforts were so successful that it was difficult to find a place in Japan where there were no believers in Nichiren Shoshu. The Sagami district is far from the center of Tokyo. For a long time, members of the Bunkyo Chapter living there had been forced to make the long ride into town for Gojukai and other ceremonies, since they had no Nichiren Shoshu temple of their own. Seeing the inconvenience this caused and observing the praiseworthy way in which the faithful members refused to allow it to dampen their religious ardor, Josei Toda had requested permission to build this temple. High Priest Nissho said that he had given permission and had requested that the missionary group responsible for the district render all possible assistance. He was happy to be able to attend ceremonies marking the completion of the building. He added this blessing: "May the great sacred founder of this sect bestow his infinite mercy on us so that the temple Shokei-ji will prosper and serve as a bulwark in our struggle for Kosen-rufu."

The high priest's words filled the people who were crowded into the temple hall and the others standing outside with a sense of sharing in an event of great joy. At the conclusion of the high priest's message, his face beaming with happiness, Toda took the rostrum. He congratulated the gathering on the completion of the fine, though relatively small, new temple, announced plans to build others in Narimasu and Takasaki, and commented that all Nichiren Shoshu temples, including this one, had been erected as the outcome of the heartfelt zeal of believers. He then said that the Reverend Ohashi, chief priest at Shokei-ji, was a man of strong will, uninterested in money, and thoroughly devoted to the pursuit of the truth. After laying special emphasis on the close unity between the Nichiren Shoshu clergy and the local members of Soka Gakkai, he concluded with the wish that Shokei-ji might serve as a basis of operations for workers in the Supreme Law and as an example for the tens and hundreds of new Nichiren Shoshu temples to be built by Soka Gakkai.

Activities of the organization were reaching a feverish pitch of intensity. And, since he believed that his personal guidance was important to the success of these undertakings, Toda, apparently indefatigable, further tightened his already hectic schedule to attend as many meetings and functions as possible. For instance, on June 10, he addressed the second conference of district chiefs from various parts of the nation. He expressed his regret that contacts between himself and the chiefs had been intermittent and less than close, especially since this group of leaders was of immense importance to the forward development of the entire society. He went on to say that Buddhism and Soka Gakkai, in which all disciples are bound together by the pure ties of faith, demand severe discipline and selfless efforts. If any of the district chiefs felt incapable of living up to these high standards, Toda urged them to leave at once. He won the total approval of all present when he reminded the district chiefs that their duty was to strive to find enlightenment, devote themselves to Kosen-rufu, love their fellow members, and do all possible to bring out the best in those for whom they were responsible.

The tenth anniversary of the death of Toda's master, Tsune-saburo Makiguchi, was to be observed in the fall of 1953. The Educators' Club that was founded by Makiguchi had long since been dissolved, but Toda wanted to do something to keep alive his master's philosophy of value and education. The step he took to this end was the establishment of the Educators' Round-Table Conferences, the initial meeting of which took place on June 23, with fifty teachers in attendance, ranging from university professors to kindergarten instructors. At the meeting, Toda announced plans to publish Makiguchi's *Philosophy of Value* in book form and to distribute it among colleges and universities. Although, as he admitted, it was still too early for most people to accept it, within a few more decades, perceptive educators would certainly understand the originality and greatness of Makiguchi's philosophy, which would come to have tremendous repercussions in educational circles. Toda felt that he had to take this step at once, for, if he failed to do so, no one would remain after his death to spread Makiguchi's doctrines throughout the world. "Though I left the educational world more than twenty years ago," he said, "I am willing to study with you and share with you all that I know about my master's theory of value."

Both the district chiefs' meetings and the educators' conferences increased the number of young fledglings who had been directly nurtured and personally trained by Toda. In spite of his cruelly busy round of duties, he gave these gatherings the best of his attention, as he did to the many other meetings taking place during May and June.

At the Bunkyo Chapter meeting, on May 16, Women's Division chief Tokiko Matsui urged her fellow female members to intensify their sense of mission and rid themselves of the petty jealousies that erode unity, which is essential for collective accomplishments. Her remarks moved Toda deeply. He commented at the time that, though the women in Soka Gakkai presented a united front to danger from without, they were threatened by danger from within in the form of just the kind of jealousy that Mrs. Matsui had mentioned. Later he had her words compiled into a precept for behavior, which was distributed among the membership for guidance.

Another important precept for guidance had been delivered at the meeting of the Sendai Chapter, held on May 24. At that time, Toda informed all the 1,300 people present that they must devote attention to their businesses and their own welfare—as well as to religious work and membership campaigns—if they intended to be worthy members of the society and believers in Nichiren Shoshu. He instructed them to remember that the *Gosho* says that doing one's utmost in any task is in itself tantamount to practicing the Lotus Sutra. Toda said, "I am happy to hear that you are in good health and prosperous. But if you remain forever in poverty and distress while practicing faith and shakubuku, you cannot call yourselves my disciples. It is to live better and to make contributions to society through our various jobs and business undertakings that we practice our faith."

Toda regarded Osaka as among the most important local chapters. He was consequently highly pleased to observe that, a little more than one year after its inauguration, the chapter had added 1,400 households to its membership and had increased its districts to a total of seven. As has already been explained in an earlier volume, the growth of the chapter was largely due to the intense efforts of Seiichiro Haruki, whom Toda appointed in 1952 to fight alone for the spread of true Buddhism in this part of the nation. Toda visited Osaka to help Haruki twice in that year, and Haruki traveled to Tokyo frequently for guidance and help. One of the ideas he evolved to attract new members was to hang out lanterns bearing the words "Site of Soka Gakkai Discussion Meetings." Osakans apparently took to these lanterns, for members steadily increased at a rate of about two hundred a month.

Most of the people attending the Osaka Chapter general meeting on June 13 were actually seeing Toda in person for the first time. During his speech, he explained that people could expect to enjoy tremendous—though not full—benefits from the Gohonzon in about three years of diligence and patient practice of faith. He went on to say that both benefits and punishments, far from depending on Soka Gakkai or its president, were determined by Nichiren Daishonin and the Gohonzon. In the upper righthand corner of the Gohonzon are words to the effect that anyone vilifying true Buddhism will have his head broken into seven pieces. In the upper lefthand corner it is written that people making offerings for the sake of true Buddhism will enjoy blessings surpassing those of a Buddha.

Toda said that the very slight affluence of most members of the Osaka Chapter indicated a need to devote great energy to shakubuku and to offerings to the Buddha. It further meant, however, that the members must not neglect business or work in their enthusiam for membership campaigns. He concluded with an exhortation to them to do their best in both religious and secular work, since doing so was in their own best interest. Finally, he expressed the hope of seeing them again in three years.

To the third general meeting of the Kamata Chapter, held

on June 21, Toda explained a highly important point about the omnipotence of the Dai-Gohonzon. "If the Dai-Gohonzon is omnipotent, why is its worship not already universal? I can explain this by referring to the sun, the light and energy of which never alters. In the morning, when the sun is rising in the eastern sky, its heat is insufficient for drying laundry. At noon, however, when the sun is high overhead, wet laundry dries quickly. The sun of the Dai-Gohonzon has been rising, but it is now high in the sky and will continue to shed its light on mankind for the next ten or twenty thousand years. All who reject faith in it are fools, because, in doing so, they lose everything.

"Since we are spreading true Buddhism in the Mappo era, we can be certain of the protection of Buddhas, Bodhisattvas, and Buddhist divinities, all of whom appreciate our efforts.

"As believers in true Buddhism, you are in a position of absolute strength, where you will enjoy great blessings and will be endowed with the power of the Buddha and the Law if you practice faith with devotion. We have heard today testimonials about benefits enjoyed by some of our fellow members, but my own benefits have been infinitely greater than any of these.

"My greatest treasure and greatest fear is the Dai-Gohonzon. I have made a pledge to it to save all poor, sick, and suffering people. I must fulfill this pledge. And, for that reason, I call on all people to accept the Gohonzon and to pay no attention to the petty criticisms leveled at what I do."

To Toda's disappointment, the Study Department was not progressing at the same rate as the general membership. But it seemed that there was nothing to be done about the situation, since it is impossible to turn out trained theologians rapidly. On June 28, 1953, however, forty-one candidates passed written examinations for admission to the Study Department. On July 12, these people were given another test and an oral examination to examine their lecturing abilities. After this rigid, three-phase examination, twenty-one candidates were admitted to the Study Department, two as assistant professors and one as a lecturer.

On June 30, at a monthly leaders' meeting at the Kyoiku Kaikan Hall in Kanda, official reports showed that during June 3,933 households had been brought into the membership, raising the national total for the first half of 1953 to 20,891. This meant that, in a six-month period, the membership had doubled. Since the year's target was 50,000, an additional 30,000 conversions would have to be made in the next six months; but, in the light of the current rate of increase, that seemed possible. Optimism reigned at the meeting.

Toda's original goal had appeared fantastic; it now seemed near attainment. He had been amazingly accurate. Of course, the senior staff members had done a great deal of work to make these startling achievements possible.

At the meeting, Toda cautioned against increasing bureaucracy as the organization grew in size. Then he gave advice to the chiefs on the way they should regard and fulfill their duties. He told them that the position of chief, the person filling it, and the Law must be a unity. Nam-myoho-renge-kyo is the Law of the Mappo era, and Nichiren Daishonin is the Buddha of that era. The two are one. People who insist that Sakyamuni, not Nam-myoho-renge-kyo, is the Law of the Mappo era create a dichotomy that inevitably gives rise to serious consequences. Just as there must be no split between the Law and Nichiren Daishonin, Buddha of the Mappo era, there must be none between the title of chief and the person bearing it. Toda went on to warn chiefs against arrogance and to commend to them the Buddhist spirit of compassion, which is the only way to earn the dignity of their titles and the respect of their followers.

The ideas that had come to Toda for personnel changes during the eighth general meeting were put into effect in May of the same year. The trio of women who had brought the

Suginami Chapter to a high place within the organization had gradually broken up and moved on to other important posts. As this happened, the leadership of the chapter declined. To do something about this, Toda reinstalled Miss Katsu Kiyohara, one of the original trio who had given the organization its matriarchal character, as chapter chief, a post she held concurrently with her job as head of the Guidance Department. Toda made the surprise move of replacing gentle, quiet Hiroshi Izumida with the dynamic Takeo Konishi as chief of the important Kamata Chapter, because he felt that a forceful personality was needed for the highly prestigious job. Izumida took the change with good grace. Though fond of all of his disciples, Toda never let personal feelings interfere with the struggle for Kosen-rufu. Other changes, including the appointment of young Chuhei Yamadaira to the Study Department and altering the name of the Local Supervision Department to the Supervision Department, together with the changes made in January, 1953, put the society in full readiness for its flight into the future.

6. TRAINING TO LEAD

IN THE autumn of 1952, to provide young people with special education in the humanities outside the general framework of Soka Gakkai, Toda set up two elite groups: the Suiko Club (or Suiko-kai) for men and the Kayo Club for women. The latter met twice a month to study politics, economics, philosophy, and the humanities—all of which were studied on the basis of the literary classics of East and West. The name of the club, which means the Flower-Sun Society, was selected because Toda wanted the revolutionary young women of Soka Gakkai to be as beautiful as flowers and as proud and shining as the sun. He hoped they would broaden both their interests and their knowledge, so as to avoid becoming fanatical, narrow-minded, or stubborn. When the meetings were dinners, Toda took the opportunity to instruct the young ladies in the proper use of Western-style tableware. At each meeting, he asked them to relax completely and to discuss any subject—even a personal matter—that was of general interest.

On one occasion, a bespectacled girl raised her hand for attention. When Toda recognized her, she said, "I used to be a Christian. We were taught that Christianity is based on love and Buddhism on compassion. But I'm not sure I understand the difference between the two. Would you be kind enough to explain it for me?"

Toda said that the question was good and asked if anyone was willing to explain. No one said anything, though ordinarily the young ladies were excellent at making small talk. Toda then asked a staff member if she would explain. The tall woman rose and hesitantly said that she found the Christian idea of loving one's enemies and turning the other cheek when injured unrealistic and fantastic. She got bogged down at about this point and was unable to go further with the discussion.

Another girl, who called herself an intuitionalist, hastily blurted out the idea that love is inferior in depth and breadth to mercy, but she was unable to elaborate. Others said that love could be classified into universal love and love directed only toward human beings. Another girl got lost in the maze of a discussion of the egoistic aspects of love.

Then Toda set them all straight: "All of you have studied the doctrines of Nichiren Daishonin and ought to understand both love and compassion in the light of the concept of *ichinen sanzen* (three thousand worlds in a single thought) and the teaching of the Ten States of Life. You should know that all human life exists always in the Ten States of hell, hunger, animality, anger, tranquility, rapture, learning, absorption, Bodhisattva-nature, and Buddha-nature—and that it is impossible for a human being to remain fixed always in any one of these states. Christianity demands that its followers remain always in the state in which love is predominant, and this means that Christians, faced with this impossibility, must either be hypocritical or develop split personalities.

"Christianity is shallow, but I do not repudiate it entirely. I was once a Christian myself, and I know what I'm talking about. Christianity, though higher than many primitive religions, is inferior to the teachings of Nichiren Daishonin. Christians can go no higher in the Ten States than rapture.

"The United States, largely a Christian nation, is therefore confined to this state and can go no higher. This means that American prosperity is doomed to regress, since it can neither remain static nor advance. The case of Italy, the seat of the papacy, illustrates my point. Today Italy can hardly be called prosperous.

"The power of Christian love, then, is limited to the state of rapture—sometimes, though not often, it may attain the state of the Bodhisattva-nature. Mercy (*jihi*), however, is the elimination of suffering and the giving of joy through the works of the Buddha nature. Christian love cannot attain the Buddhanature, which is the aim of our disciplines and training. By chanting the Daimoku to the Gohonzon, the ultimate object of worship in the universe, we are striving to acquire and put into practice the spirit of mercy and compassion. With his doctrine of love, the Christian cannot reach the Buddha state, as is evident from the Christian nations' failure to eliminate warfare, though they completely understand its evil. In order to remove suffering and bring joy to others through love—even Christian love—it is necessary to make special efforts. But all actions of a person in the Buddha state radiate mercy and compassion—indeed are themselves mercy and compassion.

"We should take a hint from the fate of Christianity, however. Before it was able to win a large global following, it and its followers suffered horrible persecutions. We who embrace the highest of all religions must realize that persecutions lie in wait for us, too, and we must be prepared to strive with the greatest possible conviction to spread true Buddhism everywhere.

"Though you may think you understand now what I have said, it is a good idea for you to ponder and think about it further when you get home. If you do, you will discover new aspects of the issue. You must devote yourselves to doctrinal study so that you can hold your own in debates with men."

Then one young girl, clearly embarrassed but deeply concerned because she was personally involved, asked Toda to explain the meaning of true marital happiness. He first explained that a woman must be prepared to devote herself entirely to her husband and must therefore select a man whom she believes to be worthy of her total devotion. Though love is paramount for women, men seem to be more concerned with honor, position,

and work, which they are often unwilling to sacrifice, even for the sake of a wife's love. Toda interpreted this as the major psychological difference between the sexes. Nothing can be done about this difference. A wife ought to love her husband and help him attain honor and a position that both of them can share. To do this, more than affection and love is necessary: faith in the Gohonzon is essential, for it enables a woman to love and play a part in her husband's career. Marital happiness depends on the ability to do both of these things.

The next topic of discussion, closely related to this one, was whether it is imperative for women to marry, or whether they can live happily in devotion to the attainment of Kosen-rufu without getting married. One woman said that she hoped to emulate Miss Katsu Kiyohara and live for nothing but their great task. Several women who felt his way remarked that marriage seemed to make their female companions backslide and work at their religious duties with diminished fervor.

Toda began by saying that Miss Kiyohara was too special to serve as an example for ordinary human beings. He then set out to put what he felt to be a mistaken approach back on the right track. "Buddhism expounds the highest philosophy. We practice it to become more vibrantly alive. Men who embrace the Buddhist faith become more masculine, and women more feminine. It is natural for girls to marry and to enjoy married life. But you should not run headlong into marriage. Remember that many of the great women revolutionaries—and there are potential religious women revolutionaries among us tonight—have usually been splendid mothers and wives as well. I do not want my disciples to take the unnatural stance that they must not get married. And, if any of your companions slack off in their religious work after marriage, keep an eye on them. See to it that they live up to the training they have had from Soka Gakkai and from me. If you look after them patiently, they will grow into fine believers in the Supreme Law under the infallible protection of the Gohonzon.

"Don't run after men. Let them chase you. But, before starting a relationship, practice faith and study to build a solid basis of good fortune for yourself. This will help you find a man who suits you and will ensure that your marriage is a blessing for everyone concerned. Even marriage depends on your good fortune. Young women like you are inexperienced and should not choose hastily. The older you are, and the more people you know, the more likely you are to find the best man for you. Love once in a lifetime and let it be the kind of love on which you are willing to stake everything.

"But, as I have said, love can go no higher in the Ten States of Life than rapture and is therefore a lower order of delight than those associated with the higher states. Life is eternal, and its laws are irrefutable. Lovers who find life too difficult to bear for some reason and decide to commit suicide together in the hope of being joined in the afterlife are going to be sadly disillusioned. Their act will plunge them into the state of hell, which they will have to endure for aeons.

"How should you judge a man? Certainly not on the basis of appearance or social position, but on the basis of his worth. For young women like you this is difficult. You must rely on the advice of your family or of older Soka Gakkai members whom you respect and trust.

"Marriage with the person you love is not the happy ending of an affair, but the start of a longer affair, one that may be filled with happiness or sufferings. Faith is the key to whether marriage is happy or sorrowful. You will be truly happy only if you select a spouse with whom you share a great faith and with whom you can work toward the accomplishment of a great goal."

At successive meetings of the Kayo Club, the discussion topics varied considerably. Sometimes the members talked about books—they had a list of required reading, including Dickens's *A Tale of Two Cities;* the Chinese *Tale of Three Kingdoms;* the novel *Botchan,* by the Japanese novelist Soseki Natsume; Burnett's *Little Lord Fauntleroy;* Gogol's *Taras Bulba;* Ibsen's *A Doll's House;* and Louisa May Alcott's *Little Women.* In all of the talks about books, Toda employed the characters and situations as sounding boards against which to analyze the characters and daily-life situations of the members of his audience. Sometimes he gave advice on cooking or cosmetics. And one evening he even shared with them his vision of building the Grand Reception Hall and the Sho-Hondo at the head temple as part of the last phase of Kosen-rufu.

"These edifices," he said, "will symbolize the salvation that man has waited for throughout this Latter Day of the Law. And you are going to be an important part in this great work. Where else in the world are young women concerning themselves with visions of global importance for the twenty-first century and the still more distant future? You may not realize how vital what you are doing as members of the Kayo Club really is; but in ten years, when your lives have been completely changed, you will see."

The young women did not actually understand that they would someday be important leaders in the Women's Division. Toda was very strict about attendance, punctuality, and lesson preparations. Nonetheless, they enjoyed their meetings and were proud of their membership in the club, which was the object of the admiration and envy of other members of the Young Women's Division.

Two years of imprisonment and great superhuman struggles during the postwar period had taken a great toll in Josei Toda's health, which began to show signs of deterioration in the autumn of 1952, just as the protracted Kasahara incident was drawing to a close. His own physical condition made him acutely aware of the need to train young people to carry on his great work, no matter what happened to him. The Kayo Club was one step in this direction. Another was the formation of what was called the Suiko Club, a hand-picked group of members of the Young Men's Division. The name of the organization derived from *Suiko-den,* the Japanese rendition of the title of the famous Ming-dynasty Chinese picaresque novel *Sui-hu-ch'uan,* or *Water Margin,* which the members studied.

The suggestion for the founding of the club came from Shin'-ichi Yamamoto, to whom Toda left all the details of planning and organizing such a group. It was agreed between them, however, that members would be carefully selected from the Young Men's Division and that the club's first project would be to read through *Water Margin.*

At the early meetings, the young men took turns reading passages from the novel, and Toda led discussions on them. He pointed out the excitingly revolutionary nature of the activities of the leading characters, a group of romantic bandits, who, driven by a corrupt government to take shelter on Mount Liang, carried out raids on the degenerate rich in the style of Robin Hood. As he did with the works read by the Kayo Club, Toda urged the young men to plumb beneath the entertaining surface narrative to find the deeper meanings of the work, and apply the situations and experiences of the characters to themselves and the people around them. He told them to read as many novels as they could from the literatures of all parts of the world, since such reading develops the ability to judge people accurately. Further, he instructed them to try to grasp the currents of the times presented in the books they read. He knew that, as adherents of the highest philosophy, they were destined to play leading roles in their own century, and he wanted them to develop through reading and personal experience a clear insight into all aspects of human life in various centuries. He did not want them to be narrow.

"We members of the Suiko Club take time from our busy schedules to meet twice monthly because we are striving for Kosen-rufu, the unprecedented religious revolution that will bring lasting peace and prosperity to mankind through reforms in all fields of society," he told them. "Religious faith is of fundamental importance, but we must not confine ourselves to religious activities alone. As my disciples, awakened to the supreme philosophy of the Supreme Law, you must make substantial contributions to society at large if you are to save the suffering masses in this Mappo era. I want to be able to entrust to you members of the Suiko Club the universal propagation of true Buddhism."

Throughout the early months of 1953, the Suiko Club grew in membership, but its morale and general tone dropped. Toda sensed this drop, and it displeased him. But matters did not come to a head until one evening toward the end of June. As they read some of the latter parts of *Water Margin,* the young men began to express inordinate interest in the feasts and drinking bouts frequently indulged in by the main hero, Sung Chiang, and his gang of bandits. Toda, who was fond of drinking, too, once briefly commented on some of the characteristic traits of the Chinese beverage called *lao-ch'iu*. Though he intended to let the matter drop with a short remark, one of the members of the group stood up and launched into an extended lecture on various Chinese alcoholic beverages. He said he knew all about them; he had been raised in China.

The young man, whose way of speaking was overly knowing and offensive, paid no heed to the little signs Toda gave to show that he wanted to proceed to more important topics. Finally, when the young man asked if he knew how to make Chinese apple wine, Toda lost patience: "Have you come here to ask me about brewing? What do you think this club is? I don't like the way things are going here tonight. Get out of the room!"

Dumbfounded, the young man stood stock still, in spite of Toda's repeated orders to leave. The other hung their heads. At last, the insensitive boy seemed to understand what was required of him and left; but Toda's anger had reached a peak: "Who is it that's ruined the Suiko Club? I'll tell you who: it's all of you. Not just that boy. And you just stood by and listened to him get scolded for something that is the fault of all of you. I'm deeply disappointed in you. I'm going home."

Toda stood. The young men hurried to the door and knelt in front of him to apologize. But, paying no attention, he stormed out in angry silence. As a senior member, Hisao Seki felt that he should try to get to the cause of the unfortunate situation. He and several other started to talk matters over, but came to no conclusion. Then Shin'ichi Yamamoto rose calmly and said, "Unless we do something, Mr. Toda may disband the Suiko Club. We ought to try to learn from this bitter experience. I'm not sure yet what we must do, but I'm thinking about it."

The others did not understand precisely what Yamamoto

had in mind, but they did know how close he was to Toda. And the idea that he was proposing remedial action relieved their minds. After a brief discussion, the group disbanded, entrusting Shin'ichi Yamamoto with the responsibility for patching things up.

As the originator of the club and as Toda's closest disciple, Yamamoto knew he had to do somthing. He understood that Toda's sudden angry outburst had been more than bad temper at being interrupted by a smart aleck talking about liquor. Toda had observed the decreasing enthusiasm of the members of the club and was both disappointed and deeply hurt, since he had taken the pains to teach these young men himself in the hope that they would become leaders. Day by day, Shin'ichi pondered the problem and chanted the Daimoku. At first he thought he would wait for Toda to make a move; but, as two weeks went by with no summons from him, though the Kayo Club continued to meet regularly, Yamamoto realized that Toda was waiting for the members of the Suiko Club to reflect deeply on what had happened and to take the initiative to make things right.

Knowing that the frivolousness of the entire membership had irritated Toda, Yamamoto decided that the quality of the group would have to be improved drastically. To achieve this, he devised a three-point oath that all members would have to take. After gaining the approval of the leading senior members of the club, he showed a draft of the oath to Toda, who agreed to forgive the club members on the condition that they never allow their meetings to degenerate again. Shin'ichi happily detected a note of eagerness in Toda's question as to when meetings of the club were to resume. Somewhat embarrassed that things were not already prepared, Yamamoto humbly asked for a week in which to make preparations and to screen out all but the most worthy members.

At a meeting with Hiroshi Yamagiwa and Hisao Seki, he decided that faith must be the major criterion for membership in the club, although individual potential, character, and personality must also be taken into account. One dissenting voice from the leaders removed a man's name from the list of eligible candidates. Out of three thousand members of the Young Men's Division, forty-three were selected. Then Akio Nakamichi, a staff member and a fine calligrapher, made a clean copy of the oath with brush and India ink.

On the night of July 21, 1953, the forty-three members gathered at the headquarters in Kanda. Having heard nothing about this project, they were puzzled to see the copy of the oath spread out on a table before the Gohonzon that had been granted to Soka Gakkai by the high priest of Nichiren Shoshu as a prayer for the attainment of Kosen-rufu through the merciful practices of shakubuku. Toda sat in a rattan chair beside the table.

As they heard it read, the young men realized that the oath they were about to sign bound them for the rest of their lives. Though tense, they knew that this paper was the essence of everything Toda had taught them; and they showed no sign of hesitation. Under the excited, but restrained, gazes of everyone in the room, Hisao Seki signed first. He was followed by Hiroshi Yamagiwa, Shin'ichi Yamamoto, Kiyoshi Jujo, Kazumasa Morikawa, Kin'ya Takimoto, Akio Nakamichi, Yusuke Yoshikawa, and the others. Beside his signature, each man placed a thumb print in vermilion. During the solemn ceremony, all of them lost track of time. They felt as if they were reconfirming in the Mappo era an oath they had been predestined to make for aeons. The oath they signed read as follows:

"1. We members of the Suiko Club pledge to the Dai-Gohonzon that we shall consecrate our lives to our religious revolution and, with united wills and minds, accomplish the great task of Kosen-rufu in the Orient.

"2. We members of the Suiko Club firmly pledge to carry on Josei Toda's avowed objective of saving mankind; we dedicate our lives to the struggle to realize his cherished goal.

"3. We members of the Suiko Club, aware that we are the advance guard of Soka Gakkai and Mr. Toda's indispensable disciples and messengers, pledge to exert our utmost efforts to accomplish the mission of this organization, no matter how times may change and no matter to what place the holy battle may take us. We further pledge never to betray our comrades."

Shin'ichi signed with mixed feelings. This step seemed to open up a new horizon and show him a glimpse of the peak of the attainment of their ultimate goal. At the same time, it put a heavy responsibility on him. From that time forward, without letting anyone know, he took the greatest care to see that everything at Suiko Club meetings went right. He assigned members to be in charge of the sessions on a rotational basis and worked out study plans for background on the novels under discussion.

The meetings resumed twice monthly, with a continued treatment of *Water Margin*. One evening they discussed the personality of Sung Chiang, leader of the band of brigands on Mount Liang. When asked why this perfectly ordinary petty functionary—who was medium in build, dark of complexion, unattractive to women, and devoted to his parents, to honesty, and to ethical codes—should have been chosen to head a group of daring, romantic bandits, the club members gave a variety of reasons, none of which covered the full situation. Then Toda went to the heart of the matter: "Sung Chiang was endowed with an extraordinary ability to see into the minds and hearts of others. He at once discerned both strengths and weaknesses in the people with whom he came into contact, and he loved and respected them for themselves. Isolated and alone in their grandeur, the hero bandits of Mount Liang treasured the friendship of a man who could understand and appreciate them. He was not perfect. Indeed, he was sometimes procrastinating and indecisive. He did not win and hold respect on the basis of authority, wealth, position, or erudition.

"In his ability to understand and influence others in spite of his own apparent mediocrity, he is something like Iwao Oyama, commander in chief of the Japanese Manchurian Army during the Russo-Japanese war of 1904–05. This unprepossessing man, who earned the nickname of the 'Dozing Marshall' from his habit of napping during conferences, even in the presence of the emperor, led formidable, often temperamental, generals to triumph over the Russians in Manchuria. I am not glorifying war by using him as an illustration. I merely want to say that Marshall Oyama, like Sung Chiang, understood men and knew how to put their talents to best use.

"But now let's turn from history to the present. Each one of us wants to be understood, though each of us keeps some things hidden. This is where I come in. I understand each one of you better than anyone else. Because of my understanding, you are able to devote yourselves to religious tasks without worry. It is my job to see to it that your abilities and talents are put to full use. What would happen if I died, and you were left on your own resources?"

Though they suddenly saw that his understanding was the source of their strength, the young men did not fully grasp Toda's magnificent vision. Some of them, however—especially Shin'ichi Yamamoto—listened to his words and absorbed them into their very beings. Yamamoto always asked questions to evoke more from Toda. He alone knew of the ill health that might mean that Toda would not live to see Kosen-rufu achieved. In drawing him out at meetings, Yamamoto seemed to be trying to get Toda to pronounce his testament.

On another occasion, a discussion of Kosen-rufu in Asia led to broader topics. Toda said that the Gohonzon is the one object of worship for all mankind and that, once it and its Supreme Law have been taken to all people throughout Japan, they will inevitably reach all corners of the globe. "People everywhere, though still unaware of the existence of the Gohonzon, are sensing the approaching end of their materialistic civilization. Sooner or later, they will come to long for the Gohonzon. And it will be the mission of people like the members of the Suiko Club and those who come later to take it to them.

"Perhaps the materialistic civilization of today will not collapse in one decade or even in two. But I am sure it will not last into the twenty-first century. Its collapse is imminent, and you are going to have to live through it."

Amidst the general intoxication caused by this daring prophecy, Yamamoto rose and asked Toda what languages they would have to study first in order to carry out their great missionary campaign with maximum speed and efficiency. Toda explained that there would be no way of setting a schedule of precedents for preferred languages, because all languages will be needed for a great movement on a global scale. Countless expert linguists will be required. The Christians of the past, in times when transportation was primitive, carried their religious message far and wide. Toda pointed out the need for Soka Gakkai members to take maximum advantage of modern improved transportation to carry true Buddhism even farther and faster than the Christians took their religion.

"There is no guarantee that the attainment of Kosen-rufu will proceed in an orderly fashion, from nation to nation. Preparations must be made for all eventualities, and languages are essential. But remember, each of you has his own individual role. Not all of you need to be linguists. You, Shin'ichi, for example, do not need to spend your time learning foreign languages. You must rely on competent interpreters and translators."

Was Toda teasing Yamamoto for his want of linguistic ability? Was he being considerate by not insisting that a person who is unlikely to master any of them study foreign tongues?

Or was he hinting at a special responsibility, requiring total impartiality, which would be impossible if Yamamoto devoted time and effort to the languages of one or two peoples?

Actually Toda was setting down in a few words the role Shin'ichi Yamamoto was going to play in the future Soka Gakkai. And from time to time at Suiko Club meetings, he made other casual allusions to this role. After Toda's death, Shin'ichi remembered these remarks with great vividness.

One evening, Takeshi Arimura, who had studied sciences at the university but had later become a somewhat Bohemian composer, asked Toda to define culture. While admitting that a brief definition of such an immense subject was difficult, Toda suggested that culture might be called wisdom converted into knowledge or wisdom given forms that are useful and beneficial to humanity. In such a case, even lowly things like diapers can be considered part of culture.

"Since culture is created by wisdom, it follows that the highest culture is the product of the highest wisdom. Nammyoho-renge-kyo, the Supreme Law," said Toda, "is the supreme wisdom. The movement to attain Kosen-rufu—that is, the movement to spread the Supreme Law to all peoples—can therefore be thought of as a supreme cultural movement. Though today the number of people who understand this is small, someday everyone, including the so-called intellectuals who now spurn true Buddhism, will be astounded and will bow their heads before its greatness."

Though up to this time Arimura's attempts to give musical expression to his faith had been less than totally successful, Toda's explanation of culture inspired the young composer to finer achievements through the knowledge that first he must strive to attain wisdom in the Supreme Law.

On successive occasions, Toda discussed all kinds of topics. For instance, he once showed that there is no incompatibility between reason and emotion on a lofty plane. Low reasoning and low emotions may conflict, but high emotions—like the spirit of Nichiren Daishonin—are completely consonant with the loftiest reasoning. This explanation was of immense value to young people who often found themselves caught in what they imagined to be a dilemma between emotional reactions and the need for rational explanations.

On another evening, Toda talked at length about his experiences in prison and interspersed his sad stories with moments of bright humor. He concluded by giving the young men a spellbinding account of the enlightenment that had come to him in his prison cell. It is impossible to relate all of the significant remarks that Toda made at these meetings; to do so would require many volumes. But all of his elaborations of the great campaign for Kosen-rufu from the political, educational, cultural, and economical standpoints were strengthened by his own will power.

After getting off to a fresh start with the 43 signers of the oath, the Suiko Club grew steadily to a membership of 120 by the third class. Until the meetings were temporarily suspended in May 1956, Toda and his young men covered a number of great literary works—*Water Margin; Tale of Three Kingdoms;* Dumas's *The Count of Monte Cristo; Of Winds and Waves,* by Shofu Miramatsu; Defoe's *Robinson Crusoe; Wind and Frost,* by Shiro Ozaki; *Taras Bulba,* by Gogol; and *Quatre-vingt-treize,* by Victor Marie Hugo—all of which provided material with which Toda taught his students his own great vision of Kosen-rufu, in the movement for which they were destined to be leaders.

7. NO TIME FOR REST

WHAT WITH the increasing number of meetings to attend and lectures to give, 1953 was one of the busiest years in Josei Toda's extraordinarily busy life. In addition to all of his many duties related to Soka Gakkai, he had to run the Daito Shoko Company, in order to make money for religious activities and general living expenses. At eight-thirty each morning, he started the day with a highly useful talk on society in general and on the ways in which his employees could make fullest use of their abilities. These talks were especially aimed at Shin'-ichi Yamamoto, who was director of the company's business department. Toda kept the office running full blast from about nine-fifteen until lunch time, when he found relief from fatigue in a high-calorie lunch and a few cigarettes.

Next door to the offices of Daito Shoko was a detached office of Soka Gakkai. The shabby room, which had a low ceiling and only one window, was separated by a concrete wall from the space occupied by the business operation. Toda never allowed these two aspects of his life to interfere with each other.

Every afternoon, members of Soka Gakkai in search of advice and counsel flocked to this little room, which looked very much like—and indeed in some respects was like—the consultation room of a country hospital. All manner of people who were sick in body or spirit came there to find help in Toda's religious philosophy. Some were half-crazy with illness or worry over debts. Many of them were pale and exhausted. The room invariably became filled with people whose troubles and ailments defied cure or solution at the hands of even the most skilled doctors or the most astute lawyers. Though sometimes staggered by the enormity of the problems confronting him, Toda never gave up. Examining all predicaments in the light of the Supreme Law, he found the right counsel—kind or severe as the case demanded—to give people the hope, confidence, or chastisement they needed. The variety of people he met in a single day gives an idea of the scope of the difficulties he was trying to solve. Seated with his back to the one window, he interviewed, one by one, the suffering human beings who sat on the wooden benches around the walls.

On the day in question, the first to ask for help was a distraught woman accompanied by a ghostly pale child with large, staring eyes. He suffered from hemophilia, and his mouth bled so constantly that the bread he put to his lips came away stained red. Knowing that there is no cure for this sickness, Toda kindly asked the woman when she had become a believer in Nichiren Shoshu. In reply, she related the story of her life.

Separated from a tyrannical husband, she had to eke out a livelihood for herself and her four children. The death of her oldest son of hemophilia drove her to despair. Through friends, she heard about Nichiren Shoshu and began to attend discussion meetings. Though completely lacking in doctrinal knowledge, she found the teachings appealing and soon became a believer. Shortly after joining Nichiren Shoshu, she found that living had become easier.

But suddenly, in February 1953, she learned to her horror that her youngest son, too, suffered from the dread disease that had killed his oldest brother. He developed a temperature and

bled so profusely that she made him sleep in his clothes on a
wooden floor. Not even these apparently cruel measures
stopped his hemorrhaging. He grew deadly pale, and blood
almost never stopped oozing from his mouth.

Deeply moved by the plight of the woman and her child,
Toda told her that, though we must leave to doctors the treatment of illnesses that their skills can cure, some illnesses are
caused by karma. In such cases, faith is the sole cure.

"You are in good luck, since you have already embraced the
Gohonzon. Pray to it with all your heart, and your son will
certainly get well. I am sure that you have already been earnest
in practicing faith, so I will ask the high priest to grant you
special protection (*gohifu*) of the kind Nichiren Daishonin
granted to his own mother, who was thereby enabled to live
four more years. Such protection, which has been handed down
as a secret from one high priest to another, is very great. You
must promise to be worthy of it by preserving your faith actively, no matter what happens. If you make that pledge, the
power of the Supreme Law will manifest itself to you."

As a follow-up to this interview, Toda did obtain special
protection from the high priest; and a few days later the
woman reported that, since accepting protection as instructed
by Toda, the child had stopped bleeding. A faint rosiness was at
last returning to his cheeks.

Next to approach on that busy day was a man in his middle
forties, who told Toda about his business that continued to
fail, even though he had accepted faith in Nichiren Shoshu.
His automobile-parts plant was going bankrupt, he had no
money to pay debts or salaries, and his employees were de-
serting him. "Ever since I joined Soka Gakkai," he said, "I
have faithfully carried out morning and evening Gongyo and
have done as much membership campaigning as I can. But I
still can't borrow the money I need to put my business back
on its feet, and I am at my wits' end."

Toda tersely instructed him to continue practicing faith.

Clearly things were as bad as they could get, and a turn for the better was certainly in the offing. Maybe being unable to borrow would turn out to be a blessing.

Since the man had joined Soka Gakkai only a few months earlier, he was not entirely convinced that Toda's advice

would do him good; but he followed it nonetheless. And, true to Toda's prediction, in a few months his affairs began looking up, as he explained to his local chapter somewhat later. "Following Mr. Toda's advice, in spite of the grim outlook, I devotedly carried out morning, evening, and even midnight Gongyo and took as large a part in membership campaigning as I could. Soon I felt a great vitality stirring inside me. Then, to my utter surprise, I received an advantageous order to manufacture a monthly quota of parts at a good profit. I didn't need to borrow to keep the business going. While I was still wondering whether I was dreaming, another offer as good as the first one came along. My eighteen employees and I work together harder and better than ever before. They seem to have been inspired by what has happened to me. Now I want to build them a comfortable dormitory.

"As Mr. Toda said, my inability to borrow when I was down has turned out to be a blessing in disguise. If I had arranged for a loan then, I would have continued to go further down on the spiral of deficit financing and probably would have ended up a suicide.

"I am deeply grateful to the Gohonzon for its miraculous power and to President Toda for his wonderfully wise guidance."

By this time there were more people standing than sitting in the crowded room, but one middle-aged housewife was conspicuous for her untidy hair, lackluster complexion, and generally unclean look. Although she claimed to have come for advice on the divorce she was contemplating, in fact, all she wanted to do was complain naggingly about her hard lot. After a while, Toda lost patience: "Who brought this woman here? She has no faith in the Gohonzon. If she had faith and nonetheless faced unsolvable problems, I would be glad to help her. But it is clear to me that she only wants to complain and completely lacks faith. I have no obligation to her." Then, turning to the woman, he told her to leave.

After a few moments of tense silence, a middle-aged man walked sheepishly forward and made the startling remark: "I am waiting to be sent to prison." It turned out that he had been tried and sentenced to eighteen months in jail for fraud. After being released on bail, he had joined Nichiren Shoshu and, because of his faith, had reformed completely. Nonetheless, he had made both practical and mental preparations to serve his sentence. With his revised view of values, he was even eager to pay his debt to society. But he still had not been summoned to prison and was wondering what to do about the situation.

Toda laughed at the novelty of the story and then, after telling him not to be in a hurry to go to such an unpleasant place as prison, explained to him and the whole group the difference between the Buddhist Law and laws of national states. The laws of national states are higher than those of the local disciplines, but the Law of Buddhism is higher than both. As this man's case indicates, ordinary laws sometimes fail to work according to plan. Buddhist Law never fails. It is absolute.

"By this, however," Toda went on, "I do not mean that followers of the Law of Buddhism are permitted to ignore the laws of the lands in which they live. Nichiren Daishonin himself said that he had never violated a secular law. But some men are fated to do illegal things and to be punished for their acts. This is the result of past karma. Belief in the Supreme Law is the only way to alter karma.

"Since transgression of the Law of Buddhism is much more severely punishable by suffering in the past, present, and the future, we must all have faith in the Gohonzon and abide by the Law in order to attain perfect happiness in this world."

"You are still young," he said to the perplexed man. "Go now and apply yourself to faith, practice, and study and wait for what is in store for you. I assure you that one day the unhappiness you are experiencing now will seem like no more than a dream."

Overjoyed that Toda had been kind and had not treated him as a criminal, the man went out to await his fate, with renewed faith and with tears streaming down his cheeks.

The next man, a poor farmer, said that he could no longer go on with shakubuku and membership-drive work. Toda had instructed the members that a faithful performance of Gongyo and the conversion of one family to Nichiren Shoshu a month should be their goals. This man had tried. He performed Gongyo regularly, but his efforts at converting other people had met with complete defeat.

Toda explained that Nichiren Daishonin himself had called shakubuku the most difficult of all tasks and insisted that the man keep on trying. But the farmer explained that his attempts had been unsuccessful because he was from the group of people known as *burakumin,* descendants of a class considered sub-human in ancient Japan because of the nature of the work they did. Even today, the *burakumin* are considered socially unacceptable by some people, and this background had spoiled the man's attempts in membership campaigns.

His story and his obvious sincerity won Toda's confidence and good will from the start. He told the man that we are all equal in Buddhism, and that he should not allow himself to be defeated by unjust social prejudices. "Even though you have apparently had no success," Toda said, "you have sown the seeds of Buddhist faith in the hearts of all who have heard you. The Gohonzon will understand, and the seeds you have sown are certain to bear fruit someday. Continue in your noble work, and you may be assured of receiving blessings.

"Remember, Nichiren Daishonin, who was the son of a poor fisherman, described himself as a *candala,* an untoucha-ble, or a member of a group lower than the lowest of the Indian castes. In saying this, he identified himself with the lowly, un-fortunate people of the Mappo era, for whom he is the com-passionate Buddha. He was a child of a *candala* family, and we are his children. We cannot allow ourselves to be troubled by the opinions of society and thereby undervalue ourselves. I am your friend and ally. When you have any problems, come to me at once. Continue striving for your human revolution and in this way serving your loved ones, friends, and offspring. Don't forget, the Gohonzon is witness to all of this."

With his coarse hands folded neatly and with a radiant smile on his face, the man said he understood. Toda, who had taken an enormous liking to the man, told his secretary to bring him a bundle of edible kelp he had just received from his hometown in Hokkaido.

"I'm the son of a fisherman myself, you know," he said. "A child of a *candala* family. And I'm proud of it. Here, take this kelp. It's from Hokkaido and it's very good. Accept it as a gift from me. And remember, practice faith without wavering and whenever you're in Tokyo, come to see me."

The humble man left the room in high spirits.

Almost every day, Toda counseled people in this way, dealing with each problem individually and in a perspicacious way and teaching that true Buddhism is the sole remedy for all human sorrows. The work was exhausting and took its toll in weariness, but Toda was relentless. And the sessions were beneficial not only to the people counseled but also to those of Toda's close disciples who sat in the corner of the room, listening and profiting by what they heard.

Counseling was supposed to last from two to four in the afternoon, but it usually ran until five o'clock. When everyone but the close disciples had gone, Toda would return to the offices of Daito Shoko to hear business reports over a quick supper brought in from a nearby restaurant. In whatever time he had left, he would work out plans for the lectures he was to give in the evenings.

The annual summer course at Taiseki-ji, starting on July 31, was a great success, with forty-five hundred people attending (three times the number who attended the preceding year). Though it kept Toda busy with lectures and counseling sessions, it also gave him, if not a rest, at least a needed change. Apparently in good health and certainly in good spirits, he enjoyed swimming and discussing all kinds of subjects with his young disciples: his experiences as a teacher in Hokkaido, his fondness for the children he had taught, the importance of vitality in all undertakings, and the relative unimportance of trying to amass a fortune. From each of these friendly, warm, and informal sessions, Toda tore himself away with the greatest reluctance.

But soon the summer course was over, and Toda returned to Tokyo and his hectic round of demanding duties. He flew to Osaka, Fukuoka, and Sapporo to help fortify the chapters in these important cities. He attended the headquarters executive meeting for August, at which it was reported that 4,623 households had been converted during the month.

In September, the *Seikyo Shimbun,* the newspaper of Soka Gakkai, became a weekly (previously it had come out three times a month) and, while increasing its circulation to twenty-one thousand, lowered its subscription rate by 20 percent.

All of the officers, who resumed their full schedules at headquarters in the autumn, were sunburned and ready to plunge into new assignments. The study department grew, and the Friday lectures on the *Gosho* were reconvened. Toda placed special emphasis on the study of Nichiren Shoshu theology, since the prewar Soka Kyoiku Gakkai had disintegrated partly due to the fact that its members were not fully acquainted with the cardinal doctrines of true Buddhism.

Rapid growth was reflected in the numbers of pilgrims to Taiseki-ji. In September, the total of more than three thousand pilgrims who went there made it necessary to institute a system whereby such trips were conducted twice monthly, on the first and second Saturdays.

In all of this growth and activity, all dedicated members were called upon to put forth their best efforts. But there was only one man who never had time to rest—Josei Toda.

8. PURITY AHEAD OF PROFIT

INTENSIFIED attention to outlying districts, one of the policies Josei Toda instigated at the New Year, 1953, was producing excellent results, and Toda himself was personally training chiefs to take charge of the work. Meetings of district organizations were held in various parts of the country, but Toda had been unable to attend any of them until he decided to go to the Karuizawa District meeting, held on September 27.

The city of Karuizawa, located at the foot of Mount Asama, in Nagano Prefecture, is today a highly popular mountain resort, where thousands of people flock to escape the heat of the Tokyo summer. But its fortunes have gone up and down with the changing times. It was popular with the rich and with the foreign community in the earlier part of the century, and during World War II it grew to a population of 50,000 as evacuees from the city—many of them foreigners—packed the many fine summer homes on the slopes of the mountains. After the war, the town was virtually depopulated, when most of these people returned either to the cities or to their own homelands. Prosperity returned to Karuizawa when the occupation authorities requisitioned the local hotels and recreational facilities for the use of their personnel. When the San Francisco

115

Peace Treaty was signed in 1952 and the occupation forces left Japan, many of the villas and homes in Karuizawa passed into the hands of profiteers, who attempted to make fast money in real estate, while the majority of the local population remained unemployed and impoverished. Both land transactions and the low income of the population are related to an incident in Karuizawa that involved Toda and Soka Gakkai.

Shoichi Mizuno, who was born into a Karuizawa family of devoted believers in the Minobu sect of Nichiren Buddhism, had had a hard life after the war. When his foundry went bankrupt, he went into the waterworks business, but this also failed. Realizing that the teachings of the Minobu sect were heretical, he became a member of Nichiren Shoshu.

Since business was slow, he had plenty of time in which to spread knowledge about Nichiren Shoshu among his relatives and friends. He visited from house to house throughout the town and before long had a small band of fellow believers. Life was hard for them all in a town that now had a population of only about two thousand households, and they found it impossible to win more than about a dozen families to Nichiren Shoshu. But they were determined to do better. Scraping together the money for train fares, they visited surrounding villages and cities—including Komoro, Ueda, and Nagano, as well as Naoetsu, Kusatsu, and other towns on the Shin'etsu and Koumi train lines. Finally their efforts began to bear fruit. As more and more families joined Soka Gakkai, it became necessary for administrative purposes to set up a district. Hiroshi Izumida came once a month from headquarters to attend district lecture meetings and to offer guidance and advice. Soon, thanks to his help, more of the members found gainful employment and began to enjoy the blessings bestowed on them by their faith in the Gohonzon. At discussion meetings and leaders' conferences, they expressed their gratitude for the happiness they were receiving.

By April 1953, the district had a membership of 300 households. The district continued to expand by about 25 percent each month until, by September, it was among the top ten most rapidly growing districts in the organization and had increased to 750 households. For a remote mountain district, this was an astounding record, which quickly caught Toda's attention. But he saw at once that the members of the Karuizawa District were suffering under a disadvantage: they had no local Nichiren Shoshu temple where they could conduct initiation ceremonies (Gojukai) and other ceremonials. Toda resolved to build them a temple, the second sponsored by Soka Gakkai after the one that was opened the previous year in Kanagawa Prefecture.

Arriving at Karuizawa Station on September 26, Toda was in the best of spirits as he greeted the crowd of members who had come to welcome him and then went to his inn to relax and enjoy the bracingly cool, autumnal mountain weather.

On the following morning, as the rest of the group went to the place where the district meeting was to be held, Toda, Mizuno, and Miss Katsu Kiyohara were driven in an automobile to inspect the proposed site for the new temple. Mizuno was proud to have been able to purchase at a reasonable price a stretch of land on a hill about twenty minutes' walk from Karuizawa station. As they enjoyed the beautiful scenery and fine air, Mizuno pointed out to Toda the many advantages of the site and then triumphantly announced his plan for financing the project. Both a merchant at heart and a man of faith, Mizuno was still religiously immature. He had been practicing the faith of Nichiren Shoshu for no more than two or three years and did not understand its intense purity. This was why he was willing to suggest that Soka Gakkai buy the land, set aside part of it for the temple, and sell the rest to members from Tokyo, who were enjoying the merits and blessings of their faith and could therefore afford such a purchase. The profits from the sale of land could be used in constructing the temple.

At first the rest of the members of the Karuizawa organization had ridiculed Mizuno's idea as a pipe dream. But they, too, were religiously immature; and, before long, Mizuno convinced them that it was the right thing to do.

Toda was by no means convinced. Indeed, he was deeply disheartened at Mizuno's crassly commercial attitude. He himself had trained the leaders who were responsible for district groups. How was it possible that such an attitude had not only appeared but had also grown to such an extent? He had always struggled to keep commercialism out of Soka Gakkai. And Mizuno's plan for making money on land ran counter to the entire spirit of the society.

They had been walking toward the car as Mizuno outlined his proposal. Suddenly, in an outburst of rage, Toda shouted, "What idiocy! What are you? A land shark? I don't like any of this at all. Driver, back to Tokyo at once!"

Mizuno was stunned. What had he done? Gradually it dawned on him that the land scheme had offended. But he did not see what was wrong with it. His religious immaturity prevented his understanding the imperative need to keep Soka Gakkai free of all impurity and commercialism.

As Toda shouted to return to Tokyo, Miss Kiyohara quietly told the driver to go at once to the public hall where the district meeting was to be held. Hiroshi Izumida was waiting for them. Getting out of the automobile, Toda raged at him, "What kind of guidance have you been giving these people? I have no intention of putting up with anything shady."

Izumida was as stunned as Mizuno had been, but after a minute's reflection he came to the conclusion that all of this must have something to do with the land for the new temple. Kiyohara quickly and quietly related to him what had transpired.

Izumida went to Toda and took all the blame. He said that it was because of his own inefficient guidance that things had gone wrong. Toda agreed and, in a calmer fashion, explained that he would have objected less if the proposal of land purchase had been made to the Daito Company. He could not tolerate the idea of attempting to profit by selling land to members or of trying to capitalize on the construction of the temple.

Though upset, Toda realized that many of the people at the meeting were completely pure of any commercial interest. He therefore agreed to take part. And he did so with the best of spirit. He counseled and advised as if the entire land transaction trouble had been completely forgotten. The meeting ended congenially, and the reception following it took place in a pleasant atmosphere. But that evening at the station, as his train was about to leave, Toda caught sight of Mizuno and said quietly but forcefully, "No more tricky business deals. Understand?"

The temple Myosho-ji, which how occupies a plot in a residential section near Karuizawa Station, was not built until the autumn of 1954. Toda allowed his plan to lapse for a while, but he was not to be kept from doing good for the members of the district by Mizuno's commercially inspired money-making scheme.

At the headquarters meeting held on September 30 at the Toshima Public Hall—the first such meeting conducted in that spacious auditorium—reports showed that the goal for the year of 50,000 households was within reach. The Kamata Chapter broke the thousand-household mark for the month, and the Yaguchi district of the Kamata Chapter, which was headed by Seiichiro Haruki, had converted 334 households. In his remarks at the meeting, Toda praised the chapter and the district and said that Haruki must be enjoying good fortune. "Good fortune," he said, "does not come to people who fail in their duties as chapter and district chiefs."

He then explained that all efforts in the great membership campaign were duties to be fulfilled and not actions to be undertaken in the hope of reward. "Our work is painful and apparently unrewarding. If you don't like it, quit now. I have come into the world as a follower of the Bodhisattvas of the Earth, in order to work during the Mappo era. I can do nothing to reward you, but eventually the Dai-Gohonzon will see to it that you get what is yours by right. And, for those who work, rewards will be great. Chant the Daimoku, pray, and work in order to obtain blessings."

He concluded his talk by reminding the leaders that, though work in the rural areas was important, they must not sacrifice to it efforts to convert people in their own home areas in the city. Both the rural and the urban areas had to be regarded as parts of a total, consolidated plan.

One interesting aspect of Soka Gakkai's advances in rural areas was that they were bringing into the fold Nichiren Shoshu believers who expressed a desire to join Soka Gakkai. Members of organizations attached to the temples Hosen-ji and Horyu-ji, for example, both in Hokkaido, were so impressed by the activities of Soka Gakkai that they asked to be admitted. Toda petitioned the head temple on their behalf and received permission to accept them into Soka Gakkai. In this way, Soka Gakkai was making itself felt in all parts of the nation.

9. A NEW HEADQUARTERS

IN 1952, the membership gave its consent to a collection of funds for the purchase of a new headquarters building to take the place of the one in Nishi Kanda, now hopelessly overcrowded. But, because of his intense faith, Toda had decided to give precedence to the repair of the five-storied pagoda at the head temple; and the purchase of a new headquarters was postponed.

In early September of 1953, however, a former ambassadorial residence in the Shinanomachi district of Tokyo came up for sale. The wooden-framed, mortar-covered building, which was built in 1935, stood on a site of eighty-three square meters and had a total floor space of roughly sixty-three square meters. On September 4, the leaders of Soka Gakkai inspected the building, learned that the price was eleven and a half million yen, and, in less than two weeks, signed a contract of purchase for the building, which was to be officially turned over to Soka Gakkai on October 10.

Drastic alterations were necessary. A large meeting hall would have to be prepared, and the rest of the building would have to be divided into smaller rooms for the Seikyo Press and other offices. An additional two million yen was allocated for reconstruction, which was to be completed in one month.

On November 13, in the presence of Josei Toda and a hundred leaders of the organization, the Gohonzon bestowed on

旧 学会本部

Soka Gakkai by the high priest of Nichiren Shoshu was officially installed in the new headquarters building. Hiroshi Yamagiwa, chief of the Young Men's Division, and Shin'ichi Yamamoto bore the Gohonzon to its new home. At the new headquarters, Takeo Konishi and several chapter chiefs, one of whom held the headquarters flag, awaited their arrival. The main hall on the second floor was packed with members. Soon the shrine for the Gohonzon arrived by open car, and Toda and his group assembled not long after. As the assembly chanted the Daimoku, Toda reverently installed the Gohonzon in the shrine and led the group in chanting. The ceremony ended at one o'clock in the afternoon. In the evening, Toda hosted a banquet in the hall, which was floored with fragrant, fresh tatami mats. Bright lights, singing, and laughter enlivened the ordinarily quiet residential district until late at night. And the bustle continued into the next few days, as members came from far and near to see the new headquarters and sit with beaming faces as they chanted the Daimoku in front of the Gohonzon.

Toda was delighted with the spacious quarters and the small garden and pond. He hoped to hear insects chirping there throughout the autumn. He worked day and night at a large desk in his office, a Japanese-style room floored with eight tatami mats and separated by only a thin wall from the neighboring hall. After a week, he discovered that the constant chanting in the hall interfered seriously with his activities and, though he did not really want to do so, found it essential to put limitations on the hours at which the hall could be used for worship.

Services to commemorate the tenth anniversary of the death of Tsunesaburo Makiguchi were held in the hall of the new headquarters on November 17. The spacious room comfortably accommodated Taiei Horigome, chief of Josen-ji temple; two priests who had been on close terms with the late Makiguchi; Mrs. Makiguchi, now well advanced in years; her grandchildren; Toda; and all Soka Gakkai leaders above the rank of district chief. After Gongyo and Daimoku and a memorial service, various members stood, one by one, to relate their memories of the great man. Toda listened with profound emotion, then stood to make his remarks.

"What you have to say brings back so many memories. As Mr. Yamadaira said just now, Makiguchi was fond of young people. I was closely associated with him from the time I was young until the age of forty-four. On many of my visits I stayed at his house until one or two in the morning. Sometimes Mrs. Makiguchi would give up and go to bed first. When she did, she would say something like, 'Scholars talk forever.' "Toda smiled at Mrs. Makiguchi when he said this.

He continued: "Mr. Makiguchi was a great man, but his nation did not appreciate his greatness. Indeed, the government put him in prison, where this man of integrity, purity, and sincerity died.

"In his introduction to Makiguchi's *Value-Creating Education Theory*, Juri Tanabe said that whereas the French government honored Fabre, a primary-school principal who dedicated his entire life to entomology, Japan forced Tsunesaburo Makiguchi, a primary-school principal who dedicated his life to the creation of an epoch-making system of education, to suffer all kinds of persecution and to die in prison. Was this the way to pay tribute to a man who was a source of pride for a nation that is supposed to be on a high level of cultural development?"

Taking up a copy of the recently published *Philosophy of Value*, by Tsunesaburo Makiguchi, Toda said, "Perhaps Mr. Makiguchi leaned a little too far in favor of his theory of value. I know how a man can do this with a philosophy that is dear to him. I myself once leaned too far in favor of the Buddhist teachings of T'ien-t'ai, and I was punished for it. My punishment makes it clear that the center of all our teachings must be the Gohonzon. For, if the Gohonzon is the heart of our approach, the value-creating system can be put to highly effective use. For ten years, I have hesitated to take positive steps to publicize the theories of Tsunesaburo Makiguchi. I now intend to launch a full-scale campaign to make them known to the world. As his disciple, I consider this my duty. Of course, my goal may not be achieved during my lifetime. If it is not, I rely on you to see the task to completion."

With this statement, Toda clarified the position of the philosophy of value in relation to Soka Gakkai. The book *Philosophy of Value* was published in Japanese in time for the tenth anniversary of Makiguchi's death. Toda was then making arrangements to have it translated into other languages, so that it could ultimately be sent to other nations.

To conclude the services, Mrs. Makiguchi spoke a few words of gratitude for what had been said and done in memory of her late husband.

10. PREMONITION

THROUGHOUT these autumn months, Toda continued to keep up his frantic schedule. In the morning session of the ninth general meeting—at which some seventy-five hundred people filled the auditorium of Chuo University, and the retired high priest Nichiko Hori made one of his rare public appearances—Toda made several vitally important remarks about happiness in life. After explaining that the Lotus Sutra teaches us to be happy, not in a relative, but in an absolute way, he said, "This absolute state of happiness is attainable only to a person with unwavering faith in the Gohonzon. The things needed for a truly happy life are money, health, and vitality. To acquire them, total faith in the Gohonzon of the Three Great Secret Laws is indispensable. The Gohonzon is the source of our happiness. If you regularly perform morning and evening Gongyo and win ten new members to Nichiren Shoshu yearly, with the help of the Gohonzon, you will acquire money, health, and vitality to enable you to lead a happy life."

During the afternoon session, announcement was made of the formation of a new chapter in the city of Sakai, not far from Osaka; Hiroshi Asada, from Osaka, was appointed chief. This brought the total number of chapters to sixteen. Then letters of commendation were awarded to people who had won more than thirty new members during the year and to the chiefs of districts that had remained in the top ten in membership drives for six consecutive months.

Chief Director Konishi made a talk about the shakubuku goal for new memberships in the coming year. Toda had set a goal of 80,000 new households. But Konishi insisted—and, judging by the applause greeting his remarks, the audience agreed with him—that the goal should be raised to 130,000 to bring the total membership to 200,000.

Next Toda discussed the eternal nature of life in the past, the present, and the future; the ruling power of karma in the lives of all beings; and the possibility of changing karma through devotion to the Gohonzon. Attainment of Buddhahood during this life through faith in the Gohonzon is the only way to prevent the law of karma from carrying present sufferings into the future.

Next he said that, though the membership was being disobedient in setting a goal of 130,000 instead of accepting his more conservative 80,000, he would permit them to do as they wished, in spite of his own skepticism about their ability to reach the target. (As it turned out, Toda was right: in 1954, new memberships amounted to only 102,820, over 27,000 short of the goal.)

At the final leaders' general meeting of the year, held at the Toshima Public Hall on December 21, it was announced that in 1953, 51,996 new membership households had been registered; this was nearly 2,000 more than the goal. The new total strength of Soka Gakkai was 74,308 households, a 250 percent increase over the 22,312 households at the beginning of the year. Success made all the leaders jubilantly convinced that they could achieve anything as long as they did their best.

The Young Men's Division held its second general meeting in the auditorium of the Hoshi College of Pharmacy, in Gotanda, Tokyo, on December 23. Only seven hundred people had

attended the general meeting on April 19. At that time, each
of the four sections of the organization had been ordered to
bring its membership up to 1,000 during the year. They had
carried out orders; and, as of December, the total membership
of the division was 5,340. Morale was very high.

Reports on studies by eight selected members took the
place of the usual testimonials. Among the talks on racial
problems, capitalistic and communistic systems, qualifications
of cultural nations, and an interpretation of the "Twenty-six
Articles of Warning" by Nichiko Shonin, the second high priest
of Nichiren Shoshu, the most moving was a talk entitled
"Though I Am but an Apprentice," delivered by Ryoichi
Sawada, a printer's apprentice. Touched by the passage in the
Gosho where Nichiren Daishonin says that, though of lowly status,
he rejoiced at having the chance to study Mahayana Buddhism,
Sawada expressed his conviction that, proud to be Josei Toda's
disciple, he saw the seed of great future success in the struggles
he was facing in his present lowly place. He felt that Toyotomi
Hideyoshi, a famous military ruler of Japan in the sixteenth
century, had succeeded partly because he had served as a
humble page to a local warlord during his youth.

Smiling as he listened to these and other speeches, Toda tacitly expressed his confidence in the young men by making only
a brief talk, in which he said he wanted them to continue to
develop and mature. At the conclusion of this short talk, something unusual happened. The master of ceremonies asked
everyone to stand, and Shin'ichi Yamamoto advanced to the
platform. Facing Toda, in a resonant voice, he made the
following presentation:

"Our Oath to President Josei Toda.
"The expectations that Josei Toda, great teacher of shakubuku in the Latter Day of the Law and one of the world's
foremost philosophers, has for us fill us with deep emotion.
On the eve of the great religious battle and in the seven hun-

dred and second year since the establishment of true Buddhism, we five thousand warriors of the Supreme Law make the following pledge:

"1. We warriors of the Young Men's Division solemnly promise the Dai-Gohonzon that we will dedicate our lives in absolute unity to the religious revolution that aims to attain Kosen-rufu.

"2. We warriors of the Young Men's Division pledge to carry out President Toda's mission of saving mankind and to devote ourselves to this great task in a way worthy of his disciples.

"3. We warriors of the Young Men's Division pledge to do our utmost to accomplish our sacred mission in complete faith with our comrades at all times and in all places and to be fully aware of our importance as the advance guard of the society and as the irreplaceable disciples of President Toda.

> December 23, 1953
> Shin'ichi Yamamoto
> Chief, First Section
> On behalf of the Young Men's Division."

As the room echoed with thunderous applause, Toda stood in silence.

Because he wanted the spirit of the Suiko Club to pervade the entire Young Men's Division, Yamamoto had modeled this oath on the one made by that hand-picked group of young men, who were receiving special training direct from Toda.

That night, at work on his novel, *Ningen Kakumei* (Human Revolution), which was appearing serially in the newspaper *Seikyo Shimbun,* and galley proofs which had to be ready the next day, Toda read the portion he had recently finished, describing his arrest by detectives. Ten years had passed since that terrible event—ten turbulent years. Toda wished that

Tsunesaburo Makiguchi were alive to see how the small society he founded so long ago had grown into an organization of 50,000 households. This year, 1953, had been the great test. If Toda succeeded in meeting his goal for this year, Kosen-rufu would be assured. He had eagerly awaited December, when the outcome of all the efforts would be known. Now that success had been proclaimed, the outlook for the future was bright. If things continued to go well, within a few years the society would probably have a membership of 750,000 households. The very idea was exciting. Feeling a strange palpitation in his heart, Toda raised his hand to his chest as he chanted the Daimoku.

Debilitated by prison and ten years of heavy labor, he knew he was in his last years. Soka Gakkai was marching forward, and his life was drawing to a close. Enlightened and in full perception of eternity, Josei Toda once again turned to the Gohonzon to perform his nightly Gongyo.

BOOK EIGHT

11. THE TIDE OF
ACTUAL PROOF

A T T H E ninth general meeting of Soka Gakkai, held in November 1953, Josei Toda told his close disciples: "We have no need to convert 180,000 new households in the coming year; 80,000 is quite enough. Numerical expansion is meaningless unless it is accompanied by doctrinal study and training to make new members capable of fulfilling their responsibilities. Without prudence, discipline, and education, our organization might collapse under the burden of excessively rapid growth in numbers alone."

Elated by the triumph they had scored that year—more than doubling the membership with a total of 51,996 new households—Toda's disciples did not understand his apparent conservatism. They wanted to keep up—even accelerate—the pace in the coming year. Consequently, at the time of the New Year, 1954, serving as president of a snow-balling religious organization presented Toda with many serious problems. Each of the 70,000 households in the membership was important to him: he was responsible for them all, both spiritually and materially. He felt that he had to ensure that they remained firm in faith in the Gohonzon. He had to see to it that they were not so heavily burdened that both their daily lives and their religious faith were imperiled. For a religious organization with a sacred mission—like that of Soka Gakkai—quality must take precedence over quantity.

Toda's superb leadership and guidance were largely responsible for the triumph Soka Gakkai experienced in 1953. But there was another inspiring force impelling its members to carry out propagation drives and membership campaigns with intense zeal. Though a large percentage of the membership was relatively young in the organization, many of them were already beginning to enjoy abundant spiritual and material rewards for their active practice of faith. When they put what Toda taught them to actual practice, difficult problems in their lives were solved, and they were given proof that the religion they embraced was the noblest possible guiding principle for human life. Their own experiences testified to the true greatness of the Gohonzon and thus dispelled any remaining cloud of doubt from the minds of those who had until then been unable to accept their own good fortune. With the realization that teaching, practice, and proof are integral parts of the Buddhism of Nichiren Daishonin, they came to see clearly that theirs was the only truly living Buddhism for our times.

At discussion meetings, members continually astounded each other by relating experiences proving the virtues of faith in their own lives. Testimonials suddenly opened for everyone a formerly unknown world of truth, vitality, and joy—a joy arising from the Gohonzon. The members spoke of their experiences with the complete conviction that only truth—the truth of the Buddhism of Nichiren Daishonin—can give and with previously unknown happiness. They were anxious to share their joy with others and by means of their testimonials set up a chain reaction that was in itself a powerful form of shakubuku.

The rewards enjoyed even by Soka Gakkai neophytes were as varied and as diverse as are the fates of human beings, but all of them marked boundaries between old ways of living and the new life after conversion to Nichiren Shoshu. Relating some of these experiences may be a fruitful way to demonstrate the power of faith in the Gohonzon.

A convincing example of a man who demanded proof of faith is to be seen in the story of Seiichi Tomita, a devoted scholar who had once studied at the University of Manchester, in England, and whose wife was the granddaughter of a noted elder statesman of the Meiji era (1867–1912). Tomita, who had served on the technological staff of the Ministry of Commerce and Industry, was in his fifties when he was overcome with a strange pancreatic necrosis. This took place in the chaotic years following World War II. Of weak physical constitution, he ultimately had to undergo surgery. Though a friend who was a member of Soka Gakkai had compassionately attempted to win him to the faith, Tomita, a scientist, insisted that he could not believe in anything that was incapable of being scientifically proven. Although the operation he underwent was pronounced successful at first, it later caused serious intestinal adhesions.

Because of the dire situation of the Japanese economy at the time, Tomita, who had a wife and three sons and who had contracted another disease by this time, was forced to look for employment. His skills at the English language enabled him to find work as a job consultant in the procurement office of the forces of the British Commonwealth. Aware of his poor health and afraid that his intestinal ailment might grow worse any day, Tomita was walking on thin ice. Finally, one day, when the doctor had given him the disturbing news that he must once again face surgery, Tomita had a visit from his Soka Gakkai friend, who earnestly entreated him to believe in Nichiren Shoshu and thus to overcome illness and misfortune. Though reluctant to do so, Tomita, who was now desperate for a way out of his sickness, agreed to make an experiment: he decided to test the faith of Nichiren Shoshu for six months. If he was cured within that period, he would consider the validity of Nichiren Shoshu teachings scientifically proved and would be willing to believe in them as something that had been scientifically established as valid. His friend agreed, with the understanding that, during the six months, Tomita would have to do as instructed in matters of faith. Tomita accepted, with the proviso that, should he not be cured, he would be allowed to sever connections with Soka Gakkai and Nichiren Shoshu.

Like a good scientist, once he had joined Soka Gakkai, Tomita conducted Gongyo daily, carried out shakubuku activities as he was taught, and took part in discussion meetings. At first skeptical, he gradually noticed, to his amazement, that his health was improving. Before the six months of this strange experiment were out, he was in such good condition that his doctor had ceased to mention surgery.

Though until recently he had known nothing about the existence of Nichiren Shoshu, the wonderful success of the experiment and the improvement in his health after long years of suffering convinced this scientist that the Supreme Law is indeed the supreme guiding principle for human life.

Tomita continued carrying out his religious duties with increased vigor and shared with others the truth that he had established for himself through scientific experiment. He took part in shakubuku activities regularly and was distressed that British strictness about working hours prevented his taking part in the rural guidance trips of his fellow Soka Gakkai members.

Before long, however, the occupation forces, who were gradually reducing their British contingent, began to dismiss Japanese employees. Among those dismissed was Tomita, who, with the New Year holiday just around the corner, found himself once again out of work. How was he to make ends meet?

In the past, when out of a job, he had suffered anguish and

anxiety. This time, he was faintly happy at the prospect. Why? As a scientifically-oriented man, he analyzed his motives and saw the answer. He had been given enough severance pay to meet his immediate needs; and, more important, the dismissal gave him the free time to participate in a guidance trip. He applied at once, received permission, and was soon on his way to Fukuoka, in Kyushu, with a group of organizational leaders headed by Miss Katsu Kiyohara. For the first time able to devote himself totally to religious work without thought of job or family, Tomita was busy and elated at the idea of helping save others from misery and misfortune.

On the afternoon of their third day in Fukuoka, Miss Kiyohara interrupted his counseling session with two ladies and asked him to go at once to Hasuike to help a member of the Young Men's Division who was in difficulty with a prospective new member. Since the order came from no one less important than the highly respected Miss Kiyohara, Tomita complied immediately. Jotting down the address and leaving the two ladies with Miss Kiyohara, he dashed out and caught a trolley headed his way.

After only a few minutes' travel under a bright blue winter sky, the trolley car began to plunge out of control down a slope. No one had had time to wonder what the matter was when, with a deafening roar, the trolley crashed into something, throwing the passengers wildly about in clouds of dust and a rain of shattered glass from the broken windows. After a few seconds, when the dust had settled, Tomita was able to examine himself and to find that he was unharmed. He was apparently the only one who had escaped totally, for most of the other passengers were bleeding and moaning in pain. Eager to discover the cause of the accident, Tomita quickly left the trolley car and saw that the vehicle had plunged into the rear of another one at the bottom of the slope. The front of his trolley was a mass of twisted metal and shattered glass. But he had no time to examine it closely before still another car came hurtling down the same slope and rammed into the rear of the one he had just left.

Tomita alone escaped unharmed from this triple collision. He knew that he had been saved by the Buddhist deities and, after explaining what had taken place to the police who were

immediately on the scene, he boarded a taxi and hastened to Hasuike to complete the task on which he had been sent. (It later turned out that fallen leaves covering the tracks had rendered the trolley brakes temporarily ineffective and caused the accident, in which many people were injured, some seriously.)

His narrow escape convinced Tomita that the Buddhist deities provide absolute protection for believers in the Gohonzon, and he dwelt on the subject at length at the discussion meeting held that evening. During this gathering, a telegram for him arrived from Tokyo. It contained the information that he had been reinstated in his job with a 10-percent pay raise. When he told Miss Kiyohara about the events of the day, she said the trolley accident had been an expiation for his sins and that his job had been restored to him immediately after it as an example of what it means to change one's karma. Acting on instructions in the telegram, much more elated than he had been when he departed, Tomita returned to Tokyo that very night.

Seiichi Tomita had received actual proof of the truth of Buddhism. The *Gosho* says: "I, Nichiren, find nothing more dependable in judging the righteousness of Buddhism than reason and theoretical proof. Still, actual proof is more valuable than reason or theoretical proof." Not merely people of a scientific turn of mind, like Tomita, but all human beings can see the truth of Buddhism. In Tomita's case, however, proof, acquired only after a rigorous test, was valid even judged on the basis of scientific criteria.

The case of the Yamakawa family reveals the dangers of obstinacy in the face of proof of the power of the Gohonzon. Mitsuyo Yamakawa, who had been repatriated from mainland China at the end of World War II, lived with her sickly husband and their children in Koto Ward, Tokyo, where she worked hard to make a living. The owner of the factory where she was employed was a group chief in Soka Gakkai.

This kindly man often attempted to convince Mrs. Yamakawa that her life would improve if she accepted the teachings of Nichiren Daishonin. But she always refused to hear of such a thing, because she and her whole family professed faith in the Shingon sect of Buddhism. The factory owner told her that Nichiren Daishonin had clearly explained that the Shingon sect could cause the "ruin of the country" and that it could well be the cause of her family's misery. He added that she, too, would understand this if she studied the truth of Buddhism

enough to learn to discriminate between true and false teachings. He usually ended his remarks by telling her that she
would find happiness in matters of everyday life if she accepted
Nichiren Shoshu teachings.

But all of this kind counsel only made her angry. Although
belief in Shingon had brought her no benefits or rewards, she
could not believe that her religion was the source of her
unhappiness. When she told her husband what her boss had
said, he at first flared up indignantly that this man should
presume to disparage an ancient, well-established religious sect;
but then he professed his dislike at hearing any talk of religion
at all. A few days later, he fell and broke an arm. Not long
thereafter, the Yamakawa's five-year-old son fell and broke his
arm.

Mrs. Yamakawa's employer called on the family, offered his
condolences, and attempted to convince them that things could
get worse unless they immediately accepted the teachings of
Nichiren Daishonin. But Mr. and Mrs. Yamakawa refused
to think that the double accident in the family had been anything but a coincidence. Mrs. Yamakawa evaded the issue by
saying that she was praying to the Buddha for the fulfillment
of a certain wish and that if, by the new year, her wish had not
been answered, she might consider joining Soka Gakkai. In this
way, she issued what amounted to a challenge to Nichiren
Shoshu.

In January of the following year, her husband caught cold
and was confined to bed. Once again, Mrs. Yamakawa's employer enraged her by saying that the cold was a punishment
for her hesitation to accept the true faith. When she reported
this remark to him, in spite of his fever, her husband stormed
from his bed and house to rush to the factory owner and berate
him for making fun of their wretchedness and calling it a
punishment, as if they had done something wrong.

The factory owner explained to Mr. Yamakawa in calm,
measured words that until three years earlier he, too, had been

unable to make a clear distinction between right and false religions. Nonetheless, such a distinction exists. Nichiren Daishonin had shown that Shingon was a false religion. The Yamakawa family was unhappy, not out of their own fault, but out of the fault of a wrong religion. He went on to show that, according to Nichiren Shoshu teachings, it requires one hundred days, one year, three years, or seven years for a person to become aware of the true Buddhism. Calmly, compassionately, he warned that some grave misfortune might strike them if they persisted in their mistaken course. Though the factory owner's sincerity and calm assuaged Yamakawa's fury, he and his wife still hesitated, on the basis that they were still unconvinced.

Three months later, the Yamakawas' three-year-old daughter was hit by a motorcycle and stricken with paralyzing internal bleeding of the brain and spinal cord. The doctor at the hospital where she was receiving emergency treatment said that she could not survive.

Hearing of the accident, the factory owner hastened to the hospital and once again cautioned the Yamakawas. On this occasion, Mrs. Yamakawa decided to accept the faith; but her husband still held back.

The little girl's condition deteriorated. Yamakawa pled with the doctor to save her, but only learned that the matter was out of the hands of medical science. Still, the kindly doctor said that, some time before, an apparently hopelessly injured man had recovered because those around him devoutly practiced religious faith. Perhaps it was worth a try.

Now ready to be converted, the Yamakawas hastened to the home of the factory owner, who was delighted to have a chance to help. But it was past midnight. Gojukai initiation rites would have to wait till morning. Nonetheless, the group chief positioned the couple in front of the Gohonzon in his own home and led them in chanting Daimoku till dawn. At first light, the family rushed to the hospital to learn that their daughter had drunk a whole container of milk. The child was still in a deep sleep, but the frightened mother and father thought they saw an improvement in her condition. The doctor still shook his head in despair.

Later in the morning, the Yamakawas received a Gohonzon from a nearby Nichiren Shoshu temple. When they returned to the hospital, their child had been removed from the emergency ward and put into a private ward. They enshrined the Gohonzon by her bed and chanted Daimoku without pause.

On the following day, the factory owner, who had come to inquire about the child and who was deeply moved to see the state she was still in, said that he personally would take the mother and father to Josei Toda for guidance and counsel. Though ignorant of who Toda was, the man and wife, with sleepless, swollen eyes, did as they were told. They were willing to do anything for the sake of their daughter.

Toda was stricken with pity upon hearing about the poor little girl. He announced that the only thing for the Yamakawas to do was to save their child's life through their own deep faith. His brow clouded for an instant when he learned that the Yamakawas had joined Nichiren Shoshu only the day before. Still, if they were willing to have faith and to cling to the Gohonzon for the rest of their lives, he would administer gohifu —granted by the head temple—to them for their child. Mitsuyo Yamakawa's voice rang true when, with tear-filled eyes trained on Toda's face, she vowed to be faithful to the Gohonzon for as long as she lived.

Back at the hospital, the factory owner guided the Yamakawas in administering gohifu, which the child took in great swallows. The small group then chanted Daimoku before the Gohonzon for the rest of the night. In the morning, the doctor, who had dropped in to encourage the family from time to time throughout the dark hours, was astounded to announce the incredible truth that the child's condition was improving and that she might live.

Little by little, the girl began to move her paralyzed body. In a week, she was able to raise a rice cracker to her lips and eat it. And, fifteen days after the accident, she left the hospital.

For the first time in their lives, the overjoyed Yamakawas understood what the factory owner had meant by the omnipotence of the Gohonzon. Their very existences were changed. In time, the husband's health improved. He began to work energetically. Mitsuyo sometimes recalled then the old days when she had considered herself and all her family the most unhappy people. What a great difference the power of the Gohonzon had made. The entire family was now happy, cheerful, and full of hope for the future.

Toda often told members that belief in Nichiren Shoshu is the only hope for people whose conditions are beyond the powers of doctors or whose poverty is so great that nothing seems capable of alleviating it. And the testimonials of many people at discussion meetings proved that worshiping the Gohonzon with unquestioning faith had enabled them to call forth their own life-forces and to become strong enough to dispel the curses of illness and extreme poverty, even when all other doors to hope had been closed in their faces.

Proof of the power of the teachings of Nichiren Shoshu were turning up all over the country. In a farm village in Saitama Prefecture lived thirty-three-year-old Masayuki Makita, both of whose lungs were infected with tuberculosis. As if this were not enough, before long, illness and disaster struck other members of his family. His eldest daughter contracted pneumonia, his mother went blind, one of his younger brothers had to undergo an appendectomy, and his father was injured in an accident. His own condition deteriorated, and he had to submit to an operation for hemorrhoids.

Although Makita's family had always been believers in the Shinto Inari gods of the harvest, one of his friends, a member of Soka Gakkai, attempted to convert him to the true Buddhism. At first, Makita raised petty objections and refused. Later he saw that he had no recourse if he were to survive and to alleviate the condition of his suffering family. He became a member of Nichiren Shoshu.

By this time, however, his physical condition was so bad that he could barely chant Daimoku three times in succession, and he had to rest every ten meters when walking. The local village doctor told him that the operation he needed entailed the removal of several ribs, but that his condition was now too weak to permit anything so drastic. Still Makita managed to perform Gongyo daily and to take part in Soka Gakkai discussion meetings, because he knew this was the only way to save himself and help his family find happiness. The testimonials of others at discussion meetings convinced him that he must keep his flame of faith constantly alive and must devote his own life to the Gohonzon, the embodiment of the life of Nichiren Daishonin. He decided to perform what seemed for him the impossible task of chanting Daimoku one million times. When he had completed this, a sanatorium that had previously refused to admit him, because of the advanced state of his condition, opened its doors to him.

The doctor in charge disappointed Makita bitterly by announcing that the lobotomy on which he had placed all of his hopes for recovery would be fatal and that only a ten-year period of medical care in the sanatorium could cure him. Ten years! That was practically a death sentence!

Medical science had failed him. At first he wondered how grave his past sins must have been if even the miracles of modern medicine could do him no good. Then, from the depths of his being, welled up the conviction that he must devote himself to a still more dependable source of life and hope: the Gohonzon. He resolved that he would be cured by the day on which it was necessary for him to undergo his fifth X-ray test. He once again challenged the task of one million recitations of

Daimoku and started to try to win other patients to the true Buddhism.

No one would listen to him, however, because of his wretched physical condition. Nonetheless, he persevered. Even when a heart ailment was added to the other trials he had to bear, he continued shakubuku activities and performed Gongyo. Sometimes, as he sat reciting on his bed, he would sway because of the dizziness brought on by high fever. The other patients ridiculed him and said that he was chanting sutras because he knew his time had come. Some of them mocked him by rapping on bowls or making cacophonous sounds on guitars in accompaniment to his recitations. Out of the window next to the bed that was his world he could watch hearses carrying their sad loads to the smoking crematory on a nearby hill.

His battle was long and difficult, but he fought it. By autumn, his heart trouble had disappeared, and the pressure in his lungs had eased greatly. By the New Year, he was allowed to stay out overnight. On New Year's Day, he resolved to chant Daimoku for one million more times—this was the fourth time he was to do this. In the spring, he convinced the doctor to allow him to go to the head temple. Tears rolled down his cheeks as he worshiped the Dai-Gohonzon at Taiseki-ji. And, with this pilgrimage, his condition took a decided turn for the better. He improved day by day. By June he had chanted Daimoku a total of five million times.

On July 1, he went in for his sixth X-ray examination, and on the following morning he returned to the office with mixed feelings of hope and disquiet to hear the results. The doctor said with astonishment, "I've never seen anything like this! You're nearly well. You should be able to go to work before long. Congratulations, Makita!"

During the two years and seven months that elapsed between his joining Soka Gakkai and his dismissal from the hospital, Makita had chanted Daimoku five million times and had converted six tuberculosis patients, including one of his former tormentors, a man who had grown steadily worse until his right lung totally ceased functioning. He, too, joined Soka Gakkai, and his health became better.

At a period when most of the population of Japan was ignorant of the true Buddhism and the existence of Soka Gakkai, the teachings of Nichiren Daishonin were giving undeniable, actual proof of their validity in a sanatorium in a remote part of the nation. Once Josei Toda gave the following clear explanation of such proof: "If religious doctrines are substantiated by means of actual evidence, no matter what the age, place, race, or environment, they must be regarded as law and truth. When the prophecies of happiness or misfortune made according to a set of religious doctrines invariably come true, that religion must be accepted as an infallible, scientific law. Our age is in need of such a religion."

Toda firmly believed that the teachings of Nichiren Daishonin are scientifically valid and substantiated by actual proof and that they are not limited to such matters as illness, poverty, or family discord, but extend into all aspects of human life. He was convinced that, because this is true, the teachings of Nichiren Daishonin must ultimately win over all people.

Katsuo Ohsugi, who was in his early fifties when these events occurred, had been a fisherman for all of his life in Hakodate, on the northern island of Hokkaido. He had become the captain of a ship that fished the stormy, treacherous, icy waters off the Aleutian islands. Once a gigantic wave capsized his ship. Though he was saved by a piece of good luck, when he returned to Hakodate, he learned the sad lot of a captain who has not gone down with his ship. No one would hire him. Shipowners would have nothing to do with him. And Ohsugi was plunged into the depths of despair over the prospect of joblessness and poverty in his old age. He became misanthropic and suicidal. Formerly he had been a member of a religious sect and had faithfully worshiped a variety of Shinto and Buddhist deities, including Kompira, the guardian of seafarers, and Acala, the god of fire. After his disastrous accident at sea, he abandoned all of his former gods and came to the conclusion that, since it had done nothing to help him, religion must be powerless to do good.

The atheistic stance that he now assumed caused him to turn away from a friendly Soka Gakkai member, who offered to introduce him to Nichiren Shoshu. In August of this same year, he somehow came into possession of a pamphlet announcing a lecture on Buddhism by a group of Soka Gakkai members visiting Hakodate. Ohsugi was infuriated. Did he not know the uselessness of religion? How dare these people attempt to deceive others? Ohsugi was so angered by what he considered low deception on the part of these people that he went to the lecture meeting in order to unmask them by relating his own experiences as proof that religion is a waste of time.

For quite a while at the lecture, Ohsugi was in complete agreement with what was being said. The lecturers started out by denouncing other religions as heretical and clearly stated that the sect to which Ohsugi had formerly belonged was the most pernicious and dishonest of the lot. Up to this point, Ohsugi mentally applauded; but his attitude changed when the lecturers began to claim that Nichiren Shoshu is a true religion, indeed the only true religion. Ohsugi had never heard of Nichiren Shoshu and presumed that the people giving testimonials to its greatness were no more than a claque hired off the street for the occasion.

After the meeting, one of the speakers approached Ohsugi in a friendly way. Ohsugi at once said that he agreed with them that all religions are false, but that he did not think it was possible to prove that Nichiren Shoshu could be an exception to this general rule. The speaker, who had a mild, northeastern accent, answered that Nichiren Daishonin had devoted his life to proving the validity of his teachings seven centuries ago.

Ohsugi said he was not interested in anything that had happened seven hundred years ago. Then the speaker suggested that the testimonials offered that day might prove the truth of Nichiren Shoshu, but Ohsugi was unwilling to accept this either, since he suspected all the people who had testified of lying: what they said was too good to be true. Finally, the speaker invited Ohsugi to prove the truth of Nichiren Shoshu teachings by applying them to his own life.

Ohsugi was oddly moved by something in the voice—or perhaps it was the face—of this man, who then said: "I am willing to stake everything I have on the certainty of an improvement in your life if you accept Nichiren Shoshu. Today is a very important day—a serious turning point for you. You may accept Nichiren Daishonin's teachings or not. It's entirely up to you. But I assure you that, if you do join Nichiren Shoshu, you will come to know absolute happiness."

Ohsugi was still skeptical, but he could not dismiss this man and what he said. He was so different from all the priests Ohsugi had known in the past. He decided to hear him out. After all, the man said the decision was up to him.

Then, after briefly tracing the three-thousand-year history of Buddhism, the representative of Soka Gakkai explained that Nichiren Shoshu is the only true Buddhism for this Latter Day of the Law (Mappo era). Ohsugi found all of this new, but strangely convincing. And, if they were indeed true, the testimonials he had heard and doubted earlier attested to the orthodoxy of Nichiren Shoshu. He folded his arms and began to think in a new frame of mind.

The man from Soka Gakkai went on: "You have learned from bitter experience that the other religions with which you have come into contact have been false. You have never professed faith in Nichiren Shoshu. Therefore you cannot really know whether it is true or false. Now I, a man who does put faith in Nichiren Shoshu, am telling you that it is the only true Buddhism for our times. Since you set store by actual experience, why not try Nichiren Shoshu for yourself and see whether it is true or false? I assure you that things you now believe too good to be true will happen in your own life."

The man's gentle, unprepossessing manner pleased and convinced Ohsugi, who next asked: "What do you mean by things too good to be true?"

"Well, for one thing, the Gohonzon, the object of worship of believers in Nichiren Shoshu, gives the vitality and strength to change your own destiny."

"To be frank" said Ohsugi, "I need something to give me strength. I'm still not entirely convinced, but I'll trust you. I'll give it a try."

On the following day, at the temple Shoho-ji, in Hakodate, Ohsugi received a Gohonzon and then went home to get rid of the mountain of religious talismans he had collected over the years. He needed a cart to haul them away.

From then on, a ray of hope appeared in a life that until then had been dominated by a wish to die. Pessimism and despondency vanished, as he practiced his new religion. A captain with no ship, he had plenty of time for chanting Daimoku, hour after hour. He attended every discussion meeting and joined others in shakubuku activities. He tried to convince some of his old colleagues from the fishing fleets to join Nichiren Shoshu, but they would not take the word of a shipless skipper and even started rumors that Ohsugi was losing his mind and babbling strange things.

Ohsugi still had no job, but he was no longer in despair. He trusted in the Gohonzon and faithfully carried out his religious duties. In May of the next year, a new fishing fleet was forming in Hakodate. Boats from all over the nation were assembling, and Ohsugi wanted to join. Still no one would have him. For a few more days, he took refuge in the Gohonzon and in chanting Daimoku. Then suddenly a shipowner summoned him to serve as captain on one of his ships. Ohsugi was overjoyed. His dream had come true.

As the day for the fleet to set sail approached, other captains put out huge sums of money, paying temples and shrines to pray for their safety and prosperity. With pity for his misguided colleagues, Ohsugi prayed only to the Gohonzon—morning and night—and was thankful and unwaveringly faithful. When the

fleet set sail, each ship, including Ohsugi's, was decorated with colorful flags signifying hopes for a big catch. But Ohsugi's ship carried a Gohonzon scroll as well.

At sea for months, buffeted by winds and waves, some of the ships took big hauls on some days; on others days, the same ships took nothing. But when the fleet returned to port in the autumn and the total haul per ship was announced, Ohsugi's was at the very top of the list. In virtually no time, from the unwanted, shipless captain, he had become fishing champion of Hokkaido. His heart filled with gratitude, Ohsugi left Hokkaido on a pilgrimage to the head temple to report his triumph and to worship the Dai-Gohonzon.

The story of the widow Kiyo Mizusawa is another example of the harm that can be done by ardent faith in wrong religions. Mrs. Mizusawa's husband died when she was only twenty-four, and for more than thirty years she had managed a small restaurant, in order to provide for herself and for her only child, a daughter. Since in addition to providing meals for regular customers she was under contract to supply lunches to a local police station and a reformatory, her business went well. But she was far from rich, because she donated virtually all of her profits to a religious organization.

Suddenly one day, officials from the Bureau of Internal Revenue arrived, examined her books, went away again, and almost at once sent her a bill for a staggering amount of back taxes on the profits she had donated to the religious group. First she tried to borrow, but she could not raise enough money. The tax office continued to dun her until she went to a friend for another loan. This man, a member of Soka Gakkai, immediately told her that merely paying the back taxes would not solve her problem. She was in trouble because of the wrong beliefs of the religion she had practiced for twenty-seven years. Mrs. Mizusawa was angered by this friend, who, instead of helping her when she was down, called her religion false. "Are you going to help me or not?" she cried. "I've been a member of this religious group for all these years, and I have prospered and remained healthy. Now that I'm in a scrape this once, you want to make a fool of me and my beliefs."

Indignant, she rose and started out, when her friend said: "How happy you'd be now if you had devoted twenty-seven years to Nichiren Shoshu, instead of to this false religion!"

Still Mrs. Mizusawa remained determined not to abandon her religion. None of the people who had formerly been willing to help her would do anything for her now. To make matters worse, she suddenly found herself forced to pay a debt for a bond she had guaranteed for a friend several years earlier. Faced with the threat of having all of her property attached, she sat up late at night, desperate and unable to find relief even in weeping. Just as she was entertaining the wild idea that it would be good if the house caught on fire and burned down, she recalled the words of her Soka Gakkai friend: "How happy you'd be now. . . . "

Maybe he was right. Twenty-seven years of devotion to the other religion had only resulted in the worst crisis of her life. Maybe there was such a thing as a right and a wrong religion. She thought this way all night and by dawn had come to the conclusion that she must break ties with the religious group she had supported. Unconcerned by the early hour, she dressed and rushed to her friend. He was startled to be awakened by Mrs. Mizusawa, who looked even grayer and more weary than she had three months earlier. But he was overjoyed to hear of her decision to join Nichiren Shoshu. He quickly advised her about her financial problems and gave her detailed instructions for her conversion.

Mrs. Mizusawa at once went to her daughter's house, which was in the neighborhood of the restaurant, and persuaded her and her husband to join Nichiren Shoshu with her. They agreed, and all three underwent the necessary initiation ceremonies that same day.

The moment she enshrined the Gohonzon in her house, Kiyo Mizusawa felt as purified as if she had been exorcised of an evil spirit. She began to carry out her Nichiren Shoshu duties with the fervor of the true religious woman she was by nature. She prayed for help in her predicament. She worked hard in the restaurant, too, while carrying out all of her religious duties, performing Gongyo, and attending discussion meetings. She felt and looked better, and her business picked up. Moreover, now that she no longer donated her profits to a religious organization, she was soon able to pay off her back taxes and take care of the note and her debts. With her money worries over, Kiyo Mizusawa became deeply grateful to the Gohonzon.

But everything was not going entirely well. Her son-in-law's parents had opposed his conversion to Nichiren Shoshu from the beginning, and they continued to harass him about it over the months. Though he was serious by nature, this treatment drove him to seek an outlet for his emotions in gambling. Debt soon mounted so high that he abandoned his pregnant wife and ran away from home.

When her daughter came to live with her, Mrs. Mizusawa lamented the behavior of the runaway husband. But now the women knew what to do. Together they knelt before the Gohonzon and prayed for the young man's early return. Although for months there was no word of him, they were confident that he would come home someday.

Before long Mrs. Mizusawa's daughter gave birth to a son. The delivery was easy; the labor lasted only about fifteen minutes. But to the horror of both women, during the child's first bath, they discovered that his left foot was smaller than his right one and that it was twisted inward. At the discovery, Mrs. Mizusawa's daughter turned to the wall and burst into tears. But the new grandmother had more presence of mind. Though she realized that this tragedy was retribution for the slander she had uttered against true Buddhism during her twenty-seven years of allegiance to a false religion, she was determined to do something about it. She had not worshiped the Gohonzon long enough to change her karma, but she would spare no effort to cure her grandchild's deformity. First she made a kind of splint with absorbent cotton, bandages, and the thin wooden bottom of a lunch box. Then, and from that day forward, whenever they had a spare moment, she and her daughter prayed to Gohonzon. They kept the baby well wrapped, to prevent the secret of the deformity from being widely known.

About a week later, cautious and both hopeful and frightened, they removed the bandages from the foot, which, to their overwhelming joy, was straight, if still a little small. The mother and grandmother embraced each other and wept for joy. In another two weeks, the foot was perfectly normal and the same size as the right one. The two women chanted Daimoku together in gratitude.

Still, the runaway husband did not come home; but the women were confident that faith in the Gohonzon would solve even this problem.

Then late one rainy spring night, as Mrs. Mizusawa and her daughter were performing Gongyo, they heard a sound outside the door to the restaurant, which was in front of their living quarters. The daughter went to the front of the building, opened the door a crack, saw what appeared to be a vagabond standing drenched in the pouring rain, and called out, "Mother, he's home!"

Mrs. Mizusawa rushed forward, beckoned her son-in-law into the shelter of the dry room, and made him warmly welcome.

In a strange, subconscious desire to see his family, this sad young man had often wandered at night near the restaurant. On this occasion, he had heard the women chanting Daimoku and, unable to drag himself away, in an instant had put his hand on the doorknob. After hearing of the birth of his son and of the curing of his deformity, the new father raised his child on high and vowed to make a new start in life.

In the years immediately after World War II, countless criminal gangs mushroomed in the disturbed, desolate cities of Japan. Umon Sekimoto, while ostensibly managing a restaurant with the help of his wife and daughter, was in fact the leader of one of these bands. Irascible and willful, this man had suffered from gallstones since the prewar days. Indeed, it was the excruciating pain caused by this disease that led him to the first injection of morphine that ultimately transformed him into a drug addict. After fifteen years of drug abuse, morphine was no longer enough. He turned to cocaine; first 27 units a day sufficed, but soon this too was insufficient, and the dosage increased to the appalling sum of 200 units daily.

In the wild postwar days, he became decidedly mad and once tried to put down a rival gang with machine-gun fire. The occupation forces arrested him and sentenced him to a year and seven months' imprisonment. In the stockade, no matter how he howled in pain, the surgeons refused to give him drugs. Instead they sent him to the Tokyo University Hospital, where surgery was performed to remove thirty-two stones from his gall bladder. After his recuperation, he returned to prison to complete his sentence. He was released in 1949.

With the disease that had been the root of his trouble cured, Sekimoto could have reformed. But he did not. Before long, he was more severely addicted to drugs than ever before and turned his home into a hell for his daughter and wife. He beat them when they pled with him to give up narcotics. Though he was a brute, sometimes he would make an effort to free himself of his addiction. Unfortunately, the withdrawal symptoms were too horrible to bear. Once he decided to take a stimulant drug (Philopon) to rid himself of the need to take morphine, which is a soporific. Soon he no longer craved morphine, but was addicted to the stimulant. He forced his wife and daughter to procure drugs—even dangerous ones—and, if they refused, threatened them with ice picks and swords.

Among the customers who frequented Sekimoto's restaurant were some kindly, well-mannered members of Soka Gakkai. Seeing the horror of the lives of the family, these people attempted to win them to the teachings of Nichiren Shoshu, in the hope of inspiring them to change their hellish life for happiness; but Sekimoto refused and raged at the very idea. He threw the Soka Gakkai members out. Still, while not daring to let him know, his wife and daughter joined Soka Gakkai surreptitiously, because they were desperate to save the family from disaster. They had nowhere else to turn; relatives, friends, and acquaintances would have nothing to do with them. Enshrining the Gohonzon they received in their house, frightened though they were, wife and daughter chanted Daimoku quietly. Strangely enough, Sekimoto said nothing and showed no signs of violence. Was he too far gone to know what was happening? Had he come to see that something had to be done?

Ten days after his wife and daughter had joined Soka Gakkai, Umon Sekimoto horrified his wife by passing bloody urine. She took a specimen to the family doctor, who analyzed it and announced gravely that Sekimoto's days were numbered to not much more than a week or two. "It's a wonder he's lasted this long," said the doctor. "The only thing to do now is let him have his way for his last few days."

Daughter and wife returned home and chanted Daimoku before the Gohonzon with utmost fervor, in the hope of saving the man who, while an addict and often unkind, was all they had in the world.

But Sekimoto, unaware of his rapidly approaching death, stumbled out of the house while his wife and daughter were chanting. He fainted on a nearby bridge and, after being carried home, lay in a comatose state, without showing any signs of regaining consciousness.

A Soka Gakkai group chief hurried to the Sekimoto home as soon as he heard of this latest development. For a while, he joined the wife and daughter in chanting Daimoku. Then he suggested that, since Sekimoto seemed to be beyond medical help, they should apply for gohifu. They hastened to the chapter chief, who took an application form and then said that the brief time Mrs. Sekimoto and her daughter had been members complicated the matter: "Gohifu is usually made available only to people who have been faithful for a long time. Still this is an exceptional case. I'll request help in this if you promise to chant Daimoku ten thousand times a day for the next three days." Sekimoto's daughter quickly promised to do as he requested. Then the chapter chief said he would accept the responsibility for applying for gohifu.

At home, with her mother's help, the girl began her task. They prayed for a cure for the ill man. The mother requested that he be restored to health if it was destined to be so and that he smile at her and give her a few warm words if he was destined to die. The doctor visited regularly, but, seeing that Sekimoto remained in a coma, persisted in diagnosing imminent death.

When the thirty thousand chants of Daimoku had been performed, the group chief brought gohifu, which was immediately administered to the patient. Nonetheless, he continued in a comatose state. With his body horribly disfigured by scars and suppurating sores from injections, the drug addict still craved narcotics and moaned deliriously for them. But his body rejected both the drugs given him when they were available and the water that was used as a substitute when they were unavailable. Before long, however, he began to keep down small amounts of roasted fish or grated radish.

Forty-seven days later, on a fine autumn afternoon, Sekimoto regained a degree of consciousness. He heard his wife and daughter chanting Daimoku. The drug withdrawal symptoms were almost gone. At last emerging from an apparently endless infernal tunnel, he knew what was happening. His wife and daughter watched overjoyed as he weakly brought his hands together in a sign of worshipful gratitude, repentance, and faith in the Gohonzon. He smiled faintly. And all three of them first wept, then joined in chanting Daimoku.

A craving to make a pilgrimage to the head temple soon filled Sekimoto's being. Though his physical condition was still weak, his wife and daughter and their friendly group chief agreed to help him make the trip as a sign of his earnest wish to start life afresh.

During the Ushitora Gongyo midnight prayer in which he

participated at the head temple, Sekimoto was unable to kneel upright in the customary position. But he was strong enough to do so on the following day at the Gokaihi ceremony. Tears of joy rolled down the face of this new man, who had been a drug fiend and a thug, as he walked unaided from the temple on his way to his home and a fuller, happier life.

After recovering, he chanted Daimoku vigorously daily. He told everyone about his incredible transformation and constantly gave thanks to the Gohonzon. With joy he engaged in shakubuku work and in five months won the amazing number of fifty-two households to Nichiren Shoshu. Umon Sekimoto was changed completely, and his transformation filled his home with smiles and hope.

These are but a few of the countless examples of objective proof of the validity of the teachings of Nichiren Shoshu that were occurring all over the country at this time, winning the attention of part of the population. It is certain that the many people who changed their karma for the better would have been unable to accomplish such a feat without the Supreme Law of the true Buddhism; but it is equally certain that they would have been unable to do so without the efficient, warm, and rigorous guidance provided by Soka Gakkai under the leadership of Josei Toda.

Through his own experience, especially the mystic enlightenment he underwent while in a prison cell during World War II, Toda was starting to make possible a human revolution for all mankind. With nothing but the Supreme Law as his shield, yet convinced of absolute victory, Toda challenged the misery and misfortune of our time and attempted to cope with problems in the face of which conventional human wisdom is powerless. His unwavering conviction and his relentless struggle resuscitated true Buddhism for the twentieth century, and, in 1953 and 1954, his efforts were bearing fruit in the form of the kinds of proof discussed in this chapter.

Nichiren Daishonin discovered the great Supreme Law of life seven hundred years ago and thus established true Buddhism to take the place of the Buddhism of Sakyamuni, which had lost all ability to save mankind. But Nichiren Daishonin bequeathed to humanity not only the Law but also the principles of religious practice through which any person can transform his destiny. Josei Toda and Soka Gakkai brought these principles of practice to the people of Japan at a time of great national trial, a time when they were direly needed.

12. A NOTEBOOK

ON A COLD day in early February, 1954, a new district chief, whose rural group had been hastily put together as part of a reorganization program, paid a visit to the new Shinanomachi headquarters of Soka Gakkai. Since being appointed to the position of district chief he had encountered all kinds of confusion and trouble. Some of the senior members of his group had resented his sudden promotion. Many of the members were new and reluctant to work with an unfamiliar person. His application for help to the chapter chief brought a letter that promised aid but told him in effect that success or failure depended entirely on the intensity and strength of his own religious faith. Then suddenly he realized that, as a district chief, he was entitled to go directly to Josei Toda for help and guidance.

Before embarking on the Tokyo trip, about which he thought for some time, he decided that he should make more detailed investigations of conditions among the members of his group, so that he could be specific when he asked Toda for help. As Chief Assistant Station Master on a private railway, he had a day off every four days. Availing himself of this leisure, he began to visit members' homes. To his surprise, he learned that many of his group were very poor and that some of them were members of Nichiren Shoshu in name only, since they participated in none of the religious activities of the organization and, in some cases, were so lax as to allow the Gohonzon—the fundamental object of worship—to lie in a corner, neglected and covered with dust.

The district chief attempted to do all he could to improve conditions and to inspire his members to a more active religious life, but the situation was beyond the scope of his inexperienced powers. Finally, making a list in his notebook of the various issues he wanted to discuss, he went to Tokyo to see the Soka Gakkai president. And, on that cold February day, trembling slightly from awe, he approached the headquarters building.

A constant stream of members went in and out of the headquarters building, which had moved from the old, crowded Nishi Kanda building only three months earlier. All kinds of religious business and other activities and, of course, Gongyo services took place in the spacious new building. Although Toda's office door was always open to Soka Gakkai officers, the press of business had forced Toda in January to stop giving interviews to general members. He appointed a dozen chapter chiefs to act as his deputies; but, when they came up against problems too difficult for them to solve, Toda took over personally.

In addition to other offices, the building housed the editorial department of the newspaper *Seikyo Shimbun*. When the rural district chief arrived, Toda was in conference with some of the editorial staff. They were at work on proofs of the second edition of the *Gosho*.

The district chief timidly knocked on the heavy door. No answer. Taking a deep breath, he opened the door to hear Toda say in a warm, friendly way, "Good afternoon. Please come in and sit down." The district chief shyly sat in a corner of the room, away from the table where a group of people were working. He was made even more uneasy when he realized that they were making preparations for the new edition of the *Gosho*. Feeling out of place, he took out his notebook, opened it on his knees, and tried to calm himself by looking over the points he wanted to discuss with Toda.

The people at the table were too busy to pay attention to him. Since the autumn of the preceding year, work had been going ahead on the *Gosho*, and the second edition was to be out in May. Initially, a total edition of twenty thousand copies, all to be sold by subscription, had been announced. But by January, the number of orders had reached thirty-five thousand, and the size of the edition was increased to forty thousand.

In a brisk, businesslike fashion, Toda answered the barrage of questions put to him by the proofreaders. Sometimes he would say, "Confirm that with High Priest Nichiko." At the very mention of the name of an important man like the retired high priest, the rural district chief realized that this was no place for him. He had clearly chosen the wrong day, and he was only making a nuisance of himself. Quietly closing his notebook, rising, and bowing in the direction of Toda and the group, he started to leave, when he heard someone say, "I'm glad to see you again. Please wait a little longer. I'll be with you in just a few minutes." Recognizing Toda's voice, the district chief was surprised and delighted. He had met Toda only once at the inauguration ceremonies for the new district, but the president seemed to recall who he was. Beaming, he sat down and once again opened his notebook and began poring over it.

The proofreading, which had apparently been going on for some time, continued for what seemed an eternity. Finally Toda said to the clearly exhausted staff, "All right, let's call it a day."

Then he made provisions for a trip the following day to see the retired high priest, instructing the responsible persons to be certain to get detailed explanations on all questionable points. It was important to have the high priest's views in the greatest possible exactitude, since this edition had to be absolutely authoritative. He concluded his instructions with these remarks: "There must be no mistakes. A single error would mean erroneous transmission of the true Buddhism of Nichiren Daishonin, and that would be a terrifying sacrilege. The Supreme Law can be present only when it is transmitted correctly. That is why I am determined to make this edition of the *Gosho* definitive. The work is much harder than I had thought it would be. This is the first time in seven hundred years that anyone has undertaken so monumental a project. With your help, I want to ensure absolute accuracy.

"You members of the Study Department have an important mission. In answer to our need, Nichiren Daishonin has sent us the retired high priest, without whose learning and help we would never be able to make the kind of miraculous progress we are making. We must be grateful to him and make the most of the golden opportunity we have been given.

"Keep doing your best for a little while longer, and the task will be accomplished. By the way, stop in at a good Chinese restaurant on your way home and have something nourishing to eat. Charge it to me."

When the editors had carried away their thick bundles of proofs, Toda turned to his waiting visitor and asked: "What's troubling you? You don't look very happy."

Sitting stiffly opposite Toda, the district chief, with eyes cast down, replied, "Well, I've recently been traveling around my district, calling on members, and I have found that a lot of them are not doing what they should do. Many of them leave their Gohonzons lying around the house and don't take proper care of them. Some have returned them, and some have even burned them. I don't know exactly how many families have done this kind of thing, because I haven't visited everybody yet. But I'd estimate that what I've said applies to two out of every ten families."

"As bad as that?" asked Toda. "I suspect that overly zealous members have forced the Gohonzon on these people without explaining its supreme grace to them. You see, some inexperienced members mistakenly think that any kind of shakubuku at all is good. But the Gohonzon is very strict about rewards and punishments, and people who force Gohonzons on new members, who then neglect or mistreat them, do nothing but bring misfortune on themselves and on the new members as well.

"As a district chief, especially in this era of the Latter Day of the Law, first and foremost, you must have patience. Discuss all matters with your group chiefs and assistant group chiefs. Don't try to make everything right at one time. Divide up the work. Be patient, but be firm. Remember, the compassion of the Gohonzon is more like the stern love of a father than the soft affection of a doting mother. Speak to your wayward members with sincerity and firmness. Explain the greatness of the Gohonzon. And once they know what infinite powers it possesses, none of them will ever treat it irreverently again."

The district chief nodded with gratitude and then turned to some of the itemized questions in his notebook.

"Not long ago, a couple who had been converted about two months earlier had a petty quarrel. The wife is more devout than the husband. When the fight had reached a peak, he snatched up the Gohonzon and tore it in two. The wife was terribly upset when she came to tell me what had happened. We went to the temple, chanted Daimoku as an apology, and left the damaged Gohonzon in the priest's custody. What kind of advice should I give people like that?"

Toda replied, "Of course, it's absurd for the husband to take his anger out on the Gohonzon. But I suspect that both parties are at fault, to an extent. The wife may not have been treating her husband as well as she should. I doubt the quarrel was over religious faith. Husbands usually don't argue with wives about such things—especially as long as religious faith costs them nothing. But seriously, wives often do pick fights.

And when a man becomes really irritated, he may fight back by destroying something his wife holds dear—once again, especially if the treasured object has cost him no money. Your task is to teach the husband the vital importance of the Gohonzon to faith and to show the wife where she is falling down in everyday conduct toward her husband. When the two of them have developed a firm enough faith to convince you that they will never do such a foolish thing again, they may be given the Gohonzon back. You must keep an eye on them and encourage them as much as possible.

"But let me caution you again to be patient. As the *Gosho* teaches: 'Clad yourself with the armor of endurance.' Putting this into practice is an important part of your duty as a Buddhist. I myself am short-tempered, but in matters of faith I have extreme patience. Since the days of Nichiren Daishonin, the faithful of the Supreme Law have endured hardships with patience. We cannot achieve our great aim of Kosen-rufu unless we wear the 'armor of endurance.' "

The rural district chief had another case. "Not long ago, a couple—each of them about thirty years old, I should say—who had been converted six months earlier lost their four-year-old child in an automobile accident. When I called on them, they were deeply grieved. They had heard that steadfast faith in the Gohonzon could enable them to see their dead child again during their lifetimes. Is such a thing possible?"

Toda replied, "I can't give you a definite answer. It would be partly wrong to say yes and partly wrong to say no. It all depends on the strength of their faith.

"When I was only twenty-four and had not yet devoted myself to the Gohonzon, my daughter Yasuyo died. I was overcome with grief. But I think I have seen her again since then."

Excited by recollections of the past and deeply touched, Toda paused to find the right words, then went on, "Death is a tremendous problem. I experienced it when my daughter died and again when my wife died. When I thought about my own death, I was terrified. But finally, during the war, while I was in prison, reading the Lotus Sutra helped me to solve the problem of death. Still, I can't say whether this couple will ever see their child again. As I said, it depends on their faith and the power of perception that faith gives."

Though not understanding this subtle reply in full, the district chief felt encouraged to ask more questions. By the time he had received guidance on five of the twenty issues he had prepared, he felt strong enough to deal with the rest on his own. He was strangely uplifted and inspired. Months later, he realized what had happened: Toda had clarified cardinal principles for him. And, once a person understands these basics, it becomes easier to solve problems involving them and their variations.

At this stage, the district chief hesitantly decided to pose the personal problem that had been one of his reasons for making the visit. "May I ask one personal question, Mr. Toda?"

Laughing, then puffing on his cigarette, Toda said, "Well, you've already asked more than your share, but go ahead. First, though, somebody open a window. It's stuffy in here."

Surprised to hear this order, the district chief turned and saw that, though he had been too engrossed in Toda's counseling to notice, a fairly large group of people had come into the room and had been intently listening to the proceedings. One of the women opened a window. The district chief was abashed by the presence of the others, but he went ahead with his question anyway. It turned out that he was at odds with his wife, because, some months ago, attracted by promises of high interest rates, he had deposited all of his savings in a financial firm that had later refused to return his funds, when rumors of the undertaking's financial unsoundness had prompted him to ask for them. Toda at once told him that he had been foolish to fall for a high-interest promise. "You should have come to me before you made the investment. It's too late now. I can tell a man not to commit hara-kiri beforehand, but I can't do anything once he has already cut himself open.

"Try to get back whatever you can, though that may be nothing. Still, don't think that chanting Daimoku is useless, even if you lose your savings. I can't understand how, but I know that faith does work. And you must convince yourself that, because you were once capable of making a large investment, one of these days, twice as much money will come to you from somewhere. Forget the money; regard it as a loss. Go ahead and practice your faith with devotion. Work hard; save. You'll never be cheated again this way, and your new savings will remain intact."

Discouraged at the idea of losing all his money, but encouraged by what Toda had told him to do, the man closed his notebook, bowed in thanks, and went out. His wife would not be pleased with the news. Perhaps she would not understand or believe what Toda had said. But the rural district chief decided that he had strong enough religious faith to help his wife see the truth. His step was firmer and more vital as he headed for home.

13. A NEW DRIVING FORCE

AFTER a lecture in the main hall of the headquarters building on February 8, Toda collapsed. Lying on the floor unconscious, he murmured, "Where is Shin'ichi? Where has he gone?" Shin'ichi Yamamoto was not there, but the people present did all they could to help and called for a physician. After about an hour of unconsciousness and heavy perspiration, Toda woke. The doctors told him that failing health, combined with his murderous schedule of lectures, trips, interviews, and guidance sessions for Soka Gakkai, plus his own work in the Daito Shoko company from which he derived his sole income, were taking a grave toll.

Though somewhat weary-looking, Toda showed high spirits at the meeting of the Suiko Club on the following day, when he and his young disciples went over one of the most exciting parts of the Chinese classic, *Water Margin*. As he looked at the youthful faces around him, Toda felt certain that these were the people to carry out the mission of Kosen-rufu. And this made him forget his own ill health for a while.

After the meeting had adjourned, Shin'ichi Yamamoto apologized for having been away the night before. Acting as if he were not entirely aware of the young man's meaning and making no allusion to his own fainting spell, Toda immediately told Shin'ichi that he was working on an important plan that he would relate to him, once he had it fully organized in his mind. "In the meantime," he said, "you must study hard. Don't be content with what you've achieved so far. Always strive to

improve. You must become an unsurpassed man of wisdom under the Supreme Law. Faith is vital. But, in addition, you must make yourself expert in all the affairs of the world. It's time for you to identify yourself with the destiny of the world and keep this lofty perspective in mind as you formulate your ideas. Otherwise you will be unable to carry out your mission."

Though sensing that something immensely important was taking place in Toda's mind at the time, Shin'ichi was unable to understand precisely what. Nonetheless, he listened attentively.

In January, because of his consistent emphasis on the

importance of youth, Toda had ordered the establishment of a Youth Division section in each chapter. This was an innovation, since, until then, there had been only six sections in the Young Men's Division and five in the Young Women's Division, with members in each section coming from a number of chapters. Because of the rapid growth of the organization, a Youth Division section in each chapter was imperative. Still, splitting them up in this way could weaken the divisions. Something was missing in this plan, but Toda did not know what.

The organization was growing. It was generating tremendous energy. But energy alone is not enough for forward motion. A force that plays a part comparable to that of a ship's propeller is needed if an organization is to move ahead. For years, while standing at the helm of the Soka Gakkai's ship, Toda had served as its propelling force as well. But the double task was wearing him out. He was eager to ensure that someone else could take over as propeller and steersman when he was forced to abandon the work.

He hoped that the new Youth Division sections in the individual chapters would be propelling forces. Even if they were, however, they would be only small ones; and he himself would have to continue to function as the main propeller of the organization. Trying to find a way to convert these small propellers into the large one required by the growing society was what had inspired Toda to develop the new idea about which he had hinted vaguely to Shin'ichi Yamamoto.

He went on: "I still can't discuss this with anyone, because I'm not really sure what I'm going to do. But I want all of you Youth Division members—especially you, Shin'ichi—to study hard and take good care of yourselves. Attaining Kosen-rufu is your task. To carry it out you must be in good health. How have you been feeling lately?"

Shin'ichi replied that Toda's own health was a matter of greater concern. But Toda said, "My health? I can't die yet.

I've still got work to do. Anyone who undertakes an unprecedented task has hardships to face and problems to solve. I've faced them and solved them in the past, and I will go on doing so in the future. The power of faith enables us to overcome our difficulties. And this indicates that our faith in the Gohonzon is true. I'll leave nothing undone that I must do. And the organization has no need to worry about the future as long as you young people keep studying and working." His repeated instructions to go on studying and a heavy, ponderous quality in his manner of speaking made Toda a mystery to Shin'ichi that night. But the talk was making things clearer for Toda himself. Though he did not yet know precisely what the role would be, he saw that Shin'ichi Yamamoto must be given a position in the hierarchy that would enable him to become the propelling force in the Youth Division.

But the whirl of duties soon caught Toda up again and prevented him from giving this issue the kind of attention it deserved. On February 21, he attended a meeting of the Osaka Chapter—the meeting was in effect a general conference of all of western Japan, since members from the Kansai area, Chugoku, Shikoku, and even from Yame, in Kyushu, attended. The meeting showed how Toda's plan to make Osaka a base of operations second only to Tokyo was beginning to materialize. At this time, Osaka and Sakai, where a chapter had been set up only three months earlier, were the driving forces in the region.

The gathering of two thousand enthusiastic people, whose presence and eagerness warmed the unheated hall, convinced Toda that from that time on the Osaka Chapter would be able to handle the responsibility of carrying out on its own the summer membership campaigns in western Japan. During the meeting, new Youth Division flags were presented to the sections in the Yame and Sakai chapters, the first that had been established in accordance with Toda's recently implemented policy. As he headed back to Tokyo for further busy days, Toda was content that the chapters in the Osaka-Kyoto-Kobe area were now on a par in terms of organization and operation with the chapters in Tokyo.

On February 27, the monthly leaders' meeting was held. Reports showed that 7,146 families had joined during the month and that the Kamata Chapter, with 1,551 conversions, was first, and the Adachi Chapter, with 753, was second. The remaining chapters had converted an average of 500 families each. Toda's individual guidance for district chiefs equalized the strengths of the 105 districts and in this way bridged differences among the chapters. Examinations and strict screening on the following day and oral examinations on March 8 produced ten new assistant professors and fifteen new lecturers—most of them members of the Young Men's Division—in the Study Department.

As new Youth Division corps were formed in the various chapters, Toda shaped his idea for a new propeller into its final form: a general staff, composed of the top leaders of the Young Men's and Young Women's divisions, with Shin'ichi Yamamoto as the nucleus. At the monthly leaders' meeting on March 30, after an announcement to the effect that there was now a total of thirty Young Men's and Young Women's sections in the chapters of the organization, Toda said that it was time to set up a general staff, with Shin'ichi Yamamoto as chief and Kiyoshi Jujo as deputy chief and with the following members: Kazumasa Morikawa and Kin'ya Takimoto from the Young Men's Division; and Chisako Irie, Hideko Ishikawa, Hiroko Jujo, and Teruyo Hino from the Young Women's Division.

In doing this, Toda brought to a culmination the years of special training he had given these young people. Few of the leaders or members of Soka Gakkai would realize the mission and purpose of this new general staff for some time yet.

Toda trusted his young protégés so much that he did not even outline the purpose of the general staff or define its relation to other bodies within the organizaton. He left it all to them. At a subsequent meeting, Shin'ichi Yamamoto rejected the idea that the staff members go to Toda for an explanation of their duties. He felt that the job was theirs and that they must do it on their own. They all agreed at once that one of their first tasks was to clarify relations with the leaders of the Youth Division. There must be no friction between the groups, and there would be none as long as they remembered that they were all Toda's disciples. Then Shin'ichi Yamamoto expressed his opinions: "First, we must ask ourselves why President Toda created the general staff. I am convinced that he wants us to remold the Youth Division gradually and on our own initiative. In other words, perhaps the division has not been running as smoothly and efficiently as we have assumed. We must remember the great importance he attaches to our work. In comparison with this, our relations with the present leaders of the Youth Division are a secondary consideration.

"Of course, we must clarify our position to avoid friction. But the heart of the matter is discovering what we members of the general staff are to do. When we have answered this question, all other problems will be solved automatically."

After a short period of discussion among the other members of the staff, Shin'ichi resumed: "Though technically part of the Youth Division, we are a general staff for the sake of Kosen-rufu. That is our function. As Josei Toda's followers, we are to carry out the struggle for the attainment of our goal under his direct leadership. The Youth Division is already deployed along the front lines, and it would be mean and cowardly for us to lag behind."

This simple statement clarified their role for them: a general staff to lead, not just the Youth Division, but the entire organization in the drive for Kosen-rufu. Occupying the only lighted room in the headquarters building, this group of young people discussed their tasks late into the night. Under Yamamoto's guidance, they came to see that they must act as a legislative body, drawing up long-range, comprehensive plans, which the Youth Division, as an executive body, would implement. The general staff's work had become imperative, since, in the past, many of the operations of Soka Gakkai had suffered from shortsightedness and lack of scope. Careless planning could not be permitted if they were to carry out their role in attaining Kosen-rufu. Shin'ichi called the group's attention to the long-range nature of most of the plans that Toda had been proposing recently. He explained, "Plans to handle our rapidly increasing membership must be worked out. Our responsibility is great, for, without the kind of work we must do, the Youth Division will be unable to progress steadily. Let's prove that we are equal to our task, even if none of the other members appreciates what we are doing. This is going to be a severe trial for all of us." Sweating from enthusiasm, in spite of the cold room, Shin'ichi fired the other members of the staff with eagerness to start working at once and as hard as they possibly could.

Some of the tasks they had to perform immediately were to draw up plans for the development and education of the thirty new Youth Division sections, organize the forthcoming general Youth Division meeting, plan division pilgrimages to the head temple, and work out operational plans for the Young Men's and Young Women's divisions for the whole year.

In addition to a mountain of internal problems, the general staff had to deal with trouble between Soka Gakkai and other religious organizations. For instance, they dispatched officials to Niigata, where another religious sect had attempted to obstruct Soka Gakkai shakubuku activities, causing the police to intervene. From such experiences, the young members of the general staff learned enough to enable them to make the following suggestions to the Soka Gakkai board of directors.

"1. In the light of the recent incident in Niigata, it is suggested that the following precautions be taken when membership drives are conducted in rural areas:

a. Converts themselves, and not Soka Gakkai members, should remove heretical objects of worship from their own homes before accepting the Gohonzon.
b. Written applications for the Gohonzon must be kept on file for possible future reference.

"2. Any trouble arising with other religious sects must immediately be referred to the Youth Division for action. All chapters must be advised of this, to prevent district members from acting on their own in such instances.

"3. Since the form in use at present is legally inadequate, the board of directors is requested to consider revising the form for application for the Gohonzon."

As they began their work, the members of the new general staff discovered that a great source of potential in the organization was going to waste, since information on the professions and other vital statistics of members was practically nonexistent. The only information that the Statistics Department was able to provide headquarters was the numbers of members in each village, town, and city. It could not point to people who might be useful in given circumstances because of their distinctive backgrounds, talents, or places of residence. To provide such information, the general staff requested all chapters to submit lists of the names of all members in the educational, political, or judicial fields.

But the very eagerness, success, and efficiency with which the general staff did their work and provided plan after plan and directive after directive confused the leadership of the Youth Division and even caused some hostility. It was essential to clarify the positions of both organizations. The general staff did this in a twelve-article document concerning Youth Division stipulations (June 15, 1954), which they submitted to Toda for approval. He made the following comments: "The essence of Buddhism is the Law immanent in the universe. It is a set of doctrines that everyone must accept and obey; consequently, there is no need to burden people with other rules. Still, an organization does require something like traffic regulations to prevent confusion. This set of stipulations will be effective only if you regard them as traffic regulations.

"Incidentally, I must take this chance to remind you to work selflessly and with utmost effort if you want to become the true driving force of the organization and accomplish your mission. I put my trust in you. If the Youth Division and the society grow more active and vigorous, you'll have proven your value. If their vigor falters, you must accept the responsibility. Be strict with yourselves and generous and understanding with others." These severe, but affectionate words remained imprinted on the minds of the youthful members of the general staff and inspired them for years to come.

The flags of the new sections were a glittering spectacle for the 2,500 members of the Young Men's Division and the 1,500 members of the Young Women's Division who assembled at one o'clock in the afternoon of April 29 for the general meeting of the Youth Division, held in the Chuo University auditorium. As the new section leaders, one by one, expressed their enthusiasm and resolution, Toda saw that his efforts to train his young followers were at last bearing fruit. He knew that the newly appointed leaders would prove to be valuable to the further growth of the organization.

Seated not far from Toda on the auditorium stage, Shin'ichi Yamamoto was aware of the dawning of a new era for the Youth Division, and for himself as well. He silently resolved to accomplish his mission and to transform his youthful energy into a great driving force for the attainment of Kosen-rufu.

Nearly thirty thousand members flocked to the Nihon University auditorium (then called Memorial Hall) in Ryogoku; at the time it was the only auditorium in Tokyo large enough to accommodate the vast crowd that gathered on May 3 to attend the tenth general meeting of Soka Gakkai and to celebrate the third anniversary of Toda's inauguration as president.

Halfway through the meeting, which started at noon, Toda suddenly rose and shocked the entire assembly by making two motions: one that the entire board of directors—Takeo Konishi, Hiroshi Izumida, Koichi Harayama, Katsu Kiyohara, Hisao Seki, Koji Morikawa, Katsuzo Oba, and Joji Kanda— be dismissed; and another that they be replaced by a new board composed of Takeo Konishi (chairman) and Katsu Kiyohara, Yukio Ishikawa, and Yoji Haruki as members. Both motions were unanimously carried. Though the audience did not understand the reason for the reshuffle and the drastic reduction in the number of board members, a refreshing sense of change filled the air. By his selection of Yukio Ishikawa, the youngest of the chapter chiefs, and Yoji Haruki, the chief of a district that consistently produced better results than many chapters, Toda was indicating that only able, highly efficient persons were eligible for the board. The entire membership became keenly aware of a wave of new vigor, indicated by the formation of the thirty sections, the establishment of the general staff, and the selection of a new board of directors.

After this business was completed, a membership report was made. At the time, the membership stood at 102,637 households, or almost a hundred times the 1,204 households of three years earlier, when Toda had been made president. Hearing the thunderous applause, Toda, who was rising to take his place on the rostrum as the final speaker of the day, saw clearly that the organization was definitely waxing stronger.

"I won't burden you with difficult doctrinal explanations today," he began. "There are some people who consider the Soka Gakkai spirit complicated and difficult. Actually, of course, it is completely simple: all we have to do is return to the spirit of the times of Nichiren and accept and keep the Dai-Gohonzon as we identify with him.

"Some of you today may think of shakubuku as only a way of ensuring the expansion of Nichiren Shoshu and Soka Gakkai. You are mistaken. Nichiren Daishonin inscribed the Dai-Gohonzon to make all people happy, not just to make them worship."

Toda explained, however, that the degree of benefit a person receives is determined by the strength of that person's faith. Then, with the following words, he said good day to his audience: "I am sure that many of you have worries or unfulfilled wishes. I hope that you will all come back to the next general meeting and that, when you do, you will enjoy the rich benefits you will have earned from unrelenting practice of faith. Even if you don't come to the meeting, I hope you will receive the benefits."

The tenth general meeting ended on a note of appreciation for the organization's unprecedented success. The unexpected reshuffle of the board served as a warning to all who held office that positions must be earned through fervent practice of faith and actual accomplishments.

It had rained since dawn on May 9, and transportation had become so disorganized that the ceremony to culminate the Youth Division pilgrimage to the temple, which had been scheduled to begin before the main gate to the head temple at eight in the morning, was postponed until noon. The last contingent of members did not arrive until eleven-thirty. But, ultimately, fifty-five hundred young men and women from the thirty newly-formed sections gathered to renew their pledges for the march to Kosen-rufu.

Though soaked to the skin, the eager crowd was happy and cheerful. Someone quoted a famous line from a Kabuki play: "It's springtime rain. Who cares if we get wet!" And this humorous comment summarized the feelings of everyone present. The playing of a small brass band cheered the waiting young people until, finally, Toda and the top leaders of Soka Gakkai, unprotected from the downpour, and preceded by a drenched headquarters flag, entered the plaza. Yamagiwa, chief of the young Men's Division, made the opening remarks: "Today, 702 years after the establishment of Nichiren Shoshu, the full force of the Youth Division is gathered here to pledge our preparedness to confront the Three Formidable Foes, who are bound to try to hinder us. Come what may, we are determined to follow President Toda and fight for the attainment of Kosen-rufu, even at the cost of our lives. With our section flags, emblems of our noble cause, we solemnly swear to the Dai-Gohonzon to dedicate our lives to the propagation of the Supreme Law."

Taking the rostrum and looking out over the crowd of soaked, but happy, proud young people, Toda said, "I apologize to you for the rain. I feel certain that it is a sign of punishment for my own past slanders. But it could be a portent of future ordeals that our organization will have to face. I want you to recall this rainy ceremony as a reminder that you must surmount difficulties at all costs in order to ensure not only your own happiness, but that of the entire population of Japan as well."

Toda's apology to them for the rain and the apology to the Dai-Gohonzon implicit in it brought tears to the cheeks of many of his listeners.

Following the singing of some Soka Gakkai songs, led by Shin'ichi Yamamoto, the entire gathering went first to the Reception Hall, where they offered prayers for Kosen-rufu, and then to the Treasure Temple, where they worshiped the Dai-Gohonzon. Later, section leaders proceeded to the grave of the late president, Tsunesaburo Makiguchi, where they reported the events of the day.

Back in the lodging temples, weary and wet, but happy, the young people sang songs and discussed the ceremony as they stripped off their clothes, which were clingingly wet and in some cases stained by running dyes. Though the rain might portend difficulties and hardships, for sake of the attainment of Kosen-rufu, all of these brave young people were willing to do their utmost. As they dried off and watched the unabating rain slashing against the windowpanes, they felt as refreshed as if new blood were coursing through their bodies.

In his second-floor room in the Rikyobo, Toda soon heard the footsteps of the thirty section leaders and some of the other

officers coming to report to him—to his intense relief—that everyone was all right, and that no one had fallen ill as a consequence of exposure to the foul weather. Toda was so happy that he relaxed his usual taboo and offered the young men as much sakè as they wanted. He usually forbade the men to drink, because of the expense involved, but he relented on some special occasions like this day. After a pleasant time of discussions and reports, the young men left, many of them already slightly red in the face from the drink. Only the chief of the Youth Division, the chiefs of the Young Men's and Young Women's divisions, and the eight members of the general staff remained.

Toda turned to Yamamoto and said, "Shin'ichi, we can't

let the pilgrimage end like this. I suggest—this is a suggestion, not an order—that you members of the general staff give thought to organizing another general pilgrimage of the Youth Division as the big event of the fall. It should take place in October with ten thousand participants."

"I was just thinking exactly the same thing," replied Yamamoto at once. The other members of the general staff were astounded. They were all exhausted from the hard work they had put in to organizing this pilgrimage, for fifty-five hundred; and now Toda and Yamamoto, both apparently sharing the same thought at the same time, were talking about another one for nearly twice as many people, and only five months in the future. They were astounded by the idea, but they were elated, too. It meant increasing the total membership of the thirty sections of the Youth Division from ten to twenty thousand. Only with that great a membership could they hope to ensure ten thousand pilgrims. Success or failure of this taxing undertaking would determine whether the general staff could truly become the driving force of the entire organization. The look of determination he read in Shin'ichi's eyes told Toda that success was likely. "This is going to be a turbulent year," he thought, "a year in which the old gives way to the new."

14. STUDENTS IN SEARCH
OF THE TRUTH

AS THE DAMP, gloomy mists of the June rainy season swirled outside, Josei Toda, seated comfortably in one of the reception rooms in the headquarters building, was having a good time discussing the Lotus Sutra with a small group of students from Tokyo University, who rapidly and eagerly fired questions that he just as rapidly and eagerly answered with valuable information on ultimate religious and metaphysical issues.

One of the young men, Goro Watari, looked at Toda with intense earnestness as he asked the meaning of the passage in the third chapter (*Hiyubon*) of the sutra: "Do not preach this sutra among the ignorant and undiscerning. If, however, there are those who are intelligent, clever, wise, learned, of sure memory, and seekers after Buddhism, preach this sutra to them." All of the students present wondered if this meant that the Lotus Sutra could be taught only to the intelligentsia. If so, membership campaigns among the uneducated were illogical; and the attainment of Kosen-rufu would be difficult indeed. But Toda explained that, for them, fortunate as they were to live in the Latter Day of the Law, the highest wisdom was expressed in Nam-myoho-renge-kyo and that, according to the Buddhism of Nichiren Daishonin, all people who embraced the Gohonzon were counted among the wisest. In the Latter Day of the Law, the ignorant and undiscerning are people who are unaware of this ultimate wisdom. People who know and believe in it are able to understand the Lotus Sutra.

"As I always say, this is the way you must read the Lotus Sutra. In other words, the essence of the Lotus Sutra is expressed in the form of the Gohonzon. This is the ultimate understanding of the Lotus Sutra. Unless you grasp this point firmly, no matter how often you read it, you will be likely to misinterpret the Lotus Sutra grossly. Today Buddhist scholars, though they interpret each character in the sutra with all their minds, have no understanding of what they are reading.

"But everything becomes very clear when the Lotus Sutra is read from the standpoint of Nichiren Daishonin. And all the other sutras, too, become easy to understand if you read them after having read the Lotus Sutra. But, if you start with the Agama sutras or the Wisdom sutras, you will be rowing a boat against the current and will get nowhere."

Two students then started a discussion of Nichiren Daishonin's remonstrances against the government of Japan in his own time.

"Do you agree that the Daishonin must have been very disappointed after he had remonstrated with the government three times and had become the true Buddha without succeeding in his attempts to have the government change its ways?"

Goro Watari flared up at once with an answer: "It is not a question of disappointment. The Daishonin knew from the outset he would not succeed."

"Then why did he do it three times?"

"Because he felt that this would be the most effective way to teach Nam-myoho-renge-kyo to the people of the time, even if he did not succeed immediately."

"I wonder."

The two opponents seemed to be asking Toda to resolve their differences.

Toda said, "To be certain, we would have to ask Nichiren Daishonin himself, but this is my idea on the subject. Success and failure aside, I think the Daishonin was resolved to do his utmost. It was an important issue, for the sake of which he was determined to give his life. The successive high priests of Nichiren Shoshu have continued to remonstrate with governments as he did.

"At his third remonstrance, when he met Hei no Saemon on his way back from Sado, the government offered to recognize his sect and even build temples if Nichiren Daishonin would stop denouncing other sects and would pray for the defeat of the Mongols, who were threatening invasion at the time. But he refused and went to Mount Minobu, where he inscribed the Dai-Gohonzon for all mankind to worship. A passage in the *Hoon-sho* reads: 'If Nichiren's compassion for the world is truly great and encompassing, the teaching of Nammyoho-renge-kyo will prevail for ten thousand years and beyond into all eternity. It has the power to open the blind eyes of every living being in the country of Japan. It closes off the road that leads to the hell of incessant suffering.'

"This passage testifies to Nichiren Daishonin's belief in the eternal endurance of Buddhism. In comparison with this, the result of his remonstrances against the Kamakura government were minor. And I think that he himself placed much greater stress on the eternal endurance of the Supreme Law than on the success of those remonstrances."

The circumstances leading to Toda's teaching this small group of students from Tokyo University involve the spiritual and religious searches of two of its leading members: Goro Watari and Akira Fujiwara.

Goro Watari's father was a lieutenant colonel in the Manchurian Army. During World War II, when he was assigned to the secret service, he and his family lived in Feng Tien (modern Shen Yang) in northeastern China. An eccentric man, given to drink and opposed to what he considered stupid, senseless fighting, he died of illness before the end of the war. During their life in China, the members of his family, who were devoted members of the Nichiren sect, often chanted Daimoku together, and Goro himself, a middle-school student, became interested in the Lotus Sutra. As a child, from time to time he had expressed the desire to attend a military academy and become an officer, but his father always scolded him and told him to forget such plans and study hard so that, upon returning to Japan, he could enter Tokyo University, known then as Tokyo Imperial University, the most prestigious institution of higher education in the country.

At the end of the war, the Russians invaded Manchuria, and the Japanese living there fled before them. Many Japanese were killed, and Goro often helped at burials. The Russians invaded, pillaged, and looted Feng Tien. The house next to the Wataris' was plundered on ten separate occasions. The Russians chopped off the fingers of a man who was found in possession of a pistol. They shot down an entire family with their "balalaikas," as they called their automatic machine guns. One woman was so ashamed at being raped by a Russian soldier that she set fire to her house and killed both herself and the man who was molesting her. Only two houses in the neighborhood were spared— the Wataris' and one other. Both families were devout believers in Nichiren Buddhism and chanted Daimoku daily. Convinced that their salvation could not have been a mere coincidence, Goro Watari was deeply impressed by the power of Nam-myoho-renge-kyo from that time on.

Repatriated to Japan in 1946, the Watari family, now without a breadwinner, found it difficult to make ends meet. Both Goro's mother and sister went to work. Though only a middle-school student, he did outside jobs to help cover expenses. In spite of the hardships, however, he remembered his father's injunction to try to get into Tokyo University, and he studied hard. And when, after one failure, he was accepted, he seemed to be facing a new dawn of possibilities: to study the works of great thinkers, to work, to grow, to make lasting friendships, and to carve out a brilliant future for himself.

But after entering the university, he was deeply disappointed, partly with the cramped campus—especially restricting to a young man who had spent his youth in the wide spaces of the Chinese mainland—but more intensely with his petty, cold-hearted, superficially clever classmates and with his professors, who seemed to consider teaching nothing but a way to make a living. The circumstances at this time could be considered extenuating, however. Contributing greatly both to the shortcomings of the students and faculty and to the disillusion of such sensitive young men as Goro Watari was the turmoil and the moral and spiritual vacuum of the postwar period.

Not long after Goro became a university student, the occupation authorities began to purge leftist professors and to ban student movements. The ban did not halt the movements, and Goro became interested in them. Still, he could never bring himself to adopt a thoroughly leftist political stance, since he had witnessed with his own eyes the atrocities committed in China by the troops of the Soviet Union, the most important socialist nation in the world at the time.

Lonely, Goro frequently recalled the miracles that faith in Nam-myoho-renge-kyo had worked for his family in Feng Tien. One day, in the late autumn of 1950, he happened to visit the temple Honmon-ji, in Ikegami, Tokyo, where he saw a yellow-robed monk with a small drum, chanting Daimoku, quoting from Nichiren Daishonin, and advocating the Gandhian principles of passive resistance and nonviolence. Daimoku and the priest's pacific thoughts appealed to Goro, who soon joined the temple—which belonged to one of the heretical Nichiren sects—and took part in their activities. This movement later developed into the National Council for the Promotion of Peace, which operated under the sponsorship of a left-wing group in the Socialist Party.

Still forced to work three days a week at laying pipes for electrical or gas installations, in order to eke out his scholarship, while studying industriously and taking part in the lectures and other activities of the group of yellow-robed monks, Watari was often exhausted. He sought respite and help in Buddhism. Usually penniless, he visited secondhand bookstores and stood for hours reading the Buddhist classics he generally could not afford to buy. And when occasionally the temptation to purchase a book was too great, he treasured it and pored over it for hours in the search for spiritual solace.

After a year, Goro was much more interested in the study of Buddhism than in his classwork. Tempted to transfer to a Buddhist university, where he would be able to devote all of of his time to this beloved field of literature and learning, he had already found out enough to realize the superiority of Mahayana over Hinayana Buddhism and to be able to say that the Lotus Sutra is the supreme work among all the Buddhist classics. He tried reading and studying it on his own, but found its difficulties and obscurities too much for him. At first, he tried to find someone who could help in the study, but when this search proved futile, he resolved to try to set up a research group devoted to the Lotus Sutra. He got three applications in reply to the notices he posted about this group on the two campuses of Tokyo University. As he was reading them over one day, he received a call from an unknown student.

This young man, whose name was Akira Fujiwara, was pale, wore glasses, and had long hair—when this was not fashionable among young men. He was a member of the liberal arts department of Tokyo University, as a prospective philosophy major. Akira had seen the notice about the study group, and because of his own interest in the Lotus Sutra, made contact with Goro. Finding that they had much in common, they soon became fast friends.

Akira Fujiwara had begun to worry about the meaning of life while recuperating from a bout of ill health brought on by over-work in preparing to take high-school entrance examinations. At the time, an older cousin discussed serious matters with him, and told him that he considered Goethe's *Faust* the most important work in Western philosophical literature, but that the literature of Buddhism was superior to it and that the Lotus Sutra was the most outstanding achievement among Buddhist teachings.

These words stayed with Akira, who tried without much success to read his father's difficult books on Buddhist topics. After he entered Tokyo University, he turned again to religion and philosophy in the hope of resolving his worries about the meaning of life and death. Renewed attempts to read the Lotus Sutra proved fruitless, and he decided that he would have to find a teacher to help him. By coincidence, a childhood friend who was a student at another university called on him and, after a discussion of religious matters and Akira's desire to study the Lotus Sutra, said that Professor Joji Kanda, an Eng-lish teacher at his school, might be just the man. "His talks on Buddhism and the way that things happening today were pre-dicted three thousand years ago by Sakyamuni are much more interesting than his lectures on English. I'll arrange a meeting with him as soon as I can," said the friend. But no word came. Then, on a day in December, Akira saw Goro's bulletin-board notice about a Buddhist research group.

The two young men set out to get the group started at once. The first thing they had to do—according to university rules—was find a faculty sponsor. After some searching, they learned that Professor Sakamoto of the Biology Department was in-terested in Buddhism and might be willing to help them. He was not only interested but eager as well, since he had studied the Lotus Sutra for years himself. Warning them that under-standing Buddhism took many years, he agreed to be their ad-visor. They decided to call their group the Lotus Sutra Research Society. But the young men who gathered at the first meeting, which took place on January 26, 1952, were bitterly disappointed to find that Professor Sakamoto was resolved to discuss not the sutra itself but its Indian philosophical background and the course of development leading up to it.

In March of that same year, Akira Fujiwara at last heard from his old friend. Until that time, Professor Kanda had been too busy to meet him—small wonder, since Kanda, whom his students jokingly called the "Lotus Sutra Maniac"—was a leading member of the Soka Gakkai Study Division and an editor on the panel that was preparing to publish the *Gosho* in commemoration of the seventh centennial of the founding of Nichiren Shoshu. But it was arranged that he would meet Fujiwara and his friend on the evening of March 17. The friend concluded, "I talked with him today. Though I have no intention of joining his sect—Nichiren Shoshu—I sensed something firm and indomitable in his faith and convictions. And he says that there is a man at Soka Gakkai who is infinitely his senior in knowledge and faith. That man's name is Josei Toda." The name was completely new to Akira.

On the evening of March 17, Akira Fujiwara found himself being closely scrutinized—long hair and all—by Professor Joji Kanda, who, after his examination was satisfactorily concluded, launched at once into a difficult treatment of the eternity of life; the Ten States of life; the Three Existences of past, present, and future; and other doctrines of true Buddhism. He then explained to the bewildered young man that the Buddhism of Nichiren Daishonin was indeed the only true Buddhism and that if he, Akira, was really in search of the truth, he should profess faith in it at once and study its doctrines.

Confused by this totally new approach, Akira attempted to bring the discussion around to his own problems by mentioning the Lotus Sutra Research Society, its faculty adviser, his own intentions of learning Sanskrit to be able to read the sutra in the original, and his hopes of majoring in philosophy. But

Professor Kanda immediately told him that he was on the wrong track. "As he prophesied himself, Sakyamuni's Lotus Sutra is invalid in the present Mappo era, or Latter Day of the Law [Kanda paused here to explain the three stages of the Buddhism of Sakyamuni—the Shoho, Zoho, and Mappo eras]; and this invalidates the need to study the Sanskrit original. The Lotus Sutra, as we have it, is of major importance; but it must be studied in the light of the teachings of Nichiren Daishonin. Any other way of studying it can lead to grave error and harm, as has happened with others in the past."

At the conclusion of their talk, Kanda invited Akira to a meeting to be held at his home on the following night, when young members of Soka Gakkai would discuss the true Buddhism. Perplexed by the idea that, if he accepted Nichiren Shoshu as the true Buddhism, he would have to abandon all he had learned and start afresh, Akira returned on the following evening. After much coaxing, he convinced one of his childhood friends to accompany him. Although Professor Kanda himself was not at home, the lively, efficient meeting dealt once again with the Ten States of Life, the philosophy of value, the criteria by means of which it is possible to discern between true and false religions, and the blessings bestowed by the Gohonzon on faithful believers.

This last point caused Akira so much concern that he asked for an explanation during the question-and-answer period following the general discussion. The group chief first expressed his willingness to devote as much time as necessary to the topic and then advised Akira that, since knowledge of the deep meanings of the true Buddhism could not be acquired in a day, it would be wise if he joined Nichiren Shoshu and took advantage of the study opportunities afforded to members.

Another newcomer left, irritated by what he considered impenetrable doctrines; and Akira, too, rose to go. But his friend tugged him by the sleeve, urging him to stay and listen a while longer. A graduate of one of the technical divisions of Tokyo

University came up to the two young men and explained how becoming a member of Nichiren Shoshu had relieved the spiritual sufferings he had experienced and how this constituted some of the blessings received from the Gohonzon. He admitted that this could not be explained in terms of contemporary science, because scientific thought of the time ignored the fundamental issues of life that are at the heart of true Buddhism. "True Buddhism could be called a science of life," he added.

Professor Kanda returned after eleven, just as the young men were getting ready to depart, and upset Akira slightly by making a comment to the effect that probably the discussion of the evening had been too difficult for him. During the next few days, the young man pondered all he had heard. He was attracted by Nichiren Shoshu doctrines—especially the mystic idea of the Gohonzon. Still, he did not know what to do. After the next meeting of the Lotus Sutra Research Society, at which Professor Sakamoto lectured in a way that Akira found especially unconvincing and empty, he asked Goro Watari to come home with him. The two of them talked for hours about religion. Akira revealed his perplexity over Nichiren Shoshu doctrines; and eager to help his tormented friend, Goro told him how chanting Daimoku had been of infinite help to him and his family during their bitter experiences in Manchuria. He further told him how he had long felt an unchanging fascination with the Lotus Sutra. "Goro is not a member of Nichiren Shoshu," Akira thought, "yet he, too, emphasizes the power of Nam-myoho-renge-kyo. There must be some tremendous strength latent in Nichiren Shoshu teachings and in the Gohonzon."

After intensive analysis of his own development, Akira came to see that his experience with Western philosophy had led him to think mistakenly that he was searching for truth and meaning in life, when actually he had been looking for happiness and the kind of value explained in Soka (Value-Creating) Gakkai philosophy. Remembering the things about value he had heard at the meeting, the timid and sensitive Akira Fujiwara decided to call on Professor Kanda again. He took his childhood friend with him this time, too.

During this visit, the conversation soon turned in the direction of an invitation for Akira and his friend to join Nichiren Shoshu. To Akira's objection that he was still half in doubt, Professor Kanda replied, "That means you halfway believe, doesn't it? I only believed halfway when I joined." Convinced, Akira promised to join. His friend hesitated until he saw the outcome of Akira's conversion.

On April 3, 1952, Akira Fujiwara was granted the Gohonzon at the Kankiryo of the present temple Shorin-ji, in Nakano. At the time, he had just entered his sophomore year at the university. For some months, until he was able to develop unquestioning faith in the Gohonzon, he said nothing about his conversion to the other members of the Lotus Sutra Research Society.

Goro Watari became disillusioned with the peace movement in which he had participated on May 1, when a large-scale demonstration became so violent that it was harshly suppressed by the police. Goro himself was injured in the leg, but escaped arrest. From that time on, though he continued studying the Buddhist scriptures, he became despondent and discouraged.

One June evening, as he and a monk of his acquaintance were leaving the Kyoku Kaikan Hall, where they had been attending a meeting of the National Council for the Promotion of Peace, they were surprised to hear enthusiastic applause coming from the auditorium. Entering, they saw an elderly man who was lecturing vigorously on Nichiren Daishonin's Buddhism to a large, eager audience. The elderly man was none other than Josei Toda, though Goro Watari did not know it at the time.

Before long, some young men approached the monk, whose

yellow robes were conspicuous, especially since he had remained standing. After a few words, they led him out of the auditorium and into a small side room. Though nothing had been said to him, Goro followed. In the small room, the young men asked the monk if he had come to hear the lecture. He said that his visit had been accidental and sneeringly added that he considered it presumptuous of a layman to lecture on the *Gosho* of Nichiren Daishonin. This criticism of Toda led to a heated argument. The young men insisted that the Gohonzon was of supreme importance, and the monk denied this assertion. Goro stood by in amazement as, with formidable knowledge of Buddhist theory, these young men demolished the argument of the priest, who belonged to a heretical Nichiren Buddhist sect.

The monk claimed that as long as a person chants Daimoku it makes no difference whether his object of worship is Sakyamuni, the twenty-eight chapters of the Lotus Sutra, Prince Shotoku, a homemade mandala, the Three Great Secret Laws, or whatever. But the young men—Yukio Ishikawa and Kin'ya Takimoto of the Youth Division, as Goro later found out—insisted that the Dai-Gohonzon only, among the many mandala inscribed by Nichiren Daishonin, bears mention of the High Sanctuary and is therefore both the sole valid object of worship for true believers and the reason why Nichiren Daishonin appeared in this world. They substantiated their argument with this quotation from *The True Object of Worship* (*Major Writings* I, p. 81): "Now is when the Bodhisattvas of the Earth will appear in this country and establish the supreme object of worship on the earth which depicts Sakyamuni Buddha of the essential teaching attending the true Buddha." One of the men went on to prove this assertion by quoting a passage from *On Persecutions Befalling the Buddha* (*Major Writings* I, p. 239): "The Buddha fulfilled the purpose of his advent in a little over forty years; T'ien-ti'ai took about thirty years; and Dengyo, some twenty years. I have repeatedly spoken of the indescribable persecutions they suffered during those years. For me it took twenty-seven years, and the persecutions I faced during this period are well known to you all." Nichiren Daishonin infers that, just as Sakyamuni, Chi-i, and Saicho had fulfilled their purpose on earth, so he, too, twenty-seven years after founding the true Buddhism of the Mappo era, had fulfilled his purpose in inscribing the Dai-Gohonzon, the only true object of worship. The same young man suggested that the yellow-robed priest was perverting true Buddhism by refusing to see these differences. Angered, the monk gulped down the tea that had been offered him and left the room defeated, with a derisive smile on his face.

This incident caused Goro Watari to doubt the monks with whom he had been associated and, in fact, to doubt the entire peace movement. Gradually he became more interested in the organization that Akira Fujiwara had been talking about. Nonetheless, Goro did all he could to keep the Lotus Research Society going.

Having joined Nichiren Shoshu, Akira Fujiwara took part eagerly in study and other activities. He began—unsuccessfully —to try to convince his friends and family to join, too. His parents were uninterested, his childhood friend was still unconvinced, the members of the Lotus Sutra Research Society were indifferent, and even Goro Watari—in spite of his surprising knowledge of Nichiren Buddhism—declined, on the grounds that he was already a member of another Nichiren sect. Akira pointed out to Goro the doctrine that the true Law has been passed undefiled and unchanged from one high priest to another in the course of the history of Nichiren Shoshu only, and that this has come about according to the heritage of Hossui-shabyo, which enables their perfect transition, just as a jar of water is poured into another jar. Goro laughed when Akira illustrated the way in which contents can be passed from vessel to vessel unchanged by pouring coffee from his cup into Goro's. But that is where the discussion stopped.

With no great results so far in his proselytizing work, Akira took part in the August summer study course at the head temple. The happy faces of the pilgrims, the beauty of the temple grounds, and the devotion he saw everywhere braced his weak constitution and enabled him to participate in group

activities. He was intellectually stimulated by lectures from the high priest Nissho and from President Toda. And the astounding testimonials he heard about the blessings and help that people had received as a result of faith in the Gohon-zon seemed to fill his formerly cool, detached mind with rich, warm, and deep human emotions. He was humbled by the comparison between his own relatively minor sufferings and the great burdens that many of the people who testified had borne. With regret that the summer course lasted only five days, he returned to Tokyo revived, refreshed, and confident that from that time on his life would be meaningful, patient, and devoted. He was a new man.

One of his first acts after the summer course was to have his long hair cut to a manageable, neat length. Another was to call on Goro Watari, who gazed with astonishment at his tidy, changed friend, who now seemed self-assured and who even spoke in a louder, firmer voice than before. Goro thought "Can this change—Akira himself seems unaware of it—be the result of conversion to Nichiren Shoshu? If so, I must think about this seriously." He did think, and the two of them talked. After a while, Goro agreed to go to see Professor Kanda, who, with the help of the graduate of the technical division who had spoken with Akira earlier, succeeded in convincing Goro. At the conclusion of the Youth Division meeting held at Kanda's house in the evening, he, too, became a member.

After a few weeks of eager work in the organization and in the Young Men's Division, these two Tokyo University students got up the courage to visit Josei Toda, the leader who towered over the entire organization.

When they arrived at the branch office, they found others waiting for personal guidance. Gauging the length of the time he spent with each person by the gravity of that person's problem, Toda enlightened and inspired them all. Goro and Akira listened, awe-stricken and attentive. At one juncture, Toda spoke to them and learned that they were from Tokyo University and that they had been members for only a short while. He asked them to wait until all the others, even people who had come after them, had gone, so that they could talk without hurrying.

When Toda finally got around to them, Goro Watari started out with a stunning question: "What is the nature of the Buddha?" Without hesitating, Toda said that, though the answer was difficult to give concisely, it could be found in a group of *gathas* (verses) in the opening chapter of the Sutra of Infinite Meaning, the prefatory part of the Lotus Sutra. They read these verses. Then Toda admitted that they were difficult to understand, and that it had taken him a long time to find out exactly what they were about. But in his prison cell, during

World War II, he had been enlightened to the truth that these verses meant that the Buddha is life itself.

As Toda stood silhouetted strongly against the red sunset sky, he carefully explained the verses to the two men. Goro was deeply touched. Though he still was incapable of penetrat-

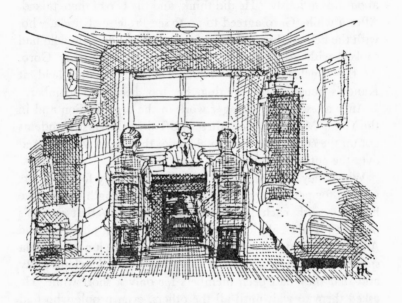

ing the true meaning of what he heard, he had decided that Josei Toda would be his master for the rest of his life.

Akira asked Toda for advice on the branch of philosophy he should study at the university, in order to understand how Nichiren Daishonin's life philosophies would be of much use to him, since, though he and other members of the Lotus Sutra Research Society had certainly devoted sincere effort to attaining highest truths, they were still only fumbling in the direction of Oriental philosophy in general and the life philosophy of Nichiren Daishonin in particular. Toda recommended the study of logic, and Akira made a mental note of that.

He then asked about Indian philosophy and Theravada Buddhism, which Toda dismissed as so-called "London Buddhism," the worldwide fame of which was the outcome of the efforts of British colonialists who had studied Indian history through documents and stone inscriptions during the period of British control of the nation. "Tragically," Toda said, "these people made the mistaken assumption that the Theravada, or Hinayana, Buddhism that survives in Southeast Asia and Sri Lanka today is the true Buddhism, and that Mahayana is not in keeping with Sakyamuni's teachings. This, of course, dismisses all of the developments Mahayana has undergone in China, Korea, and Japan. Oddly enough, many Japanese have studied in London and have come back here to teach 'London Buddhism,' especially at Tokyo University."

When the meeting was concluded with an invitation to come again, the two friends, excited both by Toda's knowledge of Buddhism and by his infallible critical sensibility, were as yet unaware that an unshakable faith in true Buddhism was already beginning to grow in their hearts.

As an outcome of their concern over the way Professor Sakamoto conducted the meetings, Watari and Fujiwara went to Toda about the Lotus Sutra Research Society. Toda agreed to send Yukio Ishikawa to talk with the faculty adviser. Sakamoto agreed reluctantly to see the young man from Soka Gakkai "this once," and then treated the group to a discussion of the Agama sutras and the possibility of attaining enlightenment by chanting the formula known as the "Stanza on Transitoriness." But the visiting Soka Gakkai member was too well informed for him and demolished his theories at once. It turned out that Professor Sakamoto was vague on the subject of the attainment of Buddhahood and wished to ignore the basic theory that all life exists through the three phases of past, present, and future. Finally, angry that he had lost the discussion, Sakamoto ended the interview.

Watari and Fujiwara, who had attended this meeting, were

now more convinced than ever that the true Buddhism they professed was superior to all others. They took new joy and secret pride in attempting to convert their friends, families, and classmates. And their redoubled efforts began to attract the attention of people around them. Goro Watari did convert two of his fellow chemistry majors: Yasushi Morinaga and Susumu Aota, who hesitated at first, but joined Nichiren Shoshu after attending a discussion meeting, where they saw how different the activities of this organization were from everything their scientific minds had formerly rejected in Buddhism.

Watari and Fujiwara convinced Morinaga and Aota to join the Lotus Sutra Research Society, but this organization was in a state of limbo since Ishikawa had put Professor Sakamoto in his place. Once again, they turned for help to Toda, who agreed to conduct their meetings for them.

And this is how Toda came to hold meetings on the Lotus Sutra for a small group of students from Tokyo University. At the meeting to discuss the first chapter of the sutra, someone read, "Thus have I heard. Once upon a time, the Buddha was staying at Rājagṛha on the Vulture Peak with a numerous assemblage. . . . " Toda stopped the reader and asked someone to read the commentary on the sentence "Thus have I heard," from the *Ongi Kuden* of Nichiren Daishonin. Aota read: "Those who do not believe cannot hear in the sense used in 'Thus have I heard.' Only votaries of the Lotus Sutra are to be called people who can hear. The first fascicle of the *Fa-hua-wen-chu* commentary on the Lotus Sutra by Chi-i says that 'Thus' connotes belief and obedience, for, through belief, a person is able to comprehend the Law and, through obedience, the way of master and disciple is established.' Therefore, only Nichiren and his disciples can be called those who have heard 'thus'!"

Toda offered the following commentary: "In this passage, Nichiren Daishonin clearly says that only votaries of the Lotus Sutra are entitled to hear Buddhism. This means that you must believe and constantly seek truth through the practice of faith, if you want to be qualified to hear the Lotus Sutra as disciples of Nichiren Daishonin.

"The great assemblages described in the introductory chapter are not to be taken literally. All of the rituals described in the sutra are representations of the Gohonzon.

"While in prison, during the war, I read the Lotus Sutra practically without stopping. And once I even visualized myself, a follower of Nichiren Daishonin, attending the great assemblage at which the Lotus Sutra was first preached. It is odd how sometimes a man can visualize something from the distant past. But, at any rate, after this experience, I found reading the *Gosho* and the Lotus Sutra much easier than it had been before. In prison, I formed a mental image of the Gohonzon. After my release, the first thing I did when I reached home was to go upstairs to see how the actual Gohonzon compared with my vision of it. They were identical. The impression this experience made on me was so strong that I shall never forget it. I wept at the time."

Toda wanted to leave after this emotional comment, because he had another appointment, but he consented to answer one last question from a young science major, who wanted to know whether he ought to choose a profession in his academic career field. Toda told him that, as Tsunesaburo Makiguchi taught, value is the criterion by which such things must be judged. He said, "In Mr. Makiguchi's words, 'It's folly to be swayed by likes and dislikes and to disregard gain and loss. On the other hand, it's evil to think of nothing but gain and loss and to ignore good and bad.' The ideal job is one that you like, one that benefits you, and one that does good for society. Choosing should be easy for you, since you can rely on the Gohonzon, the fundamental Law, which will endow you with unlimited vitality to study and improve yourself. If you are faithful and devout in worshiping the Gohonzon, and if you study and do your work without shirking, one day you are certain to find the right job.

"Each of you has a great mission to perform. Undergo the hardships and experiences that will help you cultivate vision, and don't worry about choosing an occupation. Success will depend less on the field than on the way you come to grips with the job you face."

The Lotus Sutra Research Society, which continued to meet twice monthly until Toda's twenty-sixth and last lecture on September 27, 1955, grew slowly. Its members found proselytizing on the Tokyo University campus difficult. But from the original ten, it reached a membership of thirty after opening its doors to students from other universities. Even after it disbanded, its members played an important part in the campaign for Kosen-rufu and in other fields of Soka Gakkai activity. Toda's efforts in encouraging this group—which were greater than anyone realized—were to lay the foundation for the establishment of a five-hundred-member Soka Gakkai Student Division on June 30, 1957.

15. EVENTFUL DAYS

On MARCH 1, 1954, radioactive fallout from a United States experimental hydrogen-bomb explosion on Bikini atoll contaminated the crew and catch of a Japanese fishing ship called Fukuryu-maru No. 5. It was later found that fish poisoned by the same explosion were swimming into Japanese waters. This news caused immense amounts of fish that had already been caught to be thrown away and brought such panic that many Japanese stopped buying the seafood of which they are traditionally very fond. Most of the crew members of the Fukuryu-maru were hospitalized with acute loss of hair and itching, blistering skin; one of the men died. The popular turmoil in Japan had little or no effect on the government, which, loyal to the security treaty between the two nations, insisted that the United States government was within its rights to conduct such experiments (other nations had carried out nuclear tests, too, since the conclusion of World War II). President Dwight D. Eisenhower suggested that the Japanese dismay over the tests and the contamination of the fishing ship and the seas was exaggerated. But, for the people of the first nation ever to suffer atomic attack, these tests, even at a great distance from their shores, were a terrifying menace.

Josei Toda approved of the popular petition against nuclear weapons being signed in Japan at that time. The number of signatories was to reach 670 million from all over the world by the time it was presented to the Conference for Banning Atomic and Hydrogen Bombs, held in Hiroshima on August 6, 1955. But Toda knew that only true Buddhism could bring lasting peace. According to Buddhist doctrines, the human mind is ruled by fickleness and change that cannot be controlled. The operation of the life-force commands human mental states, and a sincere, lasting desire for peace can only emerge from an absolutely peaceful state of life. This state—Buddhahood—is attainable only through belief in and practice of the teachings of Nichiren Daishonin. In fact, enabling people to attain this state is the main purpose of true Buddhism in modern times. The goal of the drive for Kosen-rufu was a revolution in the minds and lives of all individuals and a consequent establishment of total peace.

The activities of Toda and his followers were inconspicuous, but they were far more demanding than petition campaigns and promised to have a far wider effect on humanity. Although today everyone realizes that—as the preamble of the UNESCO charter says—wars begin in the minds of men, and that the minds of men must be the place in which defenses of peace are constructed, most people have no inkling of how to go about creating these defenses. Toda knew that it is the teachings of true Buddhism that can revolutionize the inner life of the individual and therefore contribute ultimately to global Kosen-rufu and peace.

Signs of how the work of Soka Gakkai was moving rapidly in that direction were shown at the leaders' meeting following the large-scale, successful summer campaign of 1954. At this time, it was learned that, during the single month of August, 12,771 new households had become members of the organization. In other words, more than one-tenth of the total membership—which stood at 120,000 households at that time—had joined in the astonishingly short period of one month.

Throughout the summer, Toda flew to many parts of the nation on campaign work and, in August, visited Hokkaido and Atsuta village, Ishikari District, where he had lived as a boy. Over a pot of Ishikari stew, in the faintly autumnal air of late August, he looked at the rough northern sea and reminisced about the past with Shin'ichi Yamamoto, who had accompanied him on the trip.

All sixty-eight members of the Suiko Club thoroughly enjoyed the camp outing they spent with Toda in the early part of September. Around a fire at night, after an evening meal of delicious pork stew and rice balls, they laughed and joked and listened attentively as Toda shared his memories of his own education with them, told them that they could all gain as much education as they needed if they only tried, and finally explained how it was not until he had joined Nichiren Shoshu and had thus found a secure orientation for his life that he was able to put to meaningful, practical use the wide knowledge of a variety of branches of learning that he had amassed until then as student and teacher. "My faith in true Buddhism acted as a catalyst," he said. "It made all the knowledge I had thought dead and useless come to life. This was a great benefit bestowed on me by the Gohonzon. And the day will come when you, too, will experience the same vitalization of what you have learned.

"Study while you are young, and, later, faith in true Buddhism will make you invincible in all undertakings. For instance, this faith enables me to go directly to the heart of any subject so quickly and completely that I can master it in a short time and can beat people who have specialized in it for years."

One of the young men asked what he should do about the quarrels he was having with his father. Toda first replied that quarrels of this kind are unworthy of his disciples, then immediately sensed that the point of contention between the two men was the son's prospective marriage.

"Consult your seniors on this important matter and do not let yourselves be carried away by women," Toda counseled. "No parent wants his child to be unhappy, and your father probably has something to say that you should hear humbly and with an open mind. Love is an untrustworthy emotion,

because it can change into resentment or hatred when exposed to different circumstances as time goes by. Physical attraction, which is a major ingredient in most young love, is even more untrustworthy. Animals can concern themselves with nothing but the propagation of their species; but this is not enough for human beings, especially for members of the Suiko Club, who are highly rational and endowed with noble emotions. When you have matured and have become more fully aware of the gifts showered on you by Nichiren Daishonin, you will be better able to judge in matters of this kind. Until then, lend a willing ear to the advice of people who are older and who know more than you do. Stop chasing around after women. When your present faith has made you outstanding young

men in the eyes of all, the right woman will come along for
you. Then you can get married with the congratulations of
everybody associated with you. Marriage is not something to
rush into."

After saying that whether one's life-force is clean or sullied
determines whether reason and emotion conflict and giving the
illustration of Nichiren Daishonin as a perfect fusion of reason,
in his sublime philosophy, and emotion, in his burning desire to save all suffering people, Toda puzzled his young listeners by saying, "I propose that we meet here in exactly ten
years. Then I'll have something important to ask you. The campaign for Kosen-rufu has just started. Everything looks relatively quiet now, but we cannot expect this situation to last.
The Three Formidable Foes are bound to stand in our way.
Soon they will attack, and we must not succumb to them. Only
the life philosophy of Nichiren Daishonin can save our defeated
nation and bring about lasting, global peace. We are the only
ones who know this. Be convinced of your mission, study hard,
and improve yourselves. I have complete confidence that you
will never weaken in faith until we hold our reunion here in a
decade."

All of the young men assured him that they would keep their
faith pure and strong. As Toda, hand raised, turned to go to his
cabin, someone started singing "Hearken to the Buddha's Will,"
and all soon joined in. In his cabin, Toda heard the group singing song after song as the moon rose in the sky and the night
grew older.

After Gongyo and breakfast the following morning, the
young men did calisthenics and played boisterous games as
Toda watched until lunch. Then, an afternoon trip took them
to the construction site of a huge dam. Always eager to help
his young followers develop, Toda took the visit to the dam as
an opportunity to make an edifying comment: "This project
is great. But the man who conceived and planned it is greater,
since he had to have both sweeping ambition and meticulous

care for the smallest things. If you are going to accomplish anything great in the future, you, too, will require these characteristics."

After a brief visit to a nearby waterfall, the party returned to Tokyo. Though the camping trip lasted only a day and a half, it was an exhilarating, fulfilling, and uplifting chance to be with Toda for all of that short time. None of the young men who attended returned to ordinary life the same as he had been on setting out.

Ever since the rain-drenched ceremonies that took place at the head temple on May 9, 1954, the Youth Division had been carrying out intensive preparations for the mammoth pilgrimage scheduled for the autumn of the same year. After the summer campaign, division leaders were happy to see that qualitative and quantitative improvements in membership made prospects for the autumn pilgrimage bright. They set October 31 as the date. Remembering the downpour of the spring, they were all eager to be able to greet Josei Toda in fine fall weather.

From midnight on the thirtieth until the early morning hours of the thirty-first, the vicinity of the main gate of Taiseki-ji was a bustling alighting place for ten thousand people, all of whom were transported from Tokyo to the head temple in a single night. All of the lodgings overflowed with joyous pilgrims. Even though the Reception Hall, the Mieido and Renzobo temples, and the Fuji Gakurin School were used, there was scarcely room for everyone. The final group to arrive from the city reached the temple at six-thirty in the morning and marched immediately to the schoolyard of the Ueno branch of the East Fujinomiya High School, where the ceremonies were to be held. This school is southwest of the head temple, not far from the gate knone as the Black Gate.

The morning air was clear and fresh. The eager young people in the schoolyard found the very chill of autumn invigorating as the sun shone on them and on sacred Mount Fuji, which seemed to be looking down benignly on the proceedings.

At seven-thirty, following the headquarters flag borne by a mounted carrier, Josei Toda rode in on a white horse. To make him easily visible to everyone, members of the Youth Division

had scoured the district for what they considered a suitable mount. With some misgivings, Toda decided that, out of respect for the endeavors of the people who had worked so hard to find the animal, he would allow it to carry him in, even though he could not actually be said to ride it.

During the preliminaries, Hisao Seki, chief of the Youth Division, reported that 6,308 young men and 4,082 young women, a total of 10,390 people, had come to the temple for the pilgrimage. They had succeeded in assembling even more than the promised 10,000. Furthermore, the autumn day was perfect. All present were jubilant.

Leaders of the Young Men's and Young Women's divisions pledged to carry on the struggle for Kosen-rufu as Toda's children, no matter what obstacles might lie in their way. Then, after short speeches by division chiefs, Toda addressed the pilgrims:

"My dear young friends, efforts being made now by politicians, economists, educators, and cultural experts to save Japan are doomed to failure, because the fields in which they work are incapable of doing what must be done, unless they are based on true Buddhism. Only true Buddhism can save our society and allow people to live in happiness."

Toda was implying that the activities of Soka Gakkai must extend into all fields of human endeavor if Kosen-rufu were to be attained.

"The writings of Nichiren Daishonin, Buddhist philosophy, and innumerable pieces of actual evidence prove conclusively that the true Buddhism is the Buddhism of Nichiren Daishonin. Some of the many religions and sects in Japan today seek profit. Others operate solely out of force of habit. Still others attempt to bluff their followers with strange prayers and services. But none of them has the power to bring happiness and stability to human beings. Obviously, none of them can instill in humanity a powerful life-force. They are so weak that their leaders put themselves in the preposterous position of compromising with other religious sects. What is the point of professing a religion if compromises with other faiths are possible? Religions that do not draw sharp distinctions among faiths are cowardly, mean, and weak. I conclude, therefore, that many religions today are interested only in prosperity and are willing to compromise to attain it.

"But we members of Nichiren Shoshu, especially we members of Soka Gakkai, will not compromise. We follow the injunction against it with faith and obedience. Seven hundred and two years ago, Nichiren Daishonin clarified the true natures of the prevalent sects of his time in his famous Four Refutations and rejected each of them in the light of orthodox Buddhist doctrines. Today, we, too, are aware that only Nam-myoho-renge-kyo can save mankind in the Latter Day of the Law. We have resolved to propagate true Buddhism throughout the world. Obviously we are without friends. Since we are determined to confront all other religions, we are necessarily surrounded by enemies. I've been prepared for this ever since I assumed the presidency. I do not mind persecution in the least. But I sincerely hope that I will see all of you absolutely happy before I die.

"Clearly, great difficulties lie in our path. That is why I want you to worship the Gohonzon, love Soka Gakkai, and develop your youthful energy so that you can meet these difficulties courageously."

After thunderous applause and the singing of a Soka Gakkai song, the pilgrims looked up to see a small airplane circling overhead. Suddenly it swooped down and dropped a small cylinder, which landed near the speakers' platform in the schoolyard. The message contained in the capsule was read aloud:

> "Hail to the youths, who stand before our master,
> The great leader of the century!
> Heralding the march toward Kosen-rufu,
> Your ten thousand voices
> And your devotion to your country
> Shake the earth and resound in the sky.
> From high above, moved by your passion,
> I wish you a great future.
>   Katsu Kiyohara
>   Chief, Guidance Department"

As the schoolyard echoed with cheers and shouts, the aircraft circled. Then, from a window of the plane appeared a white handkerchief waving a greeting. The young people below responded by waving their handkerchiefs. Then the plane flew away.

Led by Toda on his white horse, the pilgrims paraded beyond the Black Gate and the main gate to the Reception Hall, where section representatives worshiped the Gohonzon. The procession then moved to the Treasure Temple, where thirty sections, one by one, chanted Daimoku before the Dai-Gohonzon. As the remainder of the pilgrims prepared to depart, the organization leaders reported on the events of the day at the grave of the late president Tsunesaburo Makiguchi.

Over cups of sakè at the Rikyobo lodgings after the pilgrimage, Toda, who was now convinced that the general staff was capable of large undertakings, said that he counted on them for the general meeting, to be held only three days later. This meeting was of special significance, since it was to be covered by major newspapers for the first time in Soka Gakkai history. Public relations were already beginning to be an important issue.

In recent years, the press had been devoting more space to Soka Gakkai affairs, especially the minor trouble that sometimes arose when members were too enthusiastic in shakubuku activities. The reportage was not always fair. Often false, malicious comments were made about the strangeness of this religious organization and its reportedly vast budgets. Some of the people who wrote on the topic were sarcastic about the low social standing of most of the members and about their fierce evangelism. But none of the authors gave serious thought to their own lack of knowledge or shallow interpretations. Toda, who had long been fighting this kind of thing, realized that it was part of the general Japanese public ignorance about religion. The very basic concepts of Buddhism were misconstrued by most people, and Buddhist doctrinal terminology was generally used incorrectly. For instance, the word *"jobutsu,"* which means the attainment of Buddhahood, was widely thought to mean nothing but death.

The general meeting at which representatives of the general public and the press were to be present was a wonderful chance to help enlighten people who were uninformed of the natures of Buddhism and of Soka Gakkai. He would have to work over his lecture carefully. After deep thought, he decided to concentrate on the elements of Nichiren Shoshu that distinguish it from other religions and sects and make it the only true religion in the world. He would be interested to see the newspapers' reactions to what he had to say.

On November 3, the day of the eleventh general meeting, the weather was beautiful. At noon, when the proceedings were declared open, Director Ishikawa reported that between January and October, the number of new households reached 86,545, or well over the 80,000 goal for the year that Toda had set. The news that their annual target had been passed two months ahead of time delighted the audience.

Following reports from the various divisions, a special lecture by High Priest Nissho, and some testimonials, Toda rose to speak. He could see the newspaper reporters in the visitors' gallery as he started.

"A passage on page 200 of the *Gosho* reads: 'Throughout Japan, only Nichiren is aware of this.' At first encounter with this comment, I wondered what it was that Nichiren Daishonin alone knew. Then I realized the full, awe-inspiring implication. This sentence means that Nichiren Daishonin alone knew that heretical teachings make men unfortunate and unhappy.

"It necessarily follows that all religions and sects other than the Buddhism of Nichiren Daishonin are wrong. The Buddhism of Nichiren Daishonin is the only true religion; and only Nichiren Shoshu of Taiseki-ji, at the foot of Mount Fuji, has correctly and consistently preserved his teachings. All other sects and religions are likely to block our way to Kosen-rufu. We do not make enemies because we want to. We make them because of our refusal to compromise on this absolute truth.

"The more we come to know of true Buddhism, the less willing we are to remain indifferent to the existence of other religions, which bring misery on mankind. The sufferings of human society can be uprooted only when the adherents of other religions and the entire public embrace the true Buddhism. Winning them to this view is our aim. And, unavoidably, alarmed by our activities, other sects, which are ignorant of the essence of Buddhism, have become our enemies.

"No matter what difficulties stand in the way of Kosen-rufu, I ask you to believe in the absolute Dai-Gohonzon and never to forsake your faith. My one wish, my one admonition, is for each of you to attain Buddhahood, the highest happiness, and then to live in joy."

Implicitly, Toda was saying that when mankind recognizes the truth of Buddhism and when Kosen-rufu is attained, a prosperous and glorious society will become possible. For seven centuries, this truth had remained largely unknown, but in the past few years, Soka Gakkai had begun to awaken people to it. His words were charged with determination to bear the brunt of whatever ordeals might befall Soka Gakkai and to protect all its members in their pursuit of happiness, even if it cost him his life. Some members of the enthusiastic audience were moved to tears by his remarks.

Over the objections of the members of the board of directors, who considered the project expensive and inappropriate, Shin'-ichi Yamamoto and the general staff pushed through a mammoth sports meet—called the Festival of the Century—which was held on the sports field of Nihon University only four days after the general meeting. Yamamoto had insisted on going ahead with the project, since he believed it would be a distraction and a morale booster for the Youth Division after their hard, successful work for the ten-thousand-person pilgrimage. Toda gave the general staff permission to go ahead, but instructed them to raise funds on their own. They did this by purchasing various small personal articles at wholesale prices, selling them to friends and acquaintances, and using the profits to finance the meet.

At the conclusion of a range of imaginative and colorful mock cavalry battles based on Buddhist concepts—for instance the Competition of the Three Obstacles and Four Devils and the Great Buddhist War—in which hundreds of people participated, Toda addressed the immense gathering: "You have done splendidly. I am proud of your vigor and enthusiasm, which are the fruits of your daily practice of faith. Perhaps if you worked harder on studying the *Gosho*, over which I have labored with you, you might do as well with it as you have done today in games that I have never even tried to teach you."

When the laughter that his joke inspired had died down, Toda went on, "I love all of you. I would like to give each of you a prize, but there aren't enough to go around. I will present my favorite medals to the chiefs of the Young Men's and Young Women's divisions with the understanding that they are for all of you. Starting tomorrow, I want each of you to study Buddhist doctrines and work as hard as you study so that you will become future leaders of our nation."

Since this first occasion, many similar sports meets have been held in major Japanese cities. Under the banner of the Youth Division, which bears the representation of a young lion, these festivals grew larger and larger until it became necessary to hire the National Stadium in Tokyo to accommodate them. The culmination of this movement has been the Youth Division Culture Festival and the Sports Festival, which are celebrated throughout the world.

On November 10, ceremonies were held to enshrine the Gohonzon in the newly completed Myosho-ji temple in Karuizawa, over the selection of the land and initial planning for which Toda had experienced considerable unpleasantness the year before. Myosho-ji was the first temple ever built entirely under the initiative of Soka Gakkai.

At the ceremonies, the sutra was recited, and High Priest Nissho Mizutani and Soka Gakkai leaders delivered congratulatory messages to a gathering that overflowed the large, new-timber-scented main hall of the building.

After recalling the difficulties of the previous year in connection with the temple, Toda outlined the process by which Soka Gakkai tried to encourage the construction of temples throughout the country, sometimes with success and sometimes resulting in disagreements with the priesthood. He then reminded the assembly of all the hardships involved in building Myosho-ji, hardships of which most of the people there were blithely unaware. In order to impress more deeply upon them the need to take such projects as seriously as they took their faith, Toda related a few incidents, the first of which was something that had happened in Osaka in relation to the building of a temple called Honden-ji.

"After the end of World War II, three diligent parishioners of this Nichiren Shoshu temple rebuilt the main hall, which had been destroyed in an air raid. Though Honden-ji is much less imposing and much smaller than Myosho-ji, it took great faith on the part of the three men to complete the restoration project. I was happy to see that such faith was still alive. The following year, the Reverend Takano, chief priest at Honden-ji, asked for assistance in adding a room to the temple. I was happy to comply, but hesitated to undertake the job over the heads of the three parishioners whose efforts had rebuilt the temple. I met with the men, however, and asked their opinion. Even though I said I was willing to go ahead with the work, they declined my aid, because they did not want to start a new building program until all debts from the former one had been liquidated. I was deeply moved by their honest, sincere approach.

"The case was somewhat different with the two Nichiren Shoshu temples I recently visited in Asahikawa, in Hokkaido. Two local people with deep faith have been doing all within their power to revitalize these temples. I have met the men and know what they are trying to do, but they get no cooperation from the local parishioners, who have strayed so far from the path of true Buddhism that they unconcernedly display Shinto plaques and other religious talismans in their homes.

"As these two episodes demonstrate, faith, not the size or splendor of temple buildings, is the important thing. Dedicate yourselves to your temple and to the cause of Kosen-rufu. First and foremost, keep this temple pure and undefiled and practice faith with dedication and spotless hearts."

In January, 1955, another incident proved the importance of faith in connection with temples and the danger of misguided views, even among the clergy. At the conference of leaders and members of the Osaka, Sakai, and Yame chapters, held in Osaka, Toda was pleased to learn of the progress being made in the local district, but was disappointed to see that the Reverend Shimizu, head priest of the temple Renge-ji, was not present, in spite of invitations from Toda himself and from the Reverend Hosoi, and even though Shimizu had promised to attend. Toda was especially unhappy, because he had hoped that a face-to-face informal meeting with this man would iron out the differences of opinion that had been plaguing relations between Renge-ji and Soka Gakkai for some time. Since Shimizu had been absent from the two previous meetings as well, it was now obvious that he was boycotting Soka Gakkai affairs.

In 1954, Toda had visited Renge-ji and had seen the state of affairs there. The temple had burned in an air raid during the war. At this stage, the old storehouse was being used as a worship hall, where the Gohonzon was enshrined. This makeshift temple was already too cramped for the rapidly increasing membership in the Osaka area. Gojukai initiation rites were performed in inadequate space, with the result that people often had to stand outdoors during the ceremonies—protecting themselves from the rain with umbrellas as best they could. Toda made an offer to rebuild the main hall as part of his

campaign of constructing facilities for Nichiren Shoshu believers, but the Reverend Shimizu, who was profoundly prejudiced against Soka Gakkai, flatly rejected the offer. Instead
of rejoicing over progress toward Kosen-rufu, he regarded the
active laity propagation drive as impertinent and never lost
an opportunity to criticize it.

Shimizu's refusal to attend the Osaka meeting determined
Toda's course of action. Relations between Soka Gakkai and
Renge-ji were to be severed. The lay organization would build
a different temple. The new temple would serve as a center of
Osaka shakubuku activities. Toda suggested that all Soka
Gakkai members cease attending services held at Renge-ji.
Though somewhat surprised, everyone present at the meeting
agreed. Upon learning of Toda's decision, Shimizu wrote the
following letter to the chief of the Osaka chapter:

"Rumor has it that Soka Gakkai is prohibiting its members
from visiting my temple. If this is true, Soka Gakkai need
not bother to issue official instructions, for we will inform Soka
Gakkai members to stay away and will not conduct any services—including initiation rites—for them. As of January 31,
members of Soka Gakkai will be struck from the list of Renge-
ji parishioners. I request that all Gohonzons issued to these
people during the period between February 1952, and January
23, 1955, be returned to this temple immediately."

Sensing that the other priests in the Osaka area would not
side with him, Shimizu tried to stir up support of distant parishioners and of priests in remote areas who knew nothing about
the dispute. Since only the high priest of Nichiren Shoshu can
bestow or retract Gononzons, in demanding the return of some
three thousand of them, Shimizu was widely exceeding his
authority. This was a matter of grave concern to the entire sect,
and Toda felt compelled to take prompt action.

After careful thought, he and the top leaders of Soka Gakkai
requested that the high priest and other leaders of the sect
excommunicate Shimizu for his outrageous acts. In close

coordination with the leaders, members of the Youth Division visited seventy-seven Nichiren Shoshu temples during early February to explain the true circumstances surrounding the Renge-ji incident. Briefing of the remaining thirty-seven temples was finished by the middle of the month. And all of the head priests interviewed—including even Jiko Kasahara, now old and infirm, who, in 1953, had caused a great deal of trouble by advocating heresy—saw things the Soka Gakkai way.

On February 16, the Administrative Bureau of the head temple notified Toda that Soka Gakkai members need not return their Gohonzons to Renge-ji, since Shimizu's demand was unjust and doctrinally untenable.

But, without paying attention to this move, Shimizu launched an anti-Soka Gakkai campaign, in which he published documents written under the names of leading parishioners, giving distorted accounts of the dispute. He lured away a few members of Soka Gakkai to a layman's organization belonging to Renge-ji and attempted to entice more by promising them Joju Gohonzon (Gohonzon personally written by the high priest), which the high priest promptly refused to grant.

Soka Gakkai deleted from its membership eleven people who had cooperated with Shimizu, who continued his vicious campaign, overriding denunciations from priests all over the country. Matters reached such a state that the head temple demoted Shimizu and ordered him to transfer to a temple called Myojo-ji, in Shiga Prefecture, but he ignored the instructions.

Meanwhile, Toda went ahead with plans for a new temple. He purchased an inn in Osaka and speedily had it remodeled. Ceremonies to enshrine the Gohonzon were held on April 11, with the attendance of High Priest Nissho and other leading members of the clergy, as well as Osaka Chapter Chief Haruki and other local leaders. A member of Soka Gakkai who had joined the priesthood was appointed to take charge of the new temple, which was called Shoko-zan Jomyo-ji.

As far as Soka Gakkai was concerned, this solved the problem of Renge-ji; but Shimizu still refused to abide by the instructions from the head temple and thus eventually brought about his own ruin.

Because he was planning to build many more Nichiren Shoshu temples to carry out the work of the cause, Toda knew that he must instill in all the parishioners the correct attitude toward religious institutions, so that the temples could function as sanctuaries of pure faith. Furthermore, though times had improved since the early postwar period, he wanted to impress on the people the need to be completely serious about faith. Once faith becomes nonchalant and careless, it degenerates. Toda had to prevent this both among the clergy and the laity.

On November 17, Toda traveled to Akita, in the northern part of Honshu, to participate in the enshrining of a Gohonzon in the newly completed temple Myoke-ji. On December 15, he went to Takasaki for a similar ceremony at the new Shomyo-ji. His plans for new temple facilities were steadily being realized.

16. SORROW AND HOPE

TRAINS all over the nation were packed with people returning from New Year's visits home. At the Fuji Station, not far from Taiseki-ji, about three hundred members of Soka Gakkai were waiting to board the 1:10 afternoon train on January 4. The Traffic Control Division was in charge of lining people up at the white markings on the platform that indicated positions of the coach doors of the halted trains. Toshihiko Yamanouchi was a member of the group waiting to get on the second coach. But when the train arrived, six minutes late, the car and its vestibules were packed. So many people got off that the ones trying to get on were still on the platform as the train began to pull out. Yamanouchi had just managed to get the children aboard, but their parents were stranded. The children on the train began to cry, in fear of being separated from their mothers and fathers. As a member of a large family himself, Yamanouchi understood this childish terror and jumped on the train, then leaped off again with a ten-year-old boy in his arms. At once he heard the boy's twelve-year-old sister crying out to be let off too. He jumped to get her, but lost his footing and fell between the moving train and the stones of the platform.

223

The horrified people raised such a tumult that the train quickly came to a halt. Yamanouchi had already dropped to the tracks. Several station attendants and Soka Gakkai members jumped down and crawled under the train.

When he was lifted up to the platform, Yamanouchi was perfectly white. As he was being rushed to a nearby clinic, his

lips moved weakly in the Daimoku. One of his companions asked in a whisper what he wanted. In a faint, clear voice he said, "Kosen-rufu."

Though mortally wounded, the young man, who was only eighteen and who had become a believer in Nichiren Shoshu eight months ago, was in clear enough mind to answer questions that the doctors put to him before recommending that he be taken to the better-equipped Central Hospital nearby. The boy had no visible exterior wounds but was suffering from severe internal hemorrhaging and organic damage. With a pale, contorted face, he gradually lost consciousness in the cold, bleak hospital, which was almost completely empty because of the holiday season. Around his bed, fellow Soka Gakkai members chanted Daimoku with all their hearts.

Word of the accident had been sent immediately to the head temple. A young official of the Traffic Control Division named Ryoichi Sawada informed Toda, who had gohifu sent to Yamanouchi at once. "Hurry! Have him take the gohifu! Do everything possible for him. We must save him. Keep me informed of all developments." Toda's heart was torn for the boy, whom, like all members of the Youth Division, he considered one of his own children.

After gohifu was administered, touches of pink appeared on the boy's palid cheeks. To the doctor's surprise, his blood pressure rose from 60 to 120. But he remained in the coma into which he had lapsed on admission. His parents, who had been told of the accident, were on their way from Tokyo.

A blood transfusion was ordered. His blood type was O. A group of people with this type—including six members of the Youth Division from the head temple—arrived at the hospital in the evening. Throughout the transfusion, fellow members chanted Daimoku. When his parents arrived at eleven-thirty that night, he was nearly dead. Without regaining consciousness, he breathed a last faint breath at seven minutes after one on January fifth. As Ushitora Gongyo began in the Reception Hall of the head temple, Toshihiko Yamanouchi lay dead. On his face was a radiant Buddhalike smile of enlightenment; surely an indication of blessings bestowed on him as a sacrifice to the cause of the true Law.

When he heard the news, Toda closed his eyes in grief. Then, opening them again, he said to the people with him, "Toshihiko Yamanouchi died for the sake of the true Law, and he must have a chapter funeral. The Nakano Chapter will hold services for him. His ashes will be interred in my own cemetery plot."

Shin'ichi Yamamoto, who had left the head temple on January 2, called a meeting of Youth Division leaders to make arrangements for the funeral immediately upon receiving word of Yamanouchi's death. In practically no time at all, an offering of two hundred thousand yen was collected and presented to the bereaved family, Toshihiko's mother, father, and four younger brothers and sisters. Since Mr. Yamanouchi was out of work, Toshihiko had supported the family by working in a factory. His mother contributed what little she could from occasional odd jobs. One of his sisters was hospitalized with a serious heart ailment. Eight months earlier, Toshihiko had joined Nichiren Shoshu, and the rest of the family, with the exception of his mother, soon followed him in becoming members. After a great deal of persuasion, he finally convinced her that she should join, too. She did so; then his sister's heart conditions took a decided turn for the better; and, on New Year's 1955, the entire family knelt in tears of happiness in their first Daimoku all together before the Gohonzon. Overjoyed, Toshihiko went out to visit friends and, upon his return in the evening, announced his intention of going to the head temple to join the Traffic Control Division, of which he was a member.

On February 20, the day on which Toshihiko Yamanouchi's ashes were to be laid to rest in Toda's family plot at the head temple, services were held for him in the Reception Hall. For a while, an unseasonable rainstorm lashed the temple grounds and the lower slopes of the mountain. But before long, the sun broke through the clouds and revealed Mount Fuji in all its snowclad majesty. In the temple compound, plum trees were just beginning to bloom.

Services attended by the Yamanouchi family, members of the Traffic Control Division, chiefs of the Young Men's Division, the head of the Youth Division, and, of course, Toda, began at nine in the morning. The flag of the seventh section of the Young Men's Division was draped in mourning. After remarks by several others, Toda spoke. "On the train coming down here yesterday, Miss Katsu Kiyohara and I had an interesting discussion on the nature of life. In Hinayana Bud-

dhism, the major principles are *ku* (void), *mujo* (imperman-
ence), and *muga* (selflessness). In Mahayana Buddhism however, the four major principles are *jo* (eternity), *raku* (bliss or
happiness), *ga* (self), and *jo* (purity). Each of us is aware of his
ga, or self, as long as life remains, but what happens to it when
life terminates? To understand the answer to this question is to
understand all problems concerning life. Life itself is the vital
clue. Still, understanding this does not necessarily bring *raku*
(or happiness), for which the absolutely essential condition is
worship of the Gohonzon.

"Right now, radio waves transmitted from all over the world
are all around us. We do not perceive them. But they are
there, existing in harmony without interfering with each other.
Toshihiko is now dead. His life is fused with the great universal
life. And, though we do not perceive him, like the radio waves,
he is all around us, fused with all the other lives that exist in
harmony and do not interfere with each other.

"The self is permanent and eternal. Toshihiko has no body
or spirit, but he is blended with the life of the universe. He
might be said to be in a dream state.

"A violent death is like a nightmare. The person flees from
it as he would from a threatening, wild dog. He cannot escape,
however, because it is his karma. But, because the Gohonzon
is omnipotent, chanting the Daimoku changes this painful karma
into a tranquil, peaceful state, not unlike roaming happily in a
paradisiacal garden.

"Toshihiko's violent accidental death indicates that his
karma was not good. But our chanting Daimoku for him can
change that karma and permit him to wander happily in the
paradisiacal garden. This is the reality of life after death. We
must all chant for Toshihiko and live lives of devotion and
faith so that, at our deaths, we, too, will be allowed into the
garden."

While delivering these worlds, Toda was thinking of the

following passage from "Lessening the Karmic Retribution," in the *Gosho*: "If one's heavy karma from the past is not expiated within this lifetime, he must undergo the sufferings of hell in the future, but if he experiences extreme hardship in this life, the sufferings of hell will vanish instantly. When he dies, he will obtain the blessings of rapture and tranquillity, as well as those of the three vehicles and the supreme vehicle." This passage made Toda certain that, though burdened with bad karma, Toshihiko Yamanouchi had been spared the tortures of hell because of his pure-hearted faith.

Toda's speech dispelled the cloud of sorrow that had filled the Reception Hall. Finally, after several of Yamanouchi's favorite Soka Gakkai songs, the group sang "Eternal Friendship," and his close friends carried the young man's ashes to the Toda plot, where they were deposited in the gravestone chamber by Toshihiko's father.

17. PUBLIC RELATIONS

EVEN THOUGH Soka Gakkai was the sole true light in a dark society during the troubled early 1950s, most of the population was too religiously ignorant to appreciate it. Furthermore, the progress that Soka Gakkai and Nichiren Shoshu were making in many parts of the country aroused the animosity of the many new religions and sects that had sprung up like mushrooms after the war and were financially exploiting their converts. Realizing the threat that it presented to their welfare and continued expansion, the leaders of these sects launched vigorous campaigns of slander against Soka Gakkai, and especially against its energetic shakubuku activities.

While not actively stimulating them, Toda tacitly approved the religious debates that young Soka Gakkai members liked to hold with members of other religions, because he considered them effective ways of learning to appreciate the orthodoxy of Nichiren Buddhism and of fortifying their own faith. To their surprise, the young Soka Gakkai debaters found that they were invincible in these debates, though they had never been able to convert a single priest of another sect. When asked why this was the case, Toda once replied that the total corruption of the priests made it impossible for them to see or admit the truth of Nichiren Shoshu teachings.

Still such activities as debates and membership campaigns continued to win people away from many temples throughout the country, thus threatening the abandoned religious organizations with financial failure, because of loss of income from parishioners. In some cases, priests retaliated by refusing to bury the deceased relatives of people who had accepted faith in Nichiren Shoshu. The people replied by instigating court suits against the temples.

Not to be easily defeated, the priests prevailed on local newspapers to print slanderous stories about Soka Gakkai. Since the priests were ashamed to admit that financial interest had stimulated them to act, they resorted to malicious tricks and reported to the Ministry of Education that Soka Gakkai was a violent, aggressive organization. The ministry thereupon started investigations to determine whether Soka Gakkai activities ran counter to the Religious Corporation Act, Article 81, which prohibits religious activities harmful to the public welfare.

As improbable as it may sound, when it was just beginning to assert its pre-eminence, Soka Gakkai was subjected to many such distorted, hostile misrepresentations. For instance, the religious column of a certain newspaper, calling on the services of a man who, without any firm understanding of true Buddhism, headed a dubious religious group, undertook to answer readers' questions about Soka Gakkai. This writer mixed personal feelings and religious prejudices in compiling false, slanderous accounts of Soka Gakkai and its beliefs and activities.

Unable to stand passively by while this kind of thing was going on, Youth Division members submitted a protest to the newspaper and succeeded in making the columnist promise not to refer to Nichiren Shoshu as a heretical, superstitious sect. He remained hostile in his writings nonetheless.

He and a nationwide daily paper were especially malicious in their coverage of the summer membership campaign.

Faced with dwindling ranks, as many of its members converted to Nichiren Shoshu and became members of Soka Gakkai, one particular religious sect called a meeting of nearly two hundred of its priests, issued a special edition of its organ paper, and vigorously warned its readers not to be deceived by the delusive doctrines of Soka Gakkai. This and other false coverage of a similar kind caught the attention of circles beyond religious ones, and reporters from various news media began to pay harassing visits to the Soka Gakkai headquarters.

To his followers, Toda explained the meaning of the troubles they were encountering in such public relations. "This kind of thing indicates that we are beginning to confront Domonzojoman, the second of the Three Formidable Foes," he said one day to a group of his disciples. "We have already defeated the first enemy—criticism and obstruction from families, colleagues, friends, and acquaintances. The second enemy—in the form of attacks from religious leaders of hostile sects—has now started to attempt to thwart our movement. This is not surprising. In fact, we should be glad, because their actions indicate that our movement has entered its second phase.

"This is not the first time the Three Formidable Foes have appeared. During Nichiren Daishonin's time, they all three simultaneously caused him to be subjected to tyrannical persecutions, as he eloquently explains in *On the Buddha's Behavior*.

"Though exiled to the bleak island of Sado, Nichiren Daishonin carried out vigorous shakubuku activities and converted many of the islanders. Priests of the Jodo sect resented this and conferred to see what action they should take. They said, 'If we allow Nichiren to live, we will starve. Most of our parishioners have already been converted. If we are to survive, we must eliminate this priest.' They then petitioned the government in Kamakura to remove Nichiren Daishonin. 'If he remains on the island, not a single temple or priest will survive. He has already burned or cast into the river the images of Amida Buddha. . . . ' This attitude of concern over personal welfare is the major stimulus behind the actions of people slandering Soka Gakkai today, and this kind of complaint is exactly the same as those being made by other sects against us. The priests in Nichiren Daishonin's day petitioned the Kamakura shogunate; our enemies today petition the Ministry of Education or have things written in the newspapers, because of fear that, if we continue active, they will starve.

"When we have overcome the second enemy, the time will come to face the third and most formidable of all, Senshozojoman, or the hindrance from supposed sages and people who are respected in society, but who are actually frauds. This confrontation is the most difficult. If you fail to meet it successfully, all of our efforts will have been futile. The encounter with it will be a crossroads in your lives, from which one way leads to glory and the other to ruin. But there is no need to be impatient or upset as long as you continue marching forward according to the policy of Soka Gakkai."

Toda remained calm in the face of all the turmoil around the organization, which, in spite of its relatively small membership, was attracting nationwide attention. As a result of the placid, lucid interview he gave to a group of reporters on October 21 in the headquarters building, an objective, if sensational, article about Soka Gakkai, with true interpretations of the nature of shakubuku campaigns and of the financing methods of the organization, appeared on page 7 of the morning edition of a leading newspaper on October 26. Not everything about the article was satisfactory. Most important, it failed to mention the objective of Soka Gakkai and the doctrines of Nichiren Shoshu. But, in general, it was free of spiteful misrepresentation. And, if the high degree of organization of Soka Gakkai led one of the writers to refer to the group as fascist—in much the same way in which people often insist on referring to all social-welfare moves as leftist—the comments by priests of other sects added to the article's general appearance of objectivity.

On November 3, the Japan Broadcasting Corporation (popularly known as NHK, from the initials of its Japanese name) invited Toda to participate in a panel discussion with a group of scholars on its nationwide network. Although he had some misgivings, since the list of proposed questions supplied to him showed clearly that what NHK wanted to do was to examine Soka Gakkai as just another of the many social phenomena characteristic of postwar Japan, Toda finally agreed, because of the chance it offered to enlighten the general public on the nature of the organization. The scholars chosen by NHK may have studied the doctrines of the so-called established religions and may have been influenced by what Toda called the "London version" of Buddhism, but their ignorance of the vivid happiness experienced by Soka Gakkai members who apply the teachings of true Buddhism to everyday life was almost certain. Toda looked on this program as a kind of shakubuku.

On November 26, the day of the broadcast, Toda and the panel members engaged in some preliminary talk before the discussion went on the air. Toda made it clear how he and the members of Soka Gakkai felt about matters of faith. "I must tell you," he said, "that we are thoroughly prejudiced in favor of our religion. We have to fight all other religions. And for this reason, we are likely to go on making enemies. We deny all other religions."

Then a member of the NHK staff announced that the show was about to go on the air. The first question put to Toda by one of the panelists concerned the meaning of the name of Soka Gakkai, the Value-Creating Society.

"As a result of ten years of study of Dr. Kiichiro Soda's theory of value, Tsunesaburo Makiguchi, the first president of

our organization, came to the conclusion that the three greatest values are beauty, gain, and goodness, instead of truth,
goodness, and beauty, as the classical philosophers defined
them. Having discovered the philosophers' error in disregard-
ing gain, which is an object of considerable interest to econo-

mists, Makiguchi developed a new theory, according to which
the creation of the value of gain posits the creation of beauty
and goodness, and the creation of all three leads to the growth
and development of the personality.

"Mr. Makiguchi was an educator, and, when he asked me
what I thought of a title for a book he was writing, I suggested
Soka Kyoikugaku Taikei (Value-Creating Education Theory). He
agreed, and used the title. The name of our organization was
originally Soka Kyoiku Gakkai, or Value-Creating Educational Society. It was changed to the shorter Soka Gakkai in
1946.

"We do not seek new religious values. Instead we strive to
create values of beauty, gain, and goodness through the power

of religion. Everyone has a potential for creating these values. Our ideal is to employ the power of true religion to develop individual potentialities."

To the somewhat skeptical questions of the other members of the panel, Toda explained that, when a person has created the three great values through the power of faith, he becomes aware of a life force welling from the depths of his being, and then experiences the true joy of life, wherever he is and whatever he does. He next explained that only through devotion to the Gohonzon is it possible for a person to attain this kind of joy and experience the welling-up of happiness.

One of the scholars pointed out that other sects, too, have objects of worship and asked whether it was possible to attain happiness through the adoration of them. Toda replied, "The objects of worship of other sects are false, because the religious principles on which they are founded are false. It is impossible to attain true happiness through their worship."

Toda did not make doctrinal criticisms, for doing so would have entailed discussions of the Fivefold Comparison and the Threefold Secret Teachings, which he realized were beyond the shallow knowledge of Buddhism that was all he could expect from these scholars. He did make the following proposal, however, "I propose that we attempt to test the validity of various religions by setting up a committee of from thirty to fifty impartial scholars like yourselves to investigate the life conditions of one hundred households from each sect. Surveys of their living conditions could be carried out in a scientific fashion for a period of ten years. In this way, it would be possible to investigate the effects that religions have on actual daily life. The current idea that any religion is all right as long as its believers have faith in it is mistaken, as the results of an objective research project would prove."

The others on the panel insisted that, though the survey he proposed might in fact be interesting and valuable, happiness is relative, and no absolute happiness can exist. Toda stuck to his guns however: "Not a single person who does not believe in true Buddhism today can call himself happy, though in their benightedness, many think they are content. Nonetheless, I consider it my duty to awaken people to the truth and attempt to help them find real happiness for the sake of future existences, which, in accordance with Buddhist central doctrines—transmigration and the lives of past, present, and future—they are bound to face."

He related some of the countless instances in which faith had helped Soka Gakkai members overcome illness or get out of financial or other trouble. But even benefits like these are not pure joy, which is attained only when the deepest essence of life is happiness in present and future existences. "And this kind of happiness can be achieved only through true Buddhism," he said. The discussion then meandered through superficial comments on shakubuku, religious debates with other sects, and similar topics, without ever reaching a climax. In the original form of the broadcast Toda talked for about thirty minutes, but his part was pruned to twenty minutes before the program was broadcast.

Toda had avoided profound doctrinal talk and had concentrated on trying to present a coherent picture of Soka Gakaki as a lay society devoted to true Buddhism. Making the public understand was difficult. In saying that he and the organization rejected all other sects, he was running against prevailing public opinion, and he expected hostility. And when it came, without flagging under his tremendous burden, Toda continued to do what he could to deal with such reactions. On December 23, he set up a Public Relations Division, with Shin'ichi Yamamoto as its chief, to cope with public antagonism. One month earlier, he had established the Cultural Division, which, under the leadership of Minoru Suzumoto, chief of the first section of the Young Men's Division, was working out plans for a variety of activities. And, as the year drew to a close, Toda went on making one important decision after another and working relentlessly in this, the ninth year since the end of World War II and the third year of his presidency.

The first Gongyo of the new year, 1955, was held in the spacious main hall of the headquarters for all leaders above the grade of district chief. At this time, to remind his sometimes too complacent disciples that the road to the achievement of their goal was still blocked by enemies and obstacles, he read a poem he had composed.

> "Arm in arm,
> Each courage for the other,
> We march together on the
> Long, hard road to
> Kosen-rufu."

(After Toda's death, this poem was engraved on a monument to him in the garden of the Grand Lecture Hall at Taiseki-ji.)

All of the leaders present recited the brief verse over and over, and from it they gained a deeper awareness of Toda's wish that each of them could pass successfully over the thorny path to the universal propagation of the Supreme Law.

When the first Gongyo was over, the entire group left for the head temple, where leaders of the Youth Division, who had been there since New Year's Eve, awaited them at the main gate. Toda remained at the temple until January 5, since there was a heavy round of meetings and ceremonies. The many activities of the coming year demanded attention, especially discussions of the building of a temple to be called the Hoanden to enshrine the Dai-Gohonzon and to accommodate about a thousand people. In addition, he visited both the high priest and the retired high priest, held a reception for the clergy, conducted nightly question-and-answer sessions, and gave personal guidance to pilgrims with serious problems. He had scarcely a moment to rest, but the clear, unseasonably warm weather and Mount Fuji soaring in the cloudless winter sky made a paradise of the head temple.

GLOSSARY

AMIDA SUTRA: One of the three major sutras of the Jodo, or Pure Land, sect. It is a Chinese version of the Sanskrit original of the *Muryoju-kyo*.

DAI-GOHONZON: The fundamental and supreme object of worship enshrined in the Sho-Hondo (Grand Main Temple) of the Nichiren Shoshu head temple. It was inscribed by Nichiren Daishonin on October 12, 1279, to save all mankind from distress and unhappiness. The Dai-Gohonzon is the embodiment both of the profound theory of the Three Great Secret Laws and of the life of the Daishonin himself.

DAIMOKU: The invocation Nam-myoho-renge-kyo, which Nichiren Shoshu believers chant in their worship of the Gohonzon. Only by means of this invocation is it possible for a person to draw on the life-force inherent in him and thus enjoy life fully.

DENGYO THE GREAT (767–822): The founder of the Tendai sect (Japanese reading of T'ien-t'ai) in Japan. Dengyo the Great completely refuted prevalent misguided Buddhist sects in the presence of Emperor Kammu and achieved wide propagation of faith in the Lotus Sutra in the Middle Day of the Law.

DOMON-ZOJOMAN: *see* The Three Formidable Foes.

THE FIVEFOLD COMPARISON (Goju-no-Sotai): Nichiren Daishonin's analysis of religions on the basis of superiority. According to this comparison, Buddhism is superior to religions that are non-Buddhist; Mahayana Buddhism is superior to Hinayana Buddhism; actual Mahayana is superior to provisional Mahayana; Hommon (the true teachings, found in the latter half of the Lotus Sutra) is superior to Shakumon (the expedient teachings, found in the first half of the Lotus Sutra); and the Buddhism of Nichiren Daishonin is superior to that of Sakyamuni.

FOUR BODHISATTVAS: In the true teachings of the Lotus Sutra, these are the Four Bodhisattvas of the Earth who, led by Viśiṣṭa-cāritra (Jogyo in Japanese), were entrusted by Sakyamuni with the propagation of the sutra after his attainment of Nirvana. In the teachings of Nichiren Shoshu, these Bodhisattvas represent eternity, happiness, life, and purity.

THE FOUR REFUTATIONS: Nichirin Daishonin's clarification of the true natures of the prevalent sects of his time and his rejection of them.

GOHIFU: Special protection granted by the high priest of the head temple to those who are gravely ill and who have been faithful for a long time. It is protection of the kind that Nichiren Daishonin granted to his own mother, who was thereby enabled to live for four more years.

GOHONZON: The object of worship in Nichiren Shoshu, first inscribed by Nichiren Daishonin in 1279. At present it is inscribed only by the high priest of Nichiren Shoshu and bestowed upon followers. "Go" is an honorific prefix; "honzon" means object of worship.

GOJUKAI: The Gojukai is a ceremony conducted at Nichiren Shoshu temples by priests for the sake of acknowledging new converts. After having been taken to a temple by his religious sponsor, the new member promises to be faithful to the teachings of Nichiren Daishonin for the rest of his life.

GOKAIHI: The ceremony for the worshiping of the Dai-Gohonzon at Taiseki-ji, the head temple of Nichiren Shoshu. The high priest of the sect, or a senior priest representing him, conducts the service.

GONGYO: The prayer service performed by believers before the

Gohonzon every morning and evening. During Gongyo, they recite the *Hoben* and *Juryo* chapters of the Lotus Sutra and chant the Daimoku.

GOSHO: The complete works of Nichiren Daishonin, consisting of religious theses and letters containing guidance to his disciples. Followers of Nichiren Shoshu are taught to apply the precepts of the *Gosho* to everyday life in society.

HINAYANA BUDDHISM: Generally speaking, there are two main historical streams of Buddhism: Northern and Southern. Northern Buddhists call their own branch Mahayana, or the Larger Vehicle, and call the Southern branch Hinayana, or the Lesser Vehicle, because of the limitations and self-concern of its teachings. Southern Buddhists call their own school Theravada, or the Doctrine of the Elders. Hinayana Buddhism is practiced mainly in Sri Lanka, Burma, and Thailand; Mahayana Buddhism is practiced mainly in Japan, Korea, and China.

HOMMON-NO-KAIDAN (High Sanctuary): The third of the Three Secret Laws (*San Dai Hiho*) of Nichiren Shoshu, the Hommon-no-Kaidan is the high sanctuary in which the Dai-Gohonzon is enshrined. Although in the strictest meaning, the term refers to the sanctuary that will be built when the universal propagation of the true Buddhism has been attained, it applies now to the Sho-Hondo of Taiseki-ji, which houses the Dai-Gohonzon.

HOSSUI-SHABYO: The traditional heritage of the successive high priests of Nichiren Shoshu that enables the teachings of Nichiren Daishonin to be transmitted and handed down purely and perfectly, just as a jar of water is poured into another jar.

ICHINEN SANZEN: The theory according to which every single moment or thought (*ichinen*) possesses the potential to manifest the countless variety of phenomena contained within the three thousand worlds (*sanzen*). The ten factors characterizing the quality of existence in each of the ten states of life (q.v.) give rise to one thousand worlds. These worlds, multiplied by the three existences (q.v.), yield the three thousand worlds encompassing all the different forms and aspects in the universe. The concept thus indicates the inseparable relationship between each life-moment and all phenomena, and holds that all of the infinite phenomena that are possible within the entire universe are contained even in something as fleeting as a thought.

JIZO (Kṣitigarbha): A Bodhisattva who was believed to ease child-birth pains, statues of whom are considered heretical by members of Nichiren Shoshu.

KAYO CLUB: An organization set up in 1952 for women in Soka Gakkai, which met twice a month to study politics, economics, philosophy, and the humanities, on the basis of the literary classics of the East and West.

KOSEN-RUFU: The attainment of world peace and happiness through the propagation of the spirit and teachings of true Buddhism.

THE LATTER DAY OF THE LAW (Mappo era): The age that began two millenniums after the death of Sakyamuni and will last for eternity. In this age, mankind can enjoy true peace and happiness through worship of the Gohonzon and devotion to the propagation of Nichiren Daishonin's philosophy of reverence for life.

LOTUS SUTRA: The penultimate sutra expounded by Sakyamuni, it is his highest teaching, though the term also refers to the highest teaching of any Buddha, and its implications may vary with time. For instance, the Lotus Sutra of the Zoho, or Middle Day of the Law, is the Mo-ho-chih-kuan of T'ien-t'ai; and that of the Mappo, or Latter Day of the Law, is Nichiren Daishonin's Nam-myoho-renge-kyo, or the Gohonzon.

MAHA-KASYAPA: One of the ten major disciples of Sakyamuni.

MAHAYANA BUDDHISM: see Hinayana Buddhism.

MAKIGUCHI, TSUNESABURO (1871–1944): The first president of Soka Kyoiku Gakkai. Converted to Nichiren Shoshu in 1928, he published *Value-Creating Education Theory* in 1929 and established Soka Kyoiku Gakkai in 1930. Because of his antimilitaristic stand, he was arrested and imprisoned in 1943, together with Josei Toda and other leaders of Soka Kyoiku Gakkai. He died in prison in 1944.

NAM-MYOHO-RENGE-KYO: Literally, "Devotion to the Wonderful Law Lotus Sutra." Initiated by Nichiren Daishonin, the true Buddha in the Latter Day of the Law, this invocation is the basis of universal life—the most fundamental law in the universe.

NICHIREN DAISHONIN (1222–82): The founder of Nichiren Shoshu, whose teachings are the basis of Soka Gakkai. A fisherman's son, he inherited the doctrine of Sakyamuni and in 1253, at the age of thirty-one, distilled the essence of the Lotus Sutra into Nam-myoho-renge-kyo. In 1279, he exalted it to the position of the supreme guide for people living in the Latter Day of Sakyamuni's law and embodied it in the form of the Dai-Gohonzon, the ultimate object of worship of Nichiren Shoshu. Daishonin is an honorific suffix that is interpreted to mean "the true Buddha in the Latter Day of the Law."

NICHIREN SHOSHU: The Buddhist sect that has faithfully preserved the orthodox lineage of Nichiren Daishonin's Buddhism for the past seven hundred years. Its head temple is Taiseki-ji, located in Fujinomiya, Shizuoka Prefecture, on the southern slope of Mount Fuji. Soka Gakkai is the lay organization of Nichiren Shoshu.

NIKKO SHONIN: Immediate successor to Nichiren Daishonin, second high priest of Nichiren Shoshu, and founder of Taiseki-ji.

ONGI KUDEN: The oral teachings of Nichiren Daishonin written down by Nikko Shonin, the second high priest of Nichiren Shoshu. It clarifies Nichiren Daishonin's profound life philosophy by interpreting the important passages of the Lotus Sutra from the viewpoint of Buddhism of the Latter Day of the Law.

ŚĀRIPUTRA (Sharihotsu in Japanese): A contemporary of Sakyamuni, Śāriputra was known as the wisest man in India in his time. He was one of Sakyamuni's ten major disciples.

THE SECURITY OF THE LAND THROUGH THE ESTABLISHMENT OF TRUE BUDDHISM (*Rissho Ankokuron*): The treatise, written by Nichiren Daishonin in 1260, at the age of thirty-eight, that reveals the cause of disaster and unhappiness as being the proliferation of misleading religions and philosophies. This treatise is a remonstrance against the Kamakura shogunate, which then ruled Japan.

SENSHO-ZOJOMAN: *see* The Three Formidable Foes.

SHAKUBUKU: Membership campaigns and other activities conducted by Soka Gakkai members that are designed to introduce all mankind to the true faith and the happiness it brings.

SHINGON SECT: An esoteric Buddhist sect that flourished especially in the Heian period (794–1185). The word *shingon*, a Japanese translation of the Sanskrit *mantra*, meaning an incantation or prayer, suggests the importance of ritual and magic in the observances of this sect.

SUIKO CLUB (Suiko-kai): An organization set up in 1952 for a select group of members of the Young Men's Division of Soka Gakkai to discuss *Water Margin* (*Suiko-den*) and other great works of literature.

TAISEKI-JI: The head temple of Nichiren Shoshu, founded at the foot of Mount Fuji in 1290 by Nikko Shonin, the second high priest of the sect.

TENDAI SECT: The Japanese reading of the name of the Chinese T'ien-t'ai Buddhist sect founded by Chih-i the Great. The teachings of the sect were introduced into Japan in 805 by Dengyo the Great but were gradually altered by the addition of esoteric doctrines.

THE TEN STATES OF LIFE: The states of life that are manifest in both physical and spiritual aspects of all human activities. These ten states are hell, hunger, animality, anger, tranquillity, rapture, learning, absorption, Bodhisattva nature, and Buddha nature.

THE THREE EXISTENCES (Sanze): The three existences are the past, the present, and the future, which make up the continuum of individualized and universal life and are governed by the law of karma.

THE THREE FORMIDABLE FOES (Sanrui-no-goteki): The Lotus Sutra says that the worldwide propagation of true Buddhism will be preceded by the appearance of many enemies. The Three Formidable Foes, who will persecute true believers in the Latter Day of the Law, are: laymen who, without recognizing the value of true Buddhism, slander its believers (Zokushu-zojoman); heretical priests who attempt to upset the faith of believers in true Buddhism (Domon-zojoman); and government authorities or other people in high positions who persecute believers in true Buddhism who happen to fall in their sphere of control (Sensho-zojoman).

THREE GREAT SECRET LAWS: Another name for Nichiren Daishonin's Buddhism, which is composed of three vital elements: Hommon-no-Honzon (supreme object of worship as the embodiment of Nam-myoho-renge-kyo), Hommon-no-Daimoku (invocation of

Nam-myoho-renge-kyo), and Hommon-no-Kaidan (high sanctuary for the enshrinement of the Dai-Gohonzon).

USHITORA GONGYO: A religious ceremony held each night to pray for world peace and for the earliest possible attainment of worldwide propagation of true Buddhism. Since the time of Nikko Shonin, the founder of Taiseki-ji and the second high priest of Nichiren Shoshu, the Ushitora Gongyo has been conducted every night without a single lapse. At present held in the Grand Reception Hall of Taiseki-ji, it begins at midnight, although its name indicates that it was once held between the hour of the ox (*ushi*) and the hour of the tiger (*tora*). These archaic time designations correspond to two o'clock and four o'clock in the morning.

VULTURE PEAK: Mount Gṛdhrakūṭa, located near Rajgir (Rājagṛha), in the North Indian state of Bihar. The sacred mountain where Sakyamuni preached the Lotus Sutra.

ZOKUSHU-ZOJOMAN: *see* The Three Formidable Foes.

The *"weathermark"* identifies this book as a production of John Weatherhill, Inc., publishers of fine books on Asia and the Pacific. Book design and typography by Meredith Weatherby. Text composed by Samhwa Printing Co., Seoul. Printed by Kenkyusha Printing Co., Tokyo. Bound at the Makoto Binderies, Tokyo, The text is set in Baskerville *11/13*, with hand-set Baskerville for display.